Other mysteries by Mignon G. Eberhart
available in Bison Books Editions

DEATH IN THE FOG

Mignon G. Eberhart

Introduction to the Bison Books Edition
by M. K. Lorens

University of Nebraska Press
Lincoln and London

F

Introduction © 1996 by the University of Nebraska Press

⊛ The paper in this book meets the minimum requirements of
American National Standard for Information Sciences—Permanence
of Paper for Printed Library Materials, ANSI Z39.48-1984.

First Bison Books printing: 1996
Most recent printing indicated by the last digit below:
10   9   8   7   6   5   4   3   2   1

Library of Congress Cataloging-in-Publication Data
Eberhart, Mignon Good, 1899–
[Dark garden]
Death in the fog / Mignon G. Eberhart; introduction to the Bison
Books edition by M. K. Lorens.
p.   cm.
"Originally published in 1933 as The dark garden."
ISBN 0-8032-6730-4 (pa: alk. paper)
I. Title.
PS3509.B453D37   1996
813'.52—dc20
96-6153   CIP

Originally published in 1933 as *The Dark Garden* by Doubleday,
Doran & Company, New York.

"Certain dank gardens cry aloud for a murder; certain old houses demand to be haunted; certain coasts are set apart for shipwreck."

—*Robert Louis Stevenson*

INTRODUCTION

M. K. Lorens

"Certain dank gardens cry aloud for a murder; certain old houses demand to be haunted; certain coasts are set apart for shipwreck."

With these lines from Robert Louis Stevenson as its epigraph, Mignon G. Eberhart's sixth novel, *Death in the Fog,* is placed from the beginning within a tradition at once similar to and very different from her previous novels.

The Nurse Keate books, a straightforward mystery series with continuing characters, had begun in 1929 with *The Patient in Room 18,* and had gained the author—born in Lincoln, Nebraska in 1899—an enviable opening to what would prove to be a long and successful career. In 1930, she was awarded Doubleday Doran's Scotland Yard Prize for a second Keate adventure, *While the Patient Slept.* In the years and decades that followed, Mrs. Eberhart's books and stories were to gain her a wide audience. They were serialized in the *Saturday Evening Post* and other fiction-publishing weeklies, and made into films in the thirties and forties.

So it is, naturally, for the Nurse Keate stories that she is best known. They are classic mystery in the Sayers-Christie tradition—rationalistic, full of lists of suspects, and the patiently sifted enumeration of clues. They use some of the same emblems you will discover in *Death in the Fog*—the old decaying building; the wealthy, infirm, and somewhat tyrannical elder who rules it as his or her kingdom; and the imprisoning weather that is the outward token of a universe out of joint. In the *Patient* novels, the choice of a hospital as milieu and a nurse as detective told us instantly that, whatever its aberrations, the scientific mind and the rational process would triumph. There is no such assurance in *Death in the Fog*.

The novel was previously published as *The Dark Garden,* and it is by that title that I persist in thinking of it, for the Dark Garden is another country, an archetypal country of its own. The novel is firmly planted in the surreal, storm-wracked world of Mr. Rochester and Jane Eyre, or of Maxim de Winter and his callow bride in Daphne du Maurier's *Rebecca*. It is a mysterious fairy tale unmitigated by rational efforts; Katie Warren, the heroine, keeps no careful notebooks of clues or lists of suspects. Guided only by her innocence and her intuition, she stumbles through the tangled garden of misread clues and masked personalities, with death a few feet beyond her in the fog. One is almost tempted to say that *Death in the Fog* is a kind of *Cymbeline* or *Winter's Tale* translated into the vocabulary of American popular fiction.

It is *almost* as much a romance about the struggle of youth, love, and beauty against tyrannical age, selfishness, and false appearance as it is a conventional mystery novel.

Almost. But not quite. For the clues are there, and premeditated death is there, and the aptly named investigator, Mr. Crafft, whose chillingly rational presence seems a threat in this emotional island in the fog, is there, too, to perform the deductive unravelling that even Katie herself seems almost to fear. Mr. Crafft is the real detective here, but he is no hero. Nobody likes him, including the author, who presents him as "like a djinn, very old in evil wisdom, very sly, diabolically crafty. Not for one instant . . . to be trusted."

Oh, yes. *Death in the Fog* is a mystery novel, written for an audience that consumed—and still consumes, in this new heyday of the genre—four or five such books a week, always demanding something new, something with a hook to keep the interest, a book you can't put down, a page-turner.

Mignon Eberhart knew her audience for popular fiction, and she gave them what they wanted, and in that talent for reading the tastes of her marketplace lies part of the reason for her success. Perhaps, therefore, it was because, then as now, a large part of the mystery-reading public is female that *Death in the Fog* is, at its rather bitter and lonely heart, a book about women.

There is Charlotte Weinberg—grasping, hateful, frustrated, angry, bound into her narrow life of manipulations and petty punishments like the black ribbon she wears bound around her thin neck, "to conceal and hold up sagging muscles."

There is Mina Petrie, childless, infirm, believed to be dying, yet strangely vital. Mina, with her "thick, white hands," a little mad, deeply silly and deeply vulnerable, clinging to the memory of a lost lover and the wealth of a dead husband. She uses this wealth to hold the loyalty of three young people impoverished by the Depression: Paul Duchane, the handsome, dependent son of her old sweetheart; Steven Petrie, her struggling-artist nephew; and Katie Warren herself, orphan daughter of Mina's best friend, and almost—but not *quite,* thanks to Charlotte's animosity—Mina's own adopted daughter and her heir.

If anyone seems to be shipwrecked on this coast—the shore of Lake Michigan—it is Katie Warren. Type of the New Woman of the twenties, single working girl, successful stockbroker until her career struck the rock of the Crash of '29, sinking when she was cheated in a bond transaction—by someone in that dark kingdom to which she returns.

Who has a better motive for murder than Katie Warren?

Ah. The alien force. Logic. Mr. Crafft's weapon, the evil wisdom, the djinn's sly manipulation. It makes Katie the belied heroine who must clear herself, like Shakespeare's Hero or Heroine. Makes her the castaway on these fogbound coasts.

"Certain coasts are set apart for shipwreck."

"Certain dank gardens cry aloud for a murder."

The dank garden—the dark garden of the former title—is the grounds of Mina's old house on a high bluff overlooking Lake Michigan. Though the place is very near to the hustle and noise of Chicago, we see it as an island in a sea of dense fog—a fog that never lifts until the novel's end. Even in the city, where we first meet Katie, driving Mina's "huge and glittering and altogether impressive" automobile with cool nerve through the wild traffic, the fog has turned things upside down.

"Taxi drivers, a perverse lot, became merry and took hairbreadth chances and shouted gayly at one another. Traffic policemen went quietly mad under their solemn, glimmering raincoats and clung to their whistles as if whistle-blowing were the only stable thing left in a ghoulish and unbelievably fluid world."

In this kind of world anything can happen, and so it does. But Katie likes driving in the fog, likes the sense of control, not realizing that it is altogether false, that she is not in control at all. She stops in a traffic tie-up as the fog turns to sleet, still unconcerned at the surreal world through which she is moving.

"Bits of automobiles loomed out of the fog here and there into confused, futuristic paths of lights; automobiles with their radiators or their rear fenders mysteriously gone. It was a kind of Cheshire-cat effect gone modern and very noisy."

Stopped behind a safety-island, her window rolled down for better visibility, Katie hears a few words carried to her by the preternatural atmosphere of the fog.

" 'I won't,' " says a voice, " 'eat grape hair. Nor yet glocks.' "

Grape hair. Glocks. They are surreal words, emerging from the unnatural day, clue to the danger Katie still does not perceive.

And the next thing to emerge is handsome Paul Duchane. Katie offers him a lift out to Mina's estate and he accepts, but she is more interested in the whereabouts of the artist, Steven Petrie, who has suddenly vanished from his studio when she calls.

Steven, whom Katie loves, though she does not know it yet.

So, then. There is the city, on the shore of the great grey lake bound by fog. There is the somber old mansion of Mina Petrie, perched on its ravine above the lake. And to get from one to the other, Katie Warren must traverse the steep, icy roads of the dark garden.

On a precipitous slope, the car begins to slide. A light glimmers in a disused summerhouse. A dark shape stumbles onto the road in front of the careening car.

A human body is smashed under the car, with Katie at the wheel. But what was anyone doing in the foggy ravine at such an hour? The victim appears like the disembodied fenders and radiators—surreal, and will not be seen whole until the truth is pieced together.

Grape hair. Glocks. A mad world in which sane, bright, innocent Katie Warren has been shipwrecked.

And so has Steven Petrie, who loves her. These two thread their way together through the maze of complex personalities, strangely dependent on one another, locked into a final struggle for control. Anything can happen, including murder.

Is Aunt Mina—stronger than she seems, fiercely angry, hiding her secrets as she hides the horoscopes that rule her life—a killer?

Or Paul Duchane, who wanted Mina's money?

Or Steven, who disappears for most of the central section of the book, casting suspicion upon himself?

Or Chris, Mina's lawyer, secretly in debt?

Or the poor relations, Clarence and Fanny Siskinsen, who wish to ingratiate themselves with Mina?

Or Jenks, the butler?

Or Melissa, the maid?

In the end, of course, it is all sorted out. Logic, the djinn out of a bottle, proves not to be the enemy, and we even find out the nature of grape hair and glocks. The surreal becomes mundane, rational, real.

And the world is at last restored, in the classic manner of such a wintry romance, with an impending marriage.

DEATH IN THE FOG

CHAPTER I

CHARLOTTE WEINBERG sat listening.

There was, she realized, nothing to hear.

The whole great house was silent. Had there been any sound, particularly any stealthy, unaccustomed sound, she would have heard it at once. The room in which she was sitting was the very hub and center of the house. Into it opened the wide front entrance with only an open vestibule intervening, and from it on the opposite side opened the door leading out upon a strip of lawn ending in a white railing, broken where beach steps went downward out of sight, and then gray lake and gray sky.

And from that room branched like a tree all the other sections of the house, the main stem of which was the wide carpeted walnut stairway which turned over a small coatroom on its somber way to the two upper floors.

Charlotte sat with her narrow back stiffly erect in one of the shiny black wicker chairs which, with the array of ferns which lined the windows, did not look gay and frivolous as they were intended to look, but, instead, faintly funereal. On sunny days the wide windows brought the dancing blue of the lake and sky almost into the room, but on dark days, like that day, there was nothing gay in the room. The windows let you see, through spikes of green ferns, a strip of wet, brownish lawn and at its end a railing and then just gray space as if the world had dropped away there beyond the railing.

It was, thought Charlotte with irritation, a typical February fog that was creeping inexorably up from the lake. Presently it would sift through tightly closed windows and doors and would crawl silently through the house and would tickle her long, sensitive throat, and she would cough and Mina, upstairs, would grow nervous.

Across the room was a small writing desk with a mirror above it. On the desk, and directly under the pale circle of light cast by a small Lowestoft lamp, was a calendar, and Charlotte's eyes darted toward it although she already knew that it was Tuesday, the twenty-second of February.

Four more days until the twenty-sixth.

Her thin, wiry hand went to her throat and pulled a little at the black band of ribbon she always wore to conceal and hold up sagging muscles. It was not, however, the pressure of the ribbon that gave her that curious choking sensation. It was the necessity to subdue a strange rising excitement which was dreadful and yet oddly exhilarating and during the past few days had been growing more and more difficult to repress.

Then her hand stiffened as she listened.

But if there had been a sound it was not repeated, and presently Charlotte rose and walked to the windows. She paused there and glanced out into the steadily approaching gray fog wall.

She stood in the angle made by the wall and the windows so that the many entrances to the room were still within her range of vision.

Very soon the fog would envelop the house. It would be heavy, too, pressing against the windows so that the place would be an island shut in upon itself and bound about by that smothering gray blankness.

Although as to that there was always a feeling of isolation about the place which was due, perhaps, to the untidy park which lay, darkly unkempt and made wild and uneven by the ravine which twisted through it, between the house and the public road. The whole was enclosed, except on the lake side, by a high brick wall which was old and solid and, somehow, marked the feeling of remoteness and isolation which characterized the whole estate, although in point of fact it was not remote from the world at all.

Fanny and Clarence ought to be coming in soon. They were on the beach. Or in the park, walking its winding paths, or along the old carriage road which crossed the ravine and wound through the grounds to the house door and served now incongruously and rather dangerously for automobiles.

Fanny and Clarence Siskinson, unwelcome and uninvited guests and tolerated by Mina because they were relatives. But not for much longer, now.

Charlotte could still see the railing which edged the lawn. Beyond it was the sheer drop, fringed and masked by barberry bushes, to the strip of sandy beach which actually edged the lake and was lapped and sometimes beat upon by the waves. The railing was growing dim, and it was definitely darker.

She sat down again, and the wicker chair creaked dismally. How like Mina Petrie were the things she owned, thought Charlotte acidly. Anything that Mina's white, thick hands touched became promptly solid and ugly and heavy. Morose. Like the house. Like Mina.

So silent the house was. So still. Was anyone moving over those thick rugs in the crowded drawing rooms of the south wing? Was anyone approaching through the wide passage that led to them? Was a paper rustling in the small, oak-paneled bookroom, there just off the passage?

Was there no motion at all in the great dining room, opening with huge double doors directly into the lounge? Or beyond in the breakfast room and kitchen regions of the north wing? Were there no soundless feet in the corridors above approaching the heavily carpeted stairway?

No one, of course.

Charlotte rose again and moved to the desk across the room.

She sat down, took a pen and some notepaper, and began to write. She wrote swiftly, without hesitating over a word. She knew exactly what she wanted to say, for she had thought it out carefully. Every preposition, every comma had its place and its significance.

But even as she wrote, her neck was stiff and straight and rigid, and she paused now and then to listen again.

There was a mirror, heavily framed in gilt, above the desk, and by lifting her eyes from the paper she could see the reflection of the room and the objects behind her and beyond the open double doors into the cavernous shadows of the dining room. Once she caught a glimpse of herself, a smallish face that would have been sallow but for its chalk-white powder and rouged thin cheeks, defiantly black hair which was curled elaborately and pinned high on her head, and small dark eyes, penciled and artificially shadowed, with wrinkled lids that fluttered as her sharp, quick glances darted here and there—the door to the dining room, the stairway, the door to the vestibule, the entrance to the passage, the empty black wicker chairs, the windows.

No one but Charlotte Weinberg was in the room.

Her pen wrote again quickly and certainly.

It jerked to a stop, sputtering a little on the paper. Her head went up sharply, and her eyes stabbed the shadows that the mirror reflected beyond the pale circle of light, and she became taut and stiff.

There *was* a sound.

A sound from the dining room.

Her heart gave a great leap of terror. Otherwise her body was rigid and straight and taut.

Then there was a small tinkle from the dining room. One dish touching another. A cup perhaps rattling against its saucer.

Charlotte's heart throbbed and became steadier, though her body remained rigid.

That would be Jenks. Jenks bringing the tea tray. She would send him out to find Clarence and Fanny and tell them that tea was served.

Her eyes went back to the words she had written, and she felt a kind of satisfaction. She had said it rather well, she thought.

"Put the tray on the table, Jenks," she said in the thin, crisp voice she reserved for servants. "And then call Mrs. Siskinson. She's in the park." She did not, from principle, mention Clarence; it was always better, Charlotte felt, to ignore Clarence.

There was no reply.

Charlotte did not know that Jenks had a toothache and was locked in his room at the top of the house with a hot-water bottle pressed to his aching cheek.

Charlotte did not know that because Jenks had a toothache she need never again listen for sounds in that dark, silent house. Charlotte did not know that after only a short time now she would never again feel fear.

The telephone on the desk began to ring. It rang sharply and insistently.

The fog reached Michigan Boulevard and blanketed the Loop. It didn't announce its coming; all at once it was just there, gray, shifting, stifling—holding sounds and smoke and motor-exhaust gas close to the damp and glistening pavements.

Lights were on everywhere and gleamed weirdly and futilely out of thick gray veils. Traffic was impeded, pedestrians confused. Bus drivers felt their thunderous way along foot by foot. Private chauffeurs, harassed by dangers from without and instructions from within, cursed in their hearts and pretended to have gone suddenly deaf. Taxi drivers, a perverse lot, became merry and took hairbreadth chances and shouted gayly at one another. Traffic policemen went quietly mad under their solemn, glimmering raincoats and clung to their whistles as if whistle-blowing were the only stable thing left in a ghoulish and unbelievably fluid world.

The throbbing of the motors, the wailing of newsboys, the squeal of brakes, and the long, mellow notes of auto horns interwove and blended and echoed

themselves confusedly among fog walls, a shifting
pandemonium of sound, with the shrill two notes of
police whistles piercing eerily in and out and through
and above it all.

The green spot that was the traffic light disappeared, and a red glow appeared below it, and Katie
Warren shoved both feet spasmodically downward,
stopped within a few inches of the car ahead of her,
shifted to low gear, and waited, her slim foot still
on the clutch and her eyes on the traffic light.

The swirling pandemonium of sound surrounded
the long car she was driving, and Katie lifted one
hand from the wheel and grasped a silver handle and
rolled down the glass beside her. The sounds entered
the car and were louder, and the air was damp and
cold on her cheek. A faint smile tucked in the corners
of Katie's mouth. She liked driving through fog and
traffic.

It was a nice mouth, a bit strange to gayety during
the months just past, but still spirited and red and
dauntless. She turned at some suddenly shrieking
motor horn and caught a glimpse of her hat in the
small mirror above the windshield and thought that,
at any rate, her clothes and her complexion had
lasted. Doubtless she looked fairly opulent, expensively simple with just the right hat at just the right
angle driving along in Mina Petrie's huge and glittering and altogether impressive car.

Well, the brown hat was Patou and the gray suit
with its brown furred cape was Chanel at her superb
best, but neither was paid for. Nor was apt to be paid
for.

It was a too familiar thought.

Katie tugged impatiently at her brown glove and looked at the dashboard clock which said four-thirty and then back to the red light.

In the dim light her face looked very white and her blue eyes very dark beneath shadowed lashes and below slender, widely spreading black wings that were eyebrows. Her hair was soft and dark and shadowy with short curls clustered at the back of her head just below the prim little pancake that was her hat. Her nose was a bit haughty against the dusk. She looked, indeed, rather like a slim and spirited young duchess —if duchesses are slim and spirited and young—and she hadn't a cent to her name and was in debt up to those very wing-like eyebrows. Terribly, sickeningly in debt.

If Aunt Mina Petrie, aunt by courtesy only, hadn't invited Katie to stay with her for a time, Katie would have been—well, where would she have been? thought Katie, looking out into the cold and fog and confusion of a great city which, that winter, was in straits.

She gave her glove another impatient little tug as if the gesture would distract her from another too familiar thought, and her crimson mouth set itself into a firm line it had only recently learned. Her thumbs ran idly along the smooth notches in the polished wheel, and under her foot the motor hummed quietly and beautifully.

She liked driving in the fog and in heavy traffic, she thought again, although she hoped, parenthetically, that the pavements would not become frozen and slippery. It gave her a sense of adventure and of mastery. She knew herself to be cool and capable, and she liked the feeling. It was one that she had not, of late, experienced. Not since the crash.

The car directly ahead edged forward a few feet, and Katie followed and stopped again. The fog was growing heavier, and there was a hint of sleet on the windshield. Bits of automobiles loomed out of the fog here and there into confused, futuristic paths of lights; automobiles with their radiators or their rear fenders mysteriously gone. It was a kind of Cheshire-cat effect gone modern and very noisy.

She had stopped this time directly beside a safety island, and as she waited a few words drifted out from one of the shadowy figures almost at her elbow.

"I won't," it said simply, "eat grape hair." It paused and then added with plaintive earnestness: "Nor yet glocks."

Katie turned.

The speaker was one of a shadowy mass on the safety island, indistinguishable from other dark blurs from which projected, here and there, a hat or an umbrella or the white folds of a newspaper. It would go down, she thought, amused, as one of life's little mysteries; she would never know why the speaker was impelled to defend himself and his stomach against grapes, hair, and, mysteriously, glocks.

A pair of shoulders looming out of the fog, a hat pulled low over high cheekbones, and a small black silk mustache above a long chin looked familiar. It was Paul—Paul Duchane, of course. He turned his head, and Katie caught a flash of his dark, close-set eyes and leaned out to call to him.

"Paul! Paul——"

Katie's voice was pretty; low and never over-emphatic, it had a persuasive quality which, in the past, had brought many dollars into Katie's then vig-orous bank account. Now everyone on the safety island turned and stared through the fog to find its owner, and among them Paul. And it seemed to Katie that, just for an instant, he did not look pleased. But before the impression became definite his face bright-ened under a smile which in its sheer flattering charm only Paul could produce.

"It's you, Katie," he said, delighted. He pushed to the car, looming wholly out of the fog, and put one gloved hand on the door. "I'd forgotten you were going to the concert this afternoon or I should have met you there. Are you going to take me home?"

"Yes, of course. Get in. The light's about to change." Katie spoke shortly, rather regretting her impulse.

"Don't you want me to drive?"

"No."

Paul smiled again. "I didn't think so," he said and disappeared. A faint orange glow appeared, and the red traffic light vanished and the green one appeared just as Paul opened the opposite door and slipped into the seat beside Katie.

"This is luck," he said, making himself, as was usual with Paul, immediately comfortable. He pulled off one loose glove and then his hat, passed his hand over his black, satin-smooth hair and high forehead, and smiled at her again in such a fashion that his whole dark face complimented her. "Sure you don't want me to drive?"

"Yes."

"Well, then, Lovely, wouldn't you better get under way? The light's changed."

Katie's mouth tightened again. She started slowly amid the grinding flood of released traffic. Paul looked with interest at the interior of the car.

"Mina's," he said as a statement rather than a question.

Katie shifted expertly and nodded.

"You must be getting into her good graces," said Paul, smiling. "I happen to know what she paid for this machine."

Katie resisted a mean impulse to tell him that anyone might know who cared to look up the price lists of that particular make, and held her own against an encroaching car.

"She's been very kind to me," she said instead, crisply.

"She has, indeed," agreed Paul graciously. "She's a dear old soul in spite of her queer ways. Generous occasionally—look at that year she gave Steven in Paris for study. And I'm sure she's paid the rent for his studio this year."

"Why not? Steven is her nephew. Real blood nephew."

"Exactly. And you and I, Katie, are only the—what shall I say?—several offspring of her girlhood friends."

Funny, thought Katie, how Paul irritates me. He never used to. Is it because he's got money and I haven't? And because he paid me such a lot of attention last year and then stopped? He had a right to stop if he wanted to. Is my vanity wounded?

Aloud she said:

"Steven has a right to take what Aunt Mina gives him. She is really his aunt, and she has no children of her own. But neither of us, Paul, has any claim at all upon Aunt Mina. I'm the daughter of one of her closest friends. And you are the son of Aunt Mina's——" She hesitated. It was never possible, knowing as little as she did of Mina Petrie's inner life, to put words to that shadowy relationship, whatever it was, that existed very long ago between Mina Petrie—then Mina Weinberg, plump and spirited and rosy—and Paul's father.

"Sweetheart," supplied Paul with aplomb.

Katie accepted the "sweetheart," held her place firmly and deftly against a crowding truck, passed it triumphantly, and stopped for another traffic light at the bridge. Its black skeleton, veiled and wreathed in fog, loomed dimly ahead; headlights, yellow and dim, made wavering paths of light and swept along on east-bound traffic. Far above them lights in regular patterns pierced purple space. It was that night weirdly beautiful and unearthly. Sheer energy and power, epitomized in the roar of sounds that engulfed them in the street, had actually built all that beauty, but it looked that night completely dissociated from anything translatable in terms of ergs. It was instead just beauty, jeweled fantasia veiled in purple, entirely imponderable.

A river boat moaned hoarsely, and its moan multiplied and drowned all other sounds and sent little shivers along Katie's elbows.

Anything might happen in a fog like that. Anything and everything.

She felt all at once chilled and desolate and wished

she had not need to return to Mina's heavy, somber house. It would be dreary that night with the cold gray lake behind it and the dark park before it, and the blank fog surrounding and imprisoning the house and all it held.

Yet it had been a haven. And a haven in a storm.

But for Charlotte Weinberg it would have been her own home. Katie wondered vaguely, as she had wondered many times, why at that long-ago time when Mina Petrie, who had loved Katie's beautiful, gay, dead mother, had wanted to adopt Katie legally as her daughter, Charlotte had interfered. There was no reason for Charlotte to hate or to fear that slender, silent, long-legged child whose grave blue eyes held their first sorrow. But Charlotte had seen to it that Mina did not offer that child a home and security. Katie had often wondered why and how, but she was never in doubt as to Charlotte's feeling toward her. And since the recent affair of the bonds, Charlotte had not troubled to disguise that feeling.

"In any case," said Katie crisply, harking back to Aunt Mina, "we are both of us cadging right now."

Paul became dignified.

"I don't call it cadging," he said, "to accept her invitation to stay at her house while my flat's being decorated."

"It depends," murmured Katie wickedly, "on how long it takes."

Paul was queer that way, she thought. He really seemed to like staying in Mina's somber house. Yet he didn't seem to be devoted to Mina; it was, if anything, the other way around. And he certainly had money enough to keep up a dozen lavish apartments in town if he liked. Well, perhaps not a dozen, she amended, watching the traffic light. And Paul thought too well of money to spend it lavishly.

He had taken refuge in a silence which, subtly, raised a little barrier between them, and was fumbling in his pockets for cigarettes. Katie's sidelong glance caught a glimpse of his dark profile and black silk mustache. It was a rather handsome profile. Too handsome, especially when lit and warmed by a devastating charm which Paul could turn on and off as readily as he might an electric light. A good simile, thought Katie, pleased with herself; it was quite as easy with him, quite as simple and meant as little.

The whistle shrilled in two long notes, the light became green, and Katie swept ahead on the stream of throbbing motion.

"How are you getting on with Charlotte?" said Paul suddenly out of the dimness at her side.

Katie's mouth did something that was like a shrug.

"Oh—all right. I try not to hear her little pleasantries."

"Charlotte's got a wicked tongue."

"Aunt Mina asks me to do something for her now and then. Tries to make me feel that I'm some use to her. To salve my pride, I suppose. I'm really no earthly use there. Charlotte wouldn't let me be."

"No," said Paul. "Charlotte wouldn't let anyone edge in there. Wonder how long she's going to let Clarence and Fanny stay. Clarence—gets under her skin rather." Paul laughed, and Katie laughed also, and then, feeling obscurely ashamed, said shortly:

"Don't you think we've discussed Aunt Mina and her household quite enough?"

"Darling severe little Katie!" said Paul indulgently and caressingly. "See here, Katie, *is* Aunt Mina dying?"

"I don't know." Katie frowned. "Charlotte thinks so."

"Oh, Charlotte! She talks as if it's a matter of time only. What does the doctor say?"

"I don't know. I've never talked to him. Aunt Mina doesn't like it to be talked of."

"I'd have liked to see Charlotte's face when Fanny and Clarence arrived. Good Lord, they've been there for months now. Wonder how they got wind of Aunt Mina's approaching demise."

"I don't know. And I don't like the way you're speaking. Aunt Mina is devoted to you. And," said Katie, turning suddenly shrewish, "you know it."

She could feel Paul's look of humorous surprise and unruffled charm.

"Charlotte's sharp-tongued example is doing you no good, Katie," he said fondly. "Hey, what are you doing?"

Katie was signaling savagely to the traffic policeman and was turning at the frenzied wave of his hand through the intersection.

"Going to stop at Steven's."

"But I've just come from there," expostulated Paul. "You don't want to go there now."

Katie turned, avoided a similarly minded limousine, wove her way to the outside lane, and after a tense moment or two said:

"Why?"

"Oh—it's only that he's got several of his little pals there."

"Well? Steven's little pals are frequently quite nice."

"If you like that sort of thing, yes. When I was there they were talking of the relative merits of various kinds of cheese. All very analytically."

"What was Steven doing?"

"I don't know. Cleaning some brushes. Listening. Adding a word or two."

"I think I'll stop, anyway. You don't need to if you don't want to."

"I'll do anything to get a lift home in this fog. But Katie, do stop at that corner. I'm out of cigarettes."

Katie dropped one hand from the wheel, felt for her bag and pushed it toward him. He took the bag and opened it, sniffing as he did so.

"I like that perfume you use, Katie. I suppose it costs a frightful lot. But, my dear girl——" He stopped as if in horror and closed the bag abruptly.

"Don't you like my kind of cigarettes?"

"*Like* them!" Paul closed his eyes and shuddered effectively. "*Will* you stop on the next corner, Katie? There's a store there, and it's right across from Steven's place, anyhow, and I see a parking space."

Afterward Katie remembered with dismay how perfectly the heavy car slid to a pause under her manipulation. It was a huge thing, powerful, with every quality of perfection that human ingenuity can contrive and money can buy.

"Hydraulic brakes," murmured Paul. "You're a good driver."

Katie dropped her hands from the wheel and sighed.

"Nervous?" he said, smiling.

"No—not exactly. It's only that if I even crumpled a fender of this gorgeous thing I couldn't ever in the world pay for it. If I'd dreamed of a fog coming I wouldn't have let Aunt Mina persuade me to take it out. Go on and get your cigarettes."

"Look here, Katie, if you're nervous about driving in the fog, why don't we go straight home? It's apt to grow worse instead of better. And I believe it's beginning to freeze, which will be rather bad. And it's—" he paused to look at his watch—"it's a quarter to five right now."

Katie hesitated. Mina Petrie, though kind and generous in many ways, was also at heart a thrifty Dutch house-frau.

"Very well," she agreed. "It doesn't really matter. Get your cigarettes and we'll go on home."

Paul stepped down from the car and vanished. Katie stared into the wavering lanes of lights and then idly across the street. On the fourth floor of the building directly opposite, the lights from Steven's studio ought to shine. She looked, counted the floors, and looked again, but there were no lights there. On an impulse she turned the key in the ignition, slipped out of the car, and swiftly across the street.

It was a building of moderately priced apartments. There was a small lobby, and occasionally a desk clerk. It was, however, empty when she entered it, and she went to the row of bells and pressed the one labeled "Steven Petrie." She pressed it several times, finally letting her brown-gloved thumb remain on the bell until, had there been anything in that dark apartment above, it must have answered out of sheer exasperation. But there was no answer.

On the desk was a telephone, and she took it and dialed Steven's number. There was still no answer.

As she put down the telephone, the desk clerk materialized from some small inner office. He had been out, he said, recognizing Katie and giving the Patou hat a glance of distinct approval, and he didn't know where Mr. Petrie had gone.

CHAPTER II

WHEN Paul's figure loomed out of the fog at the door of the car and opened it, Katie was already seated at the wheel again, looking thoughtfully into the thin lanes of light ahead. He got in beside her, murmured something about having kept her waiting, jerked open a package of cigarettes and offered it to her.

"Not now," said Katie absently. She started the car, and it moved smoothly away from the curb into the ghostly twilight.

It was entirely dark now, with the fog holding smoke and darkness close to the wet pavements.

Back toward the south a faintly copper radiance, sullen-looking and threatening, marked the lights of a city's heart, sulkily defiant against this shifting, terribly quiet foe that all but blotted out their very existence.

There was more than a suggestion of sleet clinging to the windshield and further obscuring her view as Katie cautiously threaded her way in and out, avoiding other palely wavering lights, keeping well toward the center of the streets, and swerving, once or twice, as some dark moving object wavered out of the darkness and became a scurrying pedestrian, weird and unreal in the half-light. Presently she turned over again to the right, worked her way across to Lake Shore Drive and into the slow stream of traffic which, as the fog grew heavier and denser, was barely crawling along. Paul, smoking, had fallen silent and was sitting slouched down in the seat, his coat collar turned up and his hat brim over his eyes. Katie, too, was silent, engrossed for the most part in guiding the car scatheless through the dim half-world that now was alive again on all sides with the throbbing of other motors. They threaded Lincoln Park and went on along the lake. If possible the fog was heavier there, and it was cold. Katie rolled up the glass in the door beside her, and they were enclosed suddenly in a silence with the throbbing of the other motors muffled. Katie's throat was stinging, and her eyes felt hot. She reached upward to pull the collar of her furred cape closer around her throat. It eluded her groping, gloved hand, and Paul stirred.

"Need some help?" he said and, leaning so near that Katie felt the warm breath of smoke, his hands found the cape; he adjusted it so smoothly and gently that the gesture was like a lingering caress and then returned to his cigarette.

"When did you leave Steven's apartment?" asked Katie suddenly.

"Eh—why, just before I met you. Why do you ask?"

"You mean you had just come from there when I saw you?"

"Yes. It took me perhaps ten or fifteen minutes to walk from his apartment uptown. And lo, you dropped in my path and with you a ride home."

"Didn't you say that some of his friends were there when you left?"

"Yes. Several of them." She could feel that he had turned to look at her sharply. "What about it? Interested in Steven?"

"Not particularly," said Katie coolly. "It's just that his apartment was dark."

"Well?"

"I crossed the street while you were getting cigarettes and rang. No one answered."

"He must have gone just after I left," said Paul easily.

"Yes, of course," said Katie slowly. "But it didn't somehow seem just—right."

"Didn't seem *right!* Katie, you are talking nonsense."

"Yes, I suppose I am." She hesitated, both unable and unwilling to describe the uneasiness that had touched her there in the lobby of the apartment building. Later she remembered it. Remembered it and the ghostly drive homeward and her reluctance to talk of it to Paul and called it premonition. There are so many words like that which can be stretched over all those primitive tentacles of feeling which strive to warn of danger and which only succeed in being dismissed as nerves. Or, when it is too late, premonitions.

"Call it nonsense," said Katie, and there was again silence in the long powerful car nosing its elegant way through a secret and fog-masked world.

Long minutes passed, minutes during which Katie was conscious only of the dim light lanes the headlights sent futilely against the fog, the swish of tires on wet pavement, the hum of perfectly driven pistons, and of the increasing difficulty of driving.

The fog was turning into sleet and yet remained

fog, blinding and bewildering. Moisture was freezing
on the windshield and, she suspected, on the headlights, for the wavering paths of light they made were
growing fainter and fainter. She was literally feeling
her way along when she finally reached and turned off
the public road into the long private driveway which
Mina Petrie shared with her nearest neighbor, Christopher Lorrel. Katie felt the back wheels slip and
swerve as she turned from the pavement onto the
narrow, steeply climbing road which had been oiled at
some distant date and was never too good and, that
night, was a slippery, treacherous black ribbon.

The muscles at the back of Katie's knees ached and
twitched, and her hands were unsteady with weariness.
She shifted into low gear and felt her way blindly and,
she realized, dangerously.

She did manage to find the turn where the road
branched and took the right branch which led into the
Petrie estate. At the tall iron gates which marked the
entrance, she stopped suddenly.

"The gate's closed," said Paul in the same instant.
"I'll open it." He got out of the car.

The gate was never locked. Katie waited, straining
her eyes to see into the area of light ahead of the
car. She could barely see Paul as he appeared in that
small area of light, opened one half of the gate and
then the other, and vanished again into the blackness
surrounding them. Then the door opposite her opened
again and he got into the car. Under Katie's hands it
rolled gently through the gate and stopped again,
easily, on a level strip.

"We'd better close the gate again," she said to
Paul. "Perhaps Aunt Mina ordered it closed."

Paul, grumbling a little, got out once more and vanished into the impenetrable darkness.

Beyond the gate the road ran steeply downward again, twisting sharply through the tangled trees and hedges of what Mina Petrie's husband, dead and gone for twenty years, had been wont to call his park. Perhaps if he had lived more fully in a horseless and carriageless age he might have been persuaded to build a safer road, but he had not, and Mina Petrie was not one to change. She had trusted herself wholly to chauffeurs for years and possibly did not realize the danger of the narrow road which turned so sharply across the old bridge that spanned the ravine.

Katie wished, straining her eyes in a constant futile effort to see through the dense fog and darkness, that the slippery, twisting road ahead of her were safely passed.

Her hands felt cramped, and she flexed them slowly. Then Paul appeared faintly beyond the glow of the lights. He was trying, she realized, to scrape away some of the frozen sleet. It wasn't, however, a successful attempt, for the paths of light ahead were no stronger.

He opened the door again and slipped into the seat beside her.

"Tried to clean the headlights," he said disgustedly. "But it didn't help much. This road is like grease, Katie. You can hardly walk on it. For God's sake be careful on the bridge."

She started slowly in low gear, but in spite of that the weight and gathering momentum of the car upon the hideously slippery incline thrust the machine ahead with increasing speed. She dared not apply the brakes suddenly, and the heavy car slid downward faster and faster, over a greasy road through ghostly lanes into thick black fog.

Katie knew all at once that she was definitely alarmed, and in the same instant that Paul beside her had grown taut, also, with suspense. Then in the very nick of time she caught a faint reflection of lights on a curving bit of road, turned, caught a glancing reflection again from a concrete railing and pulled harder, missed the railing, felt for a lightning instant the sliding of tires, and then to her infinite relief the car straightened and rolled safely onto the bridge.

"That's that," she said.

Paul did not reply. And Katie thought: There's still this terribly steep bit of road beyond the bridge. The worst bit. I'm on it now. The car's sliding. I'm going too fast. If I only dared brake—but a skid—straight into the ravine—this damned ravine—the car's too heavy—the road's too slippery——

"Why, look!" cried Paul. "There's a light in the summerhouse."

Katie remembered that.

She remembered too, but vaguely and chaotically, how his voice changed and cracked madly upward and he shouted:

"Stop! Katie! My God! Stop!"

But it was too late. It was forever too late.

The dark moving object which rose so suddenly into the dim area of light went down as suddenly before that great black hood.

Katie knew that Paul was shouting. He was reaching across her and clutching and tugging at the hand-brake. Her feet were pressing the clutch and footbrake through the floor. Someone screamed, but she never knew whether the scream came from her own throat or from somewhere under that heavy great car.

It would not stop. It would not stop.

The road was rough, and the car jolted twice.

Then it had skidded madly sidewise and lurched and swerved to a stop.

Paul was out in the darkness and running back into the black, sinister fog. Katie's body was getting out of the car, too. Its feet were stumbling and slipping upward through damp darkness. It took a long time to return over that bit of narrow road—so terribly short to cover the immeasurable distance it had covered in one fearful moment.

Then she found Paul, a black blur with a white face, and she was suddenly Katie again and no longer a dumb ineffectual organism climbing a slippery road that had no end.

"*Paul!*"

"Go back, Katie. You can't do anything."

"*Paul!*"

"I tell you, go back."

"Who is it?"

"I can't tell. I think it's Charlotte."

Katie knew that Paul was kneeling. She crouched down, too, above a dark, moveless heap. But it was so dark. So dark.

"Paul—is she——"

"She's dead, Katie."

Darkness became light for Katie. The black swirling walls were dotted and whirling with pinwheels of flashing fire that spun all around her. The road was no longer solid under her feet; it rocked furiously and turned and spun with the pinwheels.

"Steady, Katie." Paul was standing and gripping her arms until the pain of it dragged her back from the whirling lights and into a terrible world of darkness and fog and Charlotte dead at her feet. Charlotte who had hated her. Charlotte whom she had killed.

"Look here. You've got to go for help. I'll stay here in case—you've got to go. Get a doctor. There might be a chance, you know, if you hurry. Take the path through the park, it's shorter. Hurry."

Down the slippery road, past the deadly black bulk standing there with its lights shining faintly; then off the road and groping for and finding the turf path. Into the park and running, stumbling, slipping, fighting for breath.

The path was a thick black cavern, close and blind and bound by fog. She could not see. She could not feel. Only now and then something brushed her face or clutched at her shoulder and then was left in the darkness. It was almost as if someone were there, running soundlessly with her.

With incredible suddenness she rounded a hedge, and there was the house with dim blotches of light showing windows. She took a last sobbing breath and ran across the graveled terrace, flung open the wide front door, and stumbled into the vestibule.

Across the vestibule, in the room with the ferns, a man rose at her entrance. He was a slender man, with a lithe, delicately rounded body and a grace and neatness of motion that would have done credit to a ballet dancer. His name was Clarence Siskinson, he was almost entirely sober although somewhat impatiently waiting a before-dinner cocktail then under preparation in the pantry, and he rose from a black wicker chair which creaked dismally.

"Katie!" he cried. "What is it! And, my God, what have you done to your face?"

CHAPTER III

MINA PETRIE's somber house forbade the loosening of emotions which permits disorder. Perhaps that is why the hours immediately following Charlotte Weinberg's death proceeded, after the first few moments, with a kind of order. It was almost as if the whole thing had been in some ghastly fashion rehearsed.

On the surface, that is, and after the first terrible moments.

Underneath that orderliness was something quite different.

Katie felt that dimly, even then and through the helpless despair of making them understand that they must call a doctor, that they must hurry, that it was Charlotte, that she was at the bridge, that she was——

". . . hurt," sobbed Katie, striving for coherence. ". . . hurt! . . ."

Then all at once Clarence was twinkling about, running here, running there, calling Jenks, the houseman, calling a maid, shouting for the chauffeur, demanding the doctor's telephone number. And Fanny was floating down the stairway, wisps of green chiffon and white hair flying, and beads and bracelets jingling, and pausing to lean over the railing so that the light fell full on her strong-featured, florid face, and her shining cobalt-blue eyes.

"Hush—Mina will hear you! What's happened? And what have you got on your face, Katie?"

It was Fanny, however, who knew what to do and who was always very good at telling other people what to do. The doctor was called at once, the right and nearest one, who was also the family physician. Clarence was dispatched immediately with smelling salts and brandy and a terse but stern admonition from Fanny regarding the disposition of the latter. Jenks and the chauffeur vanished with blankets and a swiftly improvised stretcher, and Melissa, the Negro housemaid, was sent to turn down Charlotte's bed and prepare things for the doctor.

"Hot water," said Fanny. "Bandages. Everything. Hurry." Her words were vague but her voice and long, gesturing hands were not and Melissa vanished, too. It was all swift, hurried and, with Fanny at the helm, orderly.

It was Fanny, too, who telephoned for Steven and did not succeed in finding him. Fanny who ordered the excited cook, peering agitatedly from the dining-room door, to delay dinner for the rest of them but to prepare Madame Petrie's meal at the usual time.

"And on no account may Madame Petrie be permitted to hear anything of the accident."

"No, ma'am," said the cook and lingered. "Is she dead, ma'am?"

Fanny glanced at Katie, dazed and numb and sick, pushing her tumbled hair back from her face with shaking hands.

"I'm sure I hope not," said Fanny. "A doctor is on the way. Bring me a wet towel, Hilda. Good heavens, Katie, how did you get so scratched and dirty?"

"Coming through the park."

"But, good gracious, did you fall? Or bump into every tree in it? Here's a bruise on your forehead. And a long scratch. And even grease. Let me rub harder. Hold still. Now I'll just pat it dry. Stop that shaking, Katie. Pull yourself together. You must have lost your hat—oh, there it is on the floor. Katie, sit there quiet for a moment."

The green wisps of chiffon floated into the dining room and presently returned.

"So long as Clarence doesn't see this," said Fanny absently. "Here, Katie, drink this." She held a small glass to Katie's lips. It sent up a pungent stinging odor, and Katie obeyed and felt for a moment sick and dizzy and then miraculously clear-headed and warm again.

"That's better," said Fanny. "It does have its uses, after all. Now I'll just telephone to Steven again. He's got a head on his shoulders, even," said Fanny dubiously, "if he is an artist. Painter, I believe, he calls it. And no sense to that, either," she concluded obscurely and went to the telephone.

Fanny's kind, said one part of Katie's mind. She's trying to keep me from thinking. Why don't they come! Charlotte's dead—Charlotte's dead. She couldn't have lived. The car is so heavy—so terribly heavy—and it wouldn't stop.

Above Fanny's wild white hair, above her dangling earrings, a mirror kept its secret. It reflected green ferns and black wicker chairs and a long length of dining room beyond a wide door—a room no longer dark and cavernous but gleaming now with lights in a crystal chandelier and shining white linen and flowers on a table already laid with silver. Nearer it reflected a tea service still standing on a small table near the ferns. It reflected Katie's own tossed dark hair and white face and blue eyes that were dark and wide with horror in their depths.

It reflected many things, but still it kept secret a thing it knew.

And then before Fanny and her trailing green chiffons had finished with the telephone it began to reflect another scene, and Fanny dropped the telephone and rose.

There were figures moving, a burden wrapped in blankets which was lowered gently—as gently as if the burden could still feel ungentle motion—on the chaise-longue below the stairway. There were men's faces with moving, jerky mouths; there was a familiar face, the doctor, whose lips moved more deliberately and precisely than the others and who came very near his own reflection when he approached the desk and took the telephone and called a number. Clarence was suddenly at his side, reflected too in the mirror's secret depths.

"The police!" cried Clarence.

"Yes, of course," said Dr. Mannsen coolly. "They've got to be notified. Miss Warren will be exonerated. She couldn't have helped it. Besides, Paul Duchane can testify for her at the inquest."

"Inquest——" said Katie in a choked voice.

"Only a matter of form," said the doctor briskly, but, somehow, kindly. "Don't let this thing get a grip on you, Miss Warren. Accidents will happen. A night like this is always bad. Hello—hello—desk sergeant? This is Dr. Mannsen——"

"Don't talk so loud," said Fanny sharply. "You'll rouse Madame Petrie."

"There's been an accident," went on Dr. Mannsen. "I'm calling from the Petrie place. What? Why, it's— what is this number?"

Clarence and Fanny and Jenks supplied it simultaneously. Katie glanced at Paul, who was standing near the chaise-longue; he had flung his hat and coat over the stair railing, and his olive face looked taut with excitement. Jenks, the sedate little houseman, his cheek curiously swollen and his coat wrinkled and muddy, was standing there, too. And in the shadow of the vestibule was the chauffeur, his eyes glittering. All of them, Fanny and Paul and Clarence and the two servants, had a singular likeness of expression. They were, Katie realized with a kind of dull shock, looking at her with a kind of excited strained sympathy. But Katie, after her first glimpse of that inert, blanketed burden, had not needed to ask a question.

". . . and be careful when you get into the grounds," the doctor was saying in the telephone. "There's a steep curve and a bridge and the road is icy. Just below the bridge is where the accident happened. Yes. Yes—I'll wait."

He put down the telephone and turned.

"We'd better get that car out of the way."

"I'll go," said Paul.

"Let the chauffeur do it. You stay here. I'm going to give Miss Warren something she needs, and you look like you need a pick-me-up too. Sit down, both of you."

The chauffeur stepped forward anxiously.

"Shall I put the car in the garage, sir?" he inquired.

"Better not," said Dr. Mannsen. "Just push it out from the road a bit. But leave it there so the police can see what's happened. Where's my bag? Now then, young lady—h'm, pulse fairly strong."

"I gave her some brandy," said Fanny, with a sharply defiant look at Clarence.

Fanny, always resourceful, and Dr. Mannsen, cool and accustomed to death, somehow kept things sane during those waiting moments. Clarence disappeared mysteriously into the dining room. Paul strolled to the winking black windows and stood there with his back to the room, smoking.

And on the chaise-longue was a thing that was Charlotte. And yet could not be Charlotte, for Charlotte was never still.

It was a relief when the police arrived and the mirror caught strange faces and broad blue shoulders with bright metal shields.

Dr. Mannsen explained the situation briefly. "So you see, Lieutenant, just how it happened," he concluded.

"Sergeant. Sergeant Caldwell, it is. Yes. We stopped there below the bridge to look things over. Your chauffeur—" with a glance at Fanny—"was there and showed us. We left the police car just outside the gate so we wouldn't mess up any tire tracks. Now let me get these names straight."

He looked worriedly at a small notebook in his hand. He was a large man, not tall but heavy-set, with a couple of extra chins and big, pale eyes which looked but were seldom surprised. He fished for a pencil from an inside pocket, touched it to his tongue, and started to write.

"What's your name, miss?"

Katie's heart leaped. She had been wondering what they would do—why they didn't do more than just lift a corner of the blanket on the chaise-longue for an instant—what would be next.

"Katie Warren," she said in a voice that seemed to belong to someone else.

"Residence?"

"Why, I—I live here. Now."

He wrote laboriously, looked up at her and said unexpectedly:

"How long have you lived here?"

"Not—very long. A few months."

"You mean this is your home?"

"Well—you see," Katie hesitated, and then, helplessly and because there was nothing else to do, explained: "You see, my—my business went all to pieces. I didn't have anything left. Aunt Mina—that is, Madame Petrie—asked me to come and live here for a while."

"What was your business?"

"I sold bonds."

Sergeant Caldwell's pale eyes favored her with a long look. Katie had seen that look often since money grew scarce. It was tinged with suspicion.

"What firm?"

She told him.

"This Mrs. Petrie—she's your aunt?" he indicated Fanny.

"No. That is, that isn't Madame Petrie. She's upstairs. And she's not my aunt, really."

Sergeant Caldwell looked blank, and Fanny jingled her bracelets and was efficient.

"I am not Madame Petrie. I am Madame Petrie's cousin, Mrs. Siskinson."

"Is Madame Petrie here?"

"She's here, yes, but she's ill. She is, in fact, dying. She must not be disturbed."

"Well, no. Not if she's dying," said the sergeant slowly and probably innocently. But Fanny bridled.

"Is all this necessary, Sergeant. Are we going to leave poor Charlotte there much longer?"

"The ambulance is on the way. What's your name again, if you please, ma'am?"

"I'm Fanny Siskinson. Mrs. Clarence Siskinson."

"Any relation to the deceased?"

"No. I am a cousin of Madame Petrie's on her mother's side. Charlotte—Charlotte Weinberg—was on the other side of the house. The Weinbergs."

Sergeant Caldwell repeated: "Char—lotte—Wein—berg," and wet his pencil and wrote slowly.

"Miss Weinberg," went on Fanny, "is—was—Madame Petrie's companion. That is, she was secretary, housekeeper, and friend. Madame Petrie has been ill for a long time."

"I see. How long had Miss Weinberg lived here?"

Fanny knew exactly how long.

"Sixteen years in May."

"Thank you, Mrs. Siskinson. Now, if you want to send any telegrams to—er—notify the relatives, you may go and do it now while I talk a little to Miss Warren."

"I'll stay here," said Fanny succinctly. "And anyway, Charlotte had no other relatives."

"Just as you please," said Sergeant Caldwell. "Now then, Miss Warren, were you driving your own car?"

"No. It belongs to Madame Petrie. She told me to take it to town this afternoon. I went to a concert."

"Used to driving a car, are you?"

"Yes, I've driven for—oh—years."

"Ever had any accidents?"

"No. That is, nothing serious."

"Have you driven this particular car before this afternoon?"

"Yes. It was easy to handle. Always. Until to-night." Katie tried to hold her back and her hands rigid enough to quell small tremulous shivers that were creeping over her. Resolutely she forced herself to meet Sergeant Caldwell's pale, surprised gaze.

He was only a man, thick and ponderous, with three chins and a little black notebook. It was, then, the force that his blue uniform represented that made him a forbidding figure. Katie felt, under that look, a strange, unjustifiable sense of guilt, as if she must defend herself against some cold, mysterious, but authoritative menace.

In the little pause Jenks appeared and glided across the room toward Fanny. He had managed to change to a fresh coat, but his cheek was still swollen and hot-looking.

"The ambulance is here, madame," he said. "It's at the side door."

Fanny glanced at Sergeant Caldwell.

"I'll see them," said he.

The customs called civilized operate completely and swiftly to shield a natural thing. In a few moments it was all over. Two men had entered quietly and, still quietly and decorously, had carried away on a sheet-covered stretcher the thing that so short a time before had been Charlotte Weinberg. Had carried it out and away from the house she had ruled in its smallest detail for sixteen years.

The mirror reflected briefly the long white stretcher, and then that page was turned. Never again would it reflect as it had so constantly during those years Charlotte's small rouged and powdered face, her elaborate dark curls, her darting eyes under their shadowed and wrinkled lids, her small, wiry, energetic figure.

At the door of the butler's pantry the small procession passed a woman who leaned to look curiously at the form on the stretcher and then went back to cooking the dinner that Charlotte had ordered. At the side door Jenks stood impassive in his clean white coat, never dreaming that the hot small lump in his cheek which sent out shooting stabs of pain had its own place in the strange pattern of events—a pattern of which the stretcher which he watched the two men slide into the long, gray ambulance was only a part. A pattern whose dreadful weaving had just begun.

Jenks, however, sighed and shivered. It was colder and sleeting now in good earnest. He closed the door and bolted it and wondered if oil of cloves would help his tooth. Miss Charlotte might have some in her medicine chest. No. *No!* Miss Charlotte was dead.

And from the terrace a man hurrying along with the sleet in his face caught a shadowy glimpse of the long, gray ambulance backing and turning, ghostly and strange in the shadows, and he paused sharply to look and then ran across the terrace and steps and flung open the wide door.

Everyone in the lounge jerked toward that furiously opened door. Steven Petrie, tall and breathless, his eyes gleaming under his low hatbrim, strode across the vestibule.

"What's happened?" he cried. "Is it Aunt Mina?"

No one answered. Katie wanted to speak, and her throat felt numb.

His gray gaze took in something of the strained atmosphere. Afterward Katie was to remember the change in his face, the way it suddenly became tight and rather grim and his eyes guarded.

He turned and quite deliberately took off his coat and hat, tossing them upon a chair. He gave a singular impression of knowing, without being told, what had happened. He didn't know, however, for he turned then again toward them.

"Why are these policemen here?" he said.

CHAPTER IV

THEN everyone spoke at once. Everyone but Katie.

She sat listening, watching Steven's face as he, too, listened, and then asked a few terse questions.

He listened gravely to the all too definite answers and turned to look at Katie and then suddenly walked toward her.

He said nothing, only stood there at her side. The mirror all at once caught and added to its pattern a lean face, young and brown, blond hair that glowed from the light above, dark gray eyes that shone from under level, rather stern eyebrows. It was a good face and head, built on good bones; a thoughtful face with a mouth that knew the good things and yet knew discipline, too.

And, just then, it was a face that was guarded in every muscle and every line.

"You're sure Aunt Mina doesn't know?" he asked finally, addressing the doctor.

"Unless she has heard some of the commotion. Mrs. Siskinson thought she had better not know to-night, and I heartily agree. That is," added Dr. Mannsen, "if it is possible to keep it from her."

"Where is she?"

"Mina? Why, upstairs, of course," said Fanny. "Where have you been, Steven?"

Steven looked at her absently.

"At home."

"But I've been telephoning steadily and no one answered."

There was a barely perceptible pause. Katie, indeed, was not certain that Steven had hesitated at all before he replied:

"But naturally. It took me a long time to drive out here. The roads are terrible. Can't see where you are going."

Sergeant Caldwell stirred restively.

"I'll get on with my report, if you don't mind," he said.

"Oh, yes, of course, Sergeant." There was a long divan against the wall just behind Katie's chair, and Steven turned and sat down, and Sergeant Caldwell coughed.

"All right now, Miss Warren. Will you tell me, please, just what happened?"

"It—you see, I couldn't stop the car," said Katie. "I didn't see Charlotte at all until just as she—went down."

"Now, now, Miss Warren," said Sergeant Caldwell, not unkindly. "Don't hurry. Suppose you begin at the beginning. You say you went to a concert. Mr. Duchane went to the concert, too?"

"No. I just happened to meet him as I was starting home. I offered him a lift."

"Don't you drive, Mr. Duchane?"

Paul swung around from the window and flicked the end of his cigarette toward an ashtray.

"Why, yes, of course, Sergeant," he said. "When I saw how bad it was going to be, I offered to do the driving. But Miss Warren preferred to drive herself. I think," added Paul gracefully, "that she felt a kind of personal responsibility about getting the machine safely home herself. After all, Madame Petrie had loaned it to her, not to me."

"Yes, Paul offered to drive," said Katie. "I wish ——" Her voice wavered upward, and she caught herself sharply on the very verge of sobbing hysteria. Steven leaned forward so his gray tweed shoulder almost touched her own shoulder and, although she did not look away from Sergeant Caldwell's pale eyes, still she was conscious of Steven's presence there, and she fought down the ache in her throat which meant tears.

"Now then, Miss Warren, you drove all the way out here through the traffic. Go on from the time you entered the private drive."

"Well, the gate was closed, and I stopped and Paul got out and opened it. It was dark and foggy, and there was sleet, too, freezing on the windshield."

"Did you close the gate after you had passed through it?"

"Yes. That is, Paul did. He tried, then, to clean the sleet off the lights, but they were no better. Then he got into the car again, and I started down the road to the ravine and the bridge."

"You were going slowly?"

"Yes. Very slowly. I was in low gear. But the car kept going faster and faster, and I didn't dare use the footbrake for fear I would skid into the ravine. I could scarcely see anything. But I did manage to make the turn at the bridge, and I got safely on it." Her voice had begun to shake again.

"Take your time, Miss Warren. No hurry." Sergeant Caldwell was writing laboriously in his little notebook.

"Well, it was just as I passed the bridge and started down that steep dangerous little curve that it happened. I was just leaving the bridge when Paul said something—something about the summerhouse—and then shouted to me to stop and—and then there was something dark, moving there just ahead of the machine. And then I—I tried to stop and I couldn't ——"

Her voice was shaking now desperately. Her hands, too. But she would not look away from Sergeant Caldwell until Steven leaned forward and took her hands firmly in his own clasp.

"Look at me, Katie. No, no, look at *me*. Now, Katie, it's hard, but he's got to know all about it. Answer me. Could you tell what it was that was moving in the lights ahead of the car?"

"No. Only that it was some person moving."

"Did you know who it was?"

"No. There wasn't time."

"What did you do?"

"I—I tried to stop."

"You mean you put your foot on the brake?"

"Yes. Both feet on clutch and brake as hard as I could. I stood on them—braced myself against the seat. Paul tried to help. He reached across me for the handbrake."

"Across?" inquired Sergeant Caldwell quickly and then answered himself: "That's right. The handbrake's on the left."

Steven's intent eyes held Katie when she would have turned again toward the sergeant.

"Did you turn the wheel in an effort to avoid striking the person in the road?" asked Steven.

Katie thought of that frantic moment.

"I think so. But there wasn't time."

"Then Charlotte was directly in the path of the car?"

"Yes. The road is narrow, you know."

"Which way was she going? Toward you or away from you?"

"I—I don't know. I can't remember anything but a dark figure just before the car—I know it was moving and that is all."

"About how far ahead of the car could you see? I mean, about how many feet would you say the lights penetrated the fog?"

If she only knew! There was only that memory of driving blindly, feeling her way along.

"I don't know. It seemed to me that I was driving blindfolded."

Steven looked at Paul.

"What would you say, Paul?"

Paul's fingers caressed his soft black mustache indecisively.

"Why, really, I can't say. It's as Katie said—it was like driving blindfolded. We couldn't see a thing. Just the glow ahead of the car—now and then a glimmer of lights on the wet road. I didn't see Charlotte at all until just a second or two before the car struck her. It's as Katie said. There was just someone moving there in the road, and I shouted to Katie to stop and reached for the handbrake. But there was nothing either of us could do. It was—all over before we could stop. Katie was driving very slowly and carefully. But it was downhill and the road like grease. And you know how heavy that car is."

"Then you didn't recognize Charlotte either?" asked Steven, his hand still holding Katie's own hands tightly.

Paul's beautifully tailored shoulders rose in a faint shrug.

"No. We only knew someone was there in the road."

Sergeant Caldwell said suddenly:

"How was the footbrake, Miss Warren? Working all right?"

"Perfectly," said Katie.

"You must have used it a good bit driving out from town, you know. It was still tight when you stopped at the gate?"

"Oh, yes," said Katie hopelessly.

"It seemed in excellent working order when I looked at the car just now. Also the steering gear." He paused and added rather wistfully: "A beautiful car.—Now, Mr. Duchane, what did you do when the car finally stopped?"

"I ran back along the road. It was dark. I found a—body there in the road but couldn't tell exactly who it was, although I thought it was Charlotte. I knew that it was—dead."

"How did you know?"

"Well, I——" Paul thrust his hands into his pockets suddenly, although his olive face remained calm and his voice pleasant and easy. "There wasn't any sound, you know. And then I groped around, trying to find a heartbeat. And my eyes got more accustomed to the darkness. And, well, I just knew she was dead. I thought it was Charlotte—her hair—you know. And the—the ribbon around her throat."

Katie's hands were clinging to Steven's warm hands, and she knew it and let them cling.

Paul moved uneasily and drew out another cigarette and lit it, and the tiny flame from the lighter glowed against his dark face and half-closed dark eyes. The flame shook a little, and all at once Fanny uttered a strangled kind of cough that was like a sob.

One of the waiting, solid blue columns that were policemen stirred, too, rather uneasily and shot a look at its fellow column which was unmoved.

"Then," went on Paul through a cloud of blue smoke, "then I sent Katie for help. I stayed there. Charlotte didn't move or make any sound. That's all, except that Katie couldn't have helped it. No human power could have stopped that car before it struck Charlotte."

"You stopped in exactly sixteen feet," said Sergeant Caldwell dryly, looking at his notebook, "I measured." He turned with a kind of congratulatory air to Katie. "That shows both that you were going very slowly and that you didn't lose your head."

He rose suddenly, closed his notebook, and slipped it into an inside pocket. A faint motion went over the room that was like a sigh.

Steven's eyes said something comforting to Katie before he released her hands and stood. Dr. Mannsen rose, too, and picked up his bag. Katie thought incredulously: Is it over? Is that all?

"I think that's about all," said Sergeant Caldwell.

"I'll report it just as it happened. Don't think you need to worry, Miss Warren. Guess it couldn't be helped."

"Worry!" said Katie inadequately. "Oh—it's horrible—" Her voice choked and stopped again, and she pressed both hands to her throat to relieve that dreadful ache of repressed sobs.

Sergeant Caldwell gave her a puzzled look.

"Oh, I didn't mean that," he said easily. "I was thinking of something else. There's a charge of manslaughter sometimes with reckless driving, you know."

"*Oh*—" Katie dropped her hands from her throat. She sprang to her feet, desperately searching Sergeant Caldwell's large surprised face. This was the meaning of the menace she felt. "You can't believe I did it purposely! You *can't* think that!"

"No, no, no! Didn't I just tell you not to worry? Sit down again. I know it was an accident. Everything points that way. That's why I told you not to worry. Why, I'm going to report it accident. Of course, I'll have to wait to get the report from the medical examiner."

Katie turned instinctively to Steven for reassurance. Afterward she realized that she was probably the only person in the room who saw the swift dark flicker in his eyes, that queer little flash of apprehension, of anxiety that was like—so dreadfully like—fear. Then it was gone and Steven's face was guarded and still again, and Katie realized that the doctor was addressing her.

". . . that'll be all right," he was saying comfortably. "There's only one report the medical examiner can make. Now then, I'm going to leave an opiate for

you, young lady. And some professional advice. You
eat some dinner, rest a while, take a long tepid bath
and two of the capsules and then bed for you. In the
morning you'll feel better." Dr. Mannsen turned to
Fanny. "See that she does all that," he said cheerfully.
"Now then—if that's all——"

"Oh, sure, Doctor. Go ahead," said Sergeant Caldwell readily. "Good-night, and thanks."

There was a little subdued confusion at the door
and a sweeping breath of damp, cold air, and then he
was gone.

But Sergeant Caldwell and the two stalwart blue
columns remained.

"One more thing," said Sergeant Caldwell slowly,
his surprised eyes, which were actually never surprised,
traveling very observantly from one to another.
"What about the deceased? Where was she going?
She wasn't dressed for the street. And you haven't
very near neighbors. She wore only a coat—no hat, no
gloves, no pocketbook. I shouldn't think," said Sergeant Caldwell with increased deliberation, "that she
would go out for a stroll on a night like this."

No one answered.

All at once the green ferns, the funereal wicker
chairs, the black windows were no quieter than the
people in the room. It was as if a moving picture reel
unwinding had suddenly stuck so that every breath,
every flicker of an eyelash, was held arrested and
transfixed.

Katie, standing so close to Steven, felt that he was
not breathing. Paul held a cigarette at his lips but did
not open his mouth to receive it. Fanny's green chiffons
were poised as if in suspended flight, and her bright

blue eyes blazed at the sergeant but did not wink. Even Jenks, who had bent to straighten a rug in the vestibule, checked himself, stooping, with his arms outstretched, to listen.

And just under the stairway the more stolid of the silent blue columns which had accompanied Sergeant Caldwell watched his superior with small, clear eyes.

Damn queer, he thought. That red-faced woman with the beads looks scared. Wonder where she got all those beads. And that young fella in gray looks kinda sick. Bet he's scared, too. But you can't tell much about fellas like him. Good-looking girl. She's scared, too. All of 'em scared. But none of 'em shedding any tears. Helluva place, this is. Looks like an undertaking parlor. If this is the way these rich folks live . . . His thoughts went pleasantly to a warm, bright little apartment waiting for him on the west side. There would be a radio going loudly, and a smell of cooking, and he wished Sergeant Caldwell would finish whatever he was getting at and leave.

"Doesn't anyone know where Miss Weinberg was going?" said Sergeant Caldwell. "Did no one see her leave?"

The reel was unstuck and moving again. Paul's lips opened for the cigarette, and Fanny floated nearer.

"I don't know," she said. "Jenks, do you?"

Jenks pulled the rug straight with a swift motion and rose. But Jenks did not know.

Neither, it developed, did anyone else know.

"We didn't even have tea together as usual," offered Fanny at last. "I'd been for a walk on the beach and was delayed by the fog. It was five o'clock when I came in. Charlotte wasn't here, and the tea was cold.

That is, I mean, she wasn't here in this room, where we usually have tea. I don't know where she was. Jenks usually serves tea between four-thirty and five."

Jenks in the background opened his mouth and closed it again, and Fanny twisted her long, strong hands among green beads that looked like jade but were not and went on without pause:

"I didn't order more tea. I went straight to my room. And I saw nothing of Charlotte."

Sergeant Caldwell had crossed again to the low table which held cups and a teapot and a covered dish of sandwiches. He stood there for a moment, and it seemed to Katie that just for an instant the look of surprise in his face became a bit fixed and real. If so, however, he kept the source of it to himself. He turned toward them again.

"Well, I guess that's all," he said. "It's just one of those accidents. God knows there's plenty of them when roads are what they are tonight. Don't you worry, Miss Warren," he said rather kindly to Katie. "You may have to attend the inquest. But don't worry." To Katie's vague astonishment he reached out a thick hand to pat her arm clumsily and impersonally as he might pat a troubled child.

"O'Brien. Getch."

The solid blue columns leaped to life. Sergeant Caldwell paused at the doorway to give the room and its occupants a last surprised look.

"I may need some more information. May have to call you," he said. There was a confusion of words from Fanny, and Steven was crossing the room swiftly and saying, "Good-night, Sergeant."

Then the outside door closed under Jenks's sedate

hands, the blue uniforms were gone, and Katie looked dazedly about her, and because the chair at the desk was nearest, sat down there. It was just then that Clarence Siskinson appeared in the dining-room doorway, wavered there a second or two, and came on into the room.

He was vaguely unsteady, and his neat, graceful legs had difficulty rounding the divan.

"Thought," said Clarence delicately. "Thought I'd jus' stay 'way till polishe were gone."

"Clarence!" said Fanny in a terrible voice.

"Didn' feel," said Clarence, "like seeing 'em. Didn' want them to see me."

"And rightly," said Fanny, biting off the words. "You're not fit to be seen."

"Now, Fanny," said Clarence with a good-natured wave of a small hand, "don't talk like that. You don't know what I've got. What I've found."

There was under his hazy blandness a curious ring of something significant. For a moment no one spoke. Finally Fanny said, smartly enough but still with a trace of indecision:

"It's plain enough what you've found, Clarence Siskinson."

"Don't call me Clarence Sish—Shish—Shush———" He gave up gracefully, with another good-natured wave of his small hand. "Hell of a name, anyway. But don't call me that. Not that way. And you *don't* know," said Clarence blandly, "what I've found. But I know. And I'm going to tell you. I'm going to tell you," said Clarence, making his motive clear, "because I think you ought to know. I found something. I found it in one of Charlotte's hands. And I took it out. Poor

Charlotte! I know you never liked her, Fanny. And she—she never liked me, Charlotte didn't!" He sighed. "But all the shame it's a same—a shame, I mean——"

The air was alive and electric. Fanny's eyes were blazing bright blue fire down into Clarence's bland face.

"Clarence, what are you talking about?"

"About Charlotte," he said with suddenly peevish dignity. "About the hair I found in her hand. Hair. Black hair." He paused to look at the frozen white faces about him and added with owlish gravity: "You know what I think? I think Charlotte was murdered. That's what I think. M-murdered."

CHAPTER V

AGAIN the reel stuck, and again the mirror over the desk caught and held forever in its secret depths a poignant second of suspended animation.

Then Fanny swirled to the divan and caught Clarence's elegantly tailored shoulders in the nervous grip of her strong, long hands, and the jewels on them flashed and she cried:

"What hair? Whose hair? Where is it? What did you do with it? Clarence Siskinson, you're drunk. You don't know what you're talking about."

"I'm drunk," assented Clarence readily. "But I know what I'm talking about. Stop shaking me, Fanny. You make me dizzy."

"Look here, Clarence, what do you mean?" It was Paul, easy and nonchalant but with a kind of sharp thread of anxiety cutting through and under the elaborate casualness of his words. He had strolled to the divan to stare, as they were all staring, at the graceful, half-reclining figure. Paul's dark eyes, veiled by his long dark eyelashes and a wisp of blue smoke, went to Fanny's strong, florid face.

"How do you manage him when he's like this, Fanny?"

"I don't," snapped Fanny irritably but still worriedly. "He's just plain drunk. He doesn't know what he's saying."

"Maybe he has found something. Look here, Clar-

ence," said Paul persuasively, "do you mean that you
found hair—*hair*—in Charlotte's hand? Some hair,"
said Paul pleasantly, "or a hair?"

"Hair," said Clarence, "just hair." He gestured
vaguely. "A bunch of it."

"Black?" insisted Paul smoothly but still with a
kind of undertone of sharp anxiety.

"All black," said Clarence with the air of a savant.
"Completely black."

There was a brief, thoughtful silence as the little
circle stared perplexedly and anxiously down at
Clarence, who was regarding the toe of one neat shoe
with the utmost detachment.

The silence grew oppressive. After all, Clarence had
said something—made some charge—it was out-
rageous, a drunken fancy. But still——

"Let me see the hair," said Fanny suddenly. "Have
you got it?"

"M'h'm," said Clarence drowsily. "But I'm not
going to give it to you."

"He's about gone, Fanny," said Steven quietly. "I
don't think he knows what he's saying."

"Steven, my boy, I know all about it. You see if I'm
not right. Time'll tell."

"Shall I get him up to his room, Fanny?" offered
Steven. Queer, thought one part of Katie's mind, that
Steven spoke so quietly and yet looked so grim.

Fanny gave Steven a look of troubled and rare indecision, and her long, capable hands came very near
to wringing themselves. It was like Clarence, said her
look, to go and get himself drunk at a time like this.

"And then," she said aloud, "for him to talk of
murder."

Katie found herself speaking. "But she couldn't have been murdered," she was saying very steadily. "I —I ran over her. She couldn't have been murdered."

"Katie, Katie!" said Steven gently. "Are you going to let Clarence's half-witted maunderings worry you? Certainly Charlotte wasn't murdered. A bit of hair in her hand would mean nothing, even if it were actually there, which I doubt. Anyway, who would murder Charlotte?"

Who would murder Charlotte? The ferns could have told him. The black wicker chairs could have told him. The mirror could have told him.

Clarence was blinking.

"Steven, my boy," he said, shaking his head regretfully and still managing by some miracle of tongue to remain intelligible, "you're too young. You and Paul, both too young. You don't know much. I've got that hair. And it was in her hand. All clenched together when I tried to rub her wrist. And if you ask me—" he looked suddenly sly and knowing and his voice lowered secretively—"if you ask me, there were plenty of people who would murder Charlotte." He paused and added pensively: "That was a woman that needed murdering."

"*Clarence!*" said Fanny in a strangled way.

"Hush——" Paul spoke sharply. He was staring up toward the stairway, and he dropped his cigarette and started forwards: "Aunt Mina!"

"Aunt Mina!" Steven whirled and also started forward. Fanny cried: "Good heavens!" and jingled as she hurried to pull out the chaise-longue and fluff up pillows. Clarence made an effort to stand and failed and sat upright. And Katie remained where she was;

she felt curiously detached, as if she were only a distant spectator, watching the whole scene.

Step by step two black-clad figures were descending the stairway. It was truly Mina Petrie, leaning heavily on the arm of a Negro maid. Mina herself, a thick, squat figure, was looking directly downward, her head bent in order to watch every step below her slow feet. But the maid flashed a liquid dark glance that was half defense, half appeal toward the faces below.

Katie, meeting the look, felt through her curious detachment something of the little shock she always felt when she looked at the Negro maid, Melissa.

She was a tall woman, with long, rangy bones and warm brown flesh. Her long, slow motions were beautiful in their easy, silent grace. She had a singular way of effacing herself as an animal does; she was just there, a part of the house, calm and tranquil, with a tread like velvet. It was almost as if a quiet, somewhat wistful and very humble primitive being had got itself into black clothes and a white cap and apron and was going about doing household tasks—and doing them well, else Charlotte would never have permitted Melissa to remain in the house—and all the time asking only for food and shelter and a modicum of kindness.

Katie wondered sometimes if a share of that humility was due to the thing that shocked you so. And that was Melissa's hair. She was, perhaps, a quadroon, and by some strange mingling of blood streams her warm brown face was spattered with freckles, her large, soft brown eyes had a reddish cast, and her crinkly, woolly hair was a bright flaming red.

Clarence looked up and in his befuddled state of

mind for once forgot that he was an agreeable, neat, and graceful little gentleman with nice manners. For he pointed upward and chuckled and said:

"There it is. That's just like the hair I found in Charlotte's hand. Fuzzy. Like Melissa's hair. Like Melissa's hair if it was black as it ought to be. Believe it or not, Charlotte was murdered."

"Clarence!" Fanny jerked out the word in a hoarse whisper. Her strong hands strained as if they would like to be at Clarence's bibulous throat. She said in cold anger: "Will you hush!"

But it was too late. Both black figures halted abruptly. The short, squat one raised her head.

No one moved. Katie thought it likely that no one breathed. Clarence belatedly perceived the enormity of what he had said and blinked and was silent.

Then Paul sprang upward to meet Mina, offering his arm in the warmly flattering manner with which Paul managed to invest his slightest gesture.

But Mina brushed him away with one lift of her thick white hand from its black draperies.

Her white face, with its skin stretched tightly over high cheekbones and a long chin, was a frame for two feverish black eyes. Her black hair, taken up so tightly that it seemed to pull the tight white skin over her temples, was wound in a big bun on top of her head. Habitually her head sunk a little between thick shoulders which were hunched a bit above a back as rounded as if she had worked terribly hard during most of her life—which, as a matter of fact, was not true.

Now her burning dark gaze swept the faces below and she said:

"Why have there been so many people in and out

of this house? What is Clarence talking about? What does he mean?" Her voice was harsh and had no resonant undertones, for it was always flat and without flexibility. It was the voice of a person long and entirely deaf, although Mina Petrie had, actually, very keen hearing. She added: "Why did he speak of murder?"

Fanny swirled forward and missed by a fractional inch Friquet, the great blue Persian cat, who had drifted like a shadow down the stairway in Mina's wake and was crossing the room on velvet, leisurely feet. There was a short, startled squawk from the cat, a flash of great, shining eyes and an enormous blue tail, and Fanny said violently:

"Clarence is drunk. Clarence does not know what he is saying. He is not responsible. Steven is going to put him to bed."

Friquet curved lightly to the desk and sat there staring wickedly at Fanny, and Mina stared at Fanny, too, and said with dogged persistence in her flat voice:

"What did he mean by somebody being murdered? Who was murdered?"

"Dear Aunt Mina," said Paul, leaping into the breach, "it's as Fanny said. Clarence is simply disgracefully drunk."

Mina's lifted white hand silenced him.

"Clarence," said Mina, without emotion, "who is murdered?"

"Clarence," began Fanny, tinkling her bracelets and beads agitatedly, "Clarence—don't you dare——"

"Be still, Fanny," said Mina flatly. "I'm waiting, Clarence."

Clarence's eyes, their whites faintly flushed with

pink, blinked upward. He passed a small hand over his wavy brown hair and touched his trim mustache. He smiled politely, tried twice to assemble himself, and a third time by a superb effort got to his feet and stood there swaying.

"Mina," he said, "I'm drunk. Don't pay any attention to me."

Friquet gave him a glance of green scorn and licked her paw delicately. Fanny let out a little breath of relief. Katie, moved by some impulse of sympathy, moved nearer Clarence, and without looking at her he took her arm and clung to it.

Mina was neither deceived nor diverted. She seldom was in the face of an out-and-out situation, for there was a touch of Dutch shrewdness in her blood, though it alternated with a mad credulity about matters of which she was ignorant. But she knew gentlemen's behavior when they were in Clarence's condition. She respected the memory of the late Mr. Petrie, but she always had felt that the less said of certain of his ways the better.

She said now flatly but judiciously:

"Yes, you're drunk, Clarence. But you are still conscious of what you are saying, and now you are trying to evade me." She dropped Melissa's arm and descended the remaining steps alone and unaided and with more certainty, as if she felt that some responsibility must be faced and the thought gave her strength. She reached the bottom of the stairway, ignored Steven's offered arm, and advanced slowly toward the center of the somber room.

The dome light above threw the fine wrinkles on her white forehead and around her deep-set eyes into sharp relief. Her black, silk crêpe gown trailed behind her and was pulled in at the waistline with some kind of black sash, so that her high full bust and heavy hips were well defined. Mina's face was rather thin, set as if thrust forward between her high shoulders, but her body was heavy and tightly corseted with laced and boned corsets, high-busted and narrow-waisted, which Katie, to her amazement, had once seen. They were made to order, for they could no longer be bought in any store.

She paused, facing Clarence and dominating the room.

"You're drunk," repeated Mina with cool, unemphatic conviction. "But you know what you are saying. Now then, what about somebody being murdered?"

"Nothing, Mina. Nothing. I was only talking."

She made a gesture that, strangely, was not impatient.

Her eyes searched the room, and she said:

"Where is Charlotte?"

Fanny's mouth opened and closed and opened, but no sound came from it. Katie gripped the back of the chair beside her and knew that she must speak. Somehow she must drag herself back through that queer protecting veil of detachment and must meet these searching burning eyes and she must speak. But what to say? How to tell of what she had done?

"Charlotte is not here," she said, putting forth every atom of will to hold her voice steady so that it should not betray the choke in her throat. "Charlotte —I must tell you something that will be a shock, Aunt Mina."

Mina's eyes plunged hotly upon Katie.

"What is it? Tell me."

Steven had stepped quickly forward and pulled a chair out toward Mina.

"I'll tell you," he said. "Sit down, Aunt Mina, won't you?"

Mina slowly turned the full hot impact of her gaze upon Steven.

"Charlotte," she said. "What have you done, Steven——"

He interrupted brusquely, cutting into her words.

"There was an accident, Aunt Mina," he said very distinctly. "An accident which no one could have avoided. Do you understand? Charlotte walked in front of the car and——"

Katie put her hand on Steven's arm.

"Wait, Steven. I did it. I was driving, Aunt Mina. I didn't see Charlotte until it was too late."

"Oh. She's dead?"

"Yes." Steven suddenly put his arm around Katie. She felt the warm strong band his arm made with a kind of gratitude. "Yes, Charlotte is dead, Aunt Mina," he went on, speaking very clearly. "It happened so quickly that she never knew what it was. Katie could not possibly have avoided it."

Silence.

Mina's face did not change in a single muscle. It remained flat and white and blank. Her eyes did not waver from Steven, and her thick white hands were entirely still in her short, black crêpe lap.

"It isn't right," said something in the back of Katie's tortured mind. "It isn't right. She was closest to Charlotte. And there's no grief, no shock, no tears."

"When did you discover it?" said Mina presently.

It was a curiously worded inquiry.

Steven said at once:

"It happened an hour or so ago. Katie was driving home from the concert."

Mina's eyes swerved to Katie speculatively for an instant and then returned to Steven.

"Yes. I loaned Katie the car. Where was Charlotte when it happened?"

"Just there below the bridge. It's always a bad place. You ought to have built a new road long ago, Aunt Mina. Tonight it was very dangerous on account of the fog and the sleet. Katie was unable to stop the car." He hesitated and then said again: "Do you understand?"

"Yes," said Mina flatly. "Yes, I understand."

Another silence. Friquet yawned in a bored way and sniffed the blotter on the desk. There was no other motion in the room except that Katie found herself leaning wearily against that warmly sustaining arm.

"Then what," said Mina suddenly, "is this talk of murder?"

Clarence uttered an unintelligible sound which conveyed only dismay. Steven said:

"Clarence says he found some hair in Charlotte's hand, when he tried to rub her wrist before the doctor arrived. He said that, therefore, she was murdered. I don't think we need consider it seriously. I don't just follow his reasoning." He glanced at Clarence and added: "If any."

Mina turned slowly to Clarence.

"Did you find—*hair*—in Charlotte's hand?"

"Yes," said Clarence, blinking under that smoldering black gaze.

Fanny swept forward, jingling, and Clarence turned waveringly to defy her before she could speak.

"I say yes, Fanny, and I mean yes. Mina," he asserted with tremendous dignity and a hiccup, "wants the truth. Mina must be given the truth."

"Give it to me," said Mina flatly.

"Eh?" Clarence looked startled.

"The hair. Give it to me at once, Clarence."

"But you—that hair—— Oh, very well. Very well." He fumbled in his pocket.

Paul came quietly down the stairs again to stand in that small, tense circle.

Clarence extended his hand palm upward, and a little incredulous gasp went over them like a cold small wind.

There on his palm lay a wisp of black hair. It was black hair as he had said. And it was woolly. Like Melissa's hair would be if it were black.

It was, that small black wisp, inexpressibly and terribly provocative.

And it was, somehow, revolting. Katie felt herself shrinking away from it and, at the same time, leaning forward to stare at it with a kind of fascinated, strange curiosity.

After all, how *had* it got in Charlotte's hand?

What possible errand could she have undertaken which would have made necessary, which by any stretch of the imagination could have included, the clutching of that bit of hair?

Her presence in the dark fog on that slippery road

was mysterious enough. The bit of woolly black hair confirmed and crystallized its mystery.

"It looks," said Clarence cheerfully, "as if it had been pulled out. Out of somebody's head——"

"Sh—sh!" hissed Fanny sharply. The more sharply because that was exactly what it looked like.

Katie herself had just been thinking, terribly, of a struggle. A gasping, breathless struggle and a woman's hand—Charlotte's wiry, nervous hand—grasping frenziedly and coming away with that dreadful bit of black hair that lay now on Clarence's pink, unsteady palm. Only, of course, that wasn't what happened.

"But it wasn't that," Katie heard herself saying in a voice that wasn't her own. "Because, you see, we— Paul and I—*we know*. We saw Charlotte moving. There, ahead of the car."

"Of course," said Steven a bit too emphatically. "The whole thing was an accident. This hair probably means just nothing at all. There's no sense in talking of murder. Let's drop this bit of hair in the fire and forget about it."

"A good plan," said Paul. "As Katie says, the suggestion of Charlotte's having been murdered is sheer nonsense. We saw her. She was walking. Moving just ahead of the car. She couldn't have been murdered."

"Unless," said Katie with stiff lips, "you call what I did——"

"Stop that, Katie!" said Steven, grim and decided. "There's no sense to talk like that either. Stop it. Here, Clarence—shall I drop this in the fire, Aunt Mi——" He looked at Mina as he spoke, and Katie saw his look become curiously fixed, and she followed and was gradually aware that her own gaze had become fixed.

For Mina was doing the most extraordinary thing.

She was standing there, her white face thrust forward between her high black shoulders so that her chin seemed to rest upon her bosom, and her feverish black eyes were traveling deliberately from that bit of hair in Clarence's palm back and forth in turn to every head in the room.

It was not a pleasant thing to see—that hot look of terribly naked speculation and conjecture.

It traveled slowly and steadily from one person to another, returning now and then as if for verification to Clarence's hand.

It went, even, to Melissa, who was yet standing in the shadow of the stairway, and it lingered there as if pure logic demanded something of the neatly combed bright hair under that small white cap.

Then Mina's own head made a motion of rather impatient negation. Quite obviously there was no one there whose hair even remotely resembled that dry, woolly wisp in Clarence's palm.

And William, thought Katie, and was horrified to find herself thinking it and yet must pursue the thought to its conclusion—William is almost entirely bald. And Hilda, the cook's hair looked like nothing so much as under-done taffy.

Mina's thick, slow white hand went out. Her fingers, fumbling a bit, pinched up the wisp of hair and lifted it. Slowly she wrapped the thing in her handkerchief, folding the delicate white linen and knotting it above the fold. She looked at it and then pushed the small white wad into her high bosom under the folds of black, where it became at once a part of that tight, unnatural contour.

For a moment her hot black eyes stared into the space above the chaise-longue fixedly as if she saw something the others did not see. And she said flatly and inexplicably:

"So. It was Charlotte. Charlotte all the time, and she didn't know."

No one moved or spoke, and Mina's eyes went slowly to Fanny.

"Will you see to the funeral arrangements, Fanny? Or, no. Perhaps it would be better for Chris to do that. It must be at a chapel, I think. Not here."

Not here. No brief epilogue of the page labeled Charlotte Weinberg would be recorded in the mirror reflecting then the very motions of Mina Petrie's dry red mouth.

"She wished to be cremated," continued Mina flatly. "We must tell Chris that. Now, I think, we'd better get on with dinner. Jenks, will you tell the cook it may be served in fifteen minutes?"

"But that hair——" said Fanny and faltered under the smoldering glance of Mina's black eyes.

"Very well, madame," said Jenks.

Katie turned blindly toward the stairway. Fifteen minutes. She had managed so far to keep a grip on herself. But she must be alone. She must somehow restore herself, summon up courage to meet them at dinner. She dared not relinquish that hold for an instant. Not yet. Not so soon.

But Steven stopped her at the foot of the stairway. "Katie," he said. "Katie——"

She paused and turned, one trim brown slipper on the lower stair and her hand upon the newel post and looking slim and pink against the rich walnut gleam.

"Yes, Steven."

Why were his gray eyes so narrow and dark and intent? Why was there a kind of set, grim look around his mouth?

"What was it you said about the summerhouse?"

"The summerhouse? Oh, yes, of course. It was Paul who saw it. Just as we got on the bridge. He said there was a light in the summerhouse."

The room was completely silent. Mina wheeled slowly and stood there squat and thick with her white chin thrust forward.

"A light in the summerhouse?" she said. "There was no light in the summerhouse."

CHAPTER VI

KATIE'S hand slowly tightened on the newel post. Clarence, momentarily forgotten and forgetting, collapsed very gently and with the utmost grace onto the divan and as gently passed into oblivion. Paul's close-set eyes went to Mina and then to Katie; he pulled cigarettes from his pocket, offered them to Steven, who took one absently, his gray eyes still intent upon Katie, and Paul said pleasantly to Mina:

"But there was a light tonight, Aunt Mina, darling. I saw it."

The slow turn of Mina's thick, squat body was always a bit ponderous and suggested a kind of unwieldy strength in spite of her weakness.

"You can't have seen a light, Paul," she said without any emotion at all. "There was none."

There was a dark flicker in Steven's gray eyes. He looked at Mina and said definitely:

"You always keep the summerhouse locked, don't you, Aunt Mina?"

"Yes," she said flatly. "And I have the only two keys."

"But I——" Paul checked himself, and his shoulders lifted in just the faintest hint of a shrug, which said: "I know what I saw. But I don't quarrel about it."

"You are sure?" asked Steven in a low voice.

"Positive," said Paul.

"Might it have been a reflection of a light against a window?"

"I don't know," said Paul slowly. "I thought it was only a glimpse of a light in the window of the summerhouse. But fog is tricky. It did surprise me, and I remember I said something about it to Katie."

"Did you turn to look?" asked Steven, turning to Katie again.

"No. No, I don't think so. I couldn't have——" A wave of terrible self-suspicion checked her. "Oh, I couldn't have done that and thus failed to see Charlotte." She heard her own voice pleading for reassurance.

Steven gave it to her calmly.

"No," he said at once. "If you had even glanced away from the road ahead of you, you would have remembered seeing the light. There's nothing you can reasonably blame yourself for. Run along upstairs and fix your hair and wash your face and you'll feel better."

"I tell you," said Mina's flat voice, commanding them all from the center of the room, "there was no light in the summerhouse. If you want to make yourself neat for dinner, Katie, you may go."

Later Katie remembered the curious perplexity of that moment, but then she wanted more than anything else to escape. She went swiftly up the familiar carpeted stairs, around the turn and out of sight of the funereal lounge and a gilt-framed mirror. Down a long, beautifully paneled corridor, and then the door to her room.

She closed the door behind her.

Fortunately Steven's admonition was still fresh in

her ears. She would not stand there, leaning against
the door, her hands clinging to the door knob and
her head thrown back wearily and her eyes closed
but seeing again, against her lids, a dark patch of
blurred, escaping roadway, and lights that tried and
failed to pierce black fog and then, terrifyingly, something black moving out from that fog—moving—going down——

No, No!

Fifteen minutes. Time for a bath and change.

The hot, scented water warmed her and was physically refreshing, for it drove away a kind of nervous
chill which had been threatening her and which she'd
had to fight to control. The familiar, mechanical motions of dressing were, too, steadying. Flurries of
powder, a comb ran swiftly through her hair pulling
it smoothly back from her forehead and back from
her ears into soft, short curls at the back of her head.
Powder on her face which felt smooth and soothing;
she leaned forward to look at the red scratches left
by some shrub into which she had fallen in the dark.
Strange that her face hadn't changed when everything
else in the world had changed for her.

There was something inexpressibly chilling in the
vista that thought opened, and she sheered away
from exploring it and took up a lipstick and made of
her mouth a small crimson badge of courage.

Clothes then, quickly. Stockings, and slippers with
slender heels and a single, soft garment which was de-
signed by a famous dressmaker and managed to fit
without a wrinkle. Her fingers met and pulled out a
gown of pale frosted blue like the lake when it was
frozen. She slipped it over her head and it fell grace-

fully, clinging to her shoulders and swirling about her feet.

It had taken twelve of the fifteen minutes. It took another three to brace herself sufficiently to open that protecting door.

It was altogether a strange dinner and an unhappy one.

In the first place, and dreadfully, Charlotte's place was vacant. Someone had made a half-hearted attempt to shift the various places about, but it only emphasized Charlotte's absence from the table where she had presided and ruled for so long.

And in the second place, and incredibly, Mina Petrie herself was there.

Even in view of her unexpected descent from her own rooms above, neither Katie, nor, probably, anyone else, had thought of her dining with them. For years it had been a settled thing that Madame Petrie took her meals in her room.

Everyone knew that she was not well and that she was not growing any better. Every bit of machinery of the household had been arranged to shield her from any disturbance, any effort, any slight responsibility. Charlotte had seen to all that, and she had done it well and thoroughly.

Fanny's bright, hard eyes were glistening as they looked at Mina Petrie and then went toward the place where Charlotte had been wont to sit, erect and wiry and alert, with her eyes darting sharply here and there, seeing everything. To sit and preside. Fanny was very attentive to Mina; more attentive than it was in Fanny's nature normally to be.

And when Katie looked on past Mina's white face

and high black bosom she could see Friquet, still sitting on the desk under the mirror, with her great shining eyes eagerly watching the ferns and the winking
black windows as if the cat were holding some secret,
speculative communication with the black fog that
was pushing and pressing and peering through the
windows.

There was no conversation. There could not be
with Mina's white face there at the head of the table,
and her chin thrust forward, and her refusal of course
after course while her black eyes smoldered and
watched them.

It was a strange and dreadful dinner, but it was,
finally, over.

Mina disappeared on Melissa's arm. And Fanny
swooped on Katie.

"Doctor's orders," she said. Her eyes were still
glistening, and she glanced quickly and competently
toward the dining room to quell the sudden rattle of
a dish in a servant's hand. "Doctor's orders, Katie.
Off to bed with you."

Katie submitted. There was nothing else to do. She
was swept upward by whirling, efficient green chiffon
and tinkling beads. At the landing she paused to
glance downward. There just below her was the
chaise-longue which had held a blanketed, inert
burden.

"Good-night, Katie," said Steven from below. His
blond hair shone and his gray eyes smiled from under
his level, sun-tanned eyebrows as if to reassure her.
He looked tall and certain of himself. But he was still
guarded and, somehow, wary.

Then Paul came from the dining room, looked up,

and smiled so that his white teeth gleamed below his black silk mustache.

"Good-night, Katie," he said caressingly.

"Good-night," said Katie and turned upward.

It was always simpler and easier to obey Fanny than to resist. She concluded her forceful ministrations by bringing two hot-water bags.

"One for your feet," she said, "and one for your stomach. Nothing like a hot-water bag on your stomach. I was never more surprised in my life than I was when Mina stayed downstairs during dinner."

"She didn't eat anything, and she usually eats," said Katie wearily.

"No," said Fanny. "Well—I guess that's all. Capsules, windows, hot-water bags. Now you go to sleep like a good girl." She paused, with one long hand on the door knob. Her strong, red features and her glistening cobalt eyes were thoughtful. Her white hair was more than usually askew, and one hand absently rattled the beads that were not jade. "I wonder," she said, "what Mina will do for someone to take Charlotte's place. She's dying—it won't be long. I suppose she'll have Chris Lorrel over in the morning."

"Chris?"

"Why, of course. Now that Charlotte's dead she'll have to change her will." Fanny paused and pondered and then added: "If she's made one. Well, good-night, Katie."

She closed the door with exaggerated caution. Two hot-water bags, and an extra pillow found the floor.

It was, Katie felt, impossible to sleep, capsules or no capsules. Hence it was with a kind of astonishment that she roused all at once to the knowledge that she had not only been asleep but dreaming. Dreaming —she shuddered away from the dream, groped through mists of drugged slumber toward reality and awoke.

It was very quiet in the house. She reached for the lamp on the bedside table, pulled on the light, and looked at the little French clock on the mantel. It was only about half-past eleven. But she'd been sleeping then for several hours.

Sleeping and dreaming. Dreaming of a car that wouldn't stop. Dreaming that her foot was pressing with all its strength on a footbrake and yet the car kept on going without the slightest check in its terrible, relentless power.

She sat upright, shivering, as the moment below the bridge returned to her with overwhelming force and with it the sick sense of helplessness she had felt. Facing it alone in the silence and cold was suddenly unendurable. She and she alone had been responsible for Charlotte's death.

What had the sergeant said when he left? He had looked as if he felt a little sorry for her. But it seemed to Katie, there in the clearness and quiet, that he had asked too much.

His strangely searching and prolonged questions stood out now as if each word were illumined by floodlights.

And then, at the last, he had said not to worry. That sometimes, in such cases, there was a charge of manslaughter.

The heavy car had jolted. Had risen over something and then dropped down again. Twice.

Katie pushed back her hair with a frantic gesture.

In another second she was standing, slim and vaguely rumpled and looking against the table light rather like a Tanagra figure in triple sheer pajamas and an eiderdown.

Then she had closed the window against the fog and cold, tossed the eiderdown back on the bed, and was fumbling for clothes. She didn't know what she intended to do, or, exactly, where she was going. She only knew that if there were human voices and companionship yet about in that house she must find them.

A moment later she opened the door.

The passage was long and dark except for a small night light burning away down at the head of the stairs. It was so dark that Katie and the black velvet robe she wore merged into the deep shadows.

It looked as if the whole household were sunk in sleep. There was, however, a faint possibility that Steven and Paul were still downstairs, playing cards in the little bookroom as was their custom when both of them spent the night in Mina's silent, unlively house.

Katie's feet on the carpeted floor made no sound. Her trailing velvet robe passed along with only the softest whisper. The place was silent, hushed, still, as if no living soul dwelt therein.

No living soul. That was Charlotte's door she was approaching. The door to the room in which, now, was only black emptiness.

Katie paused, fighting a reluctance to pass that closed, blank door. She was obliged to force herself to go on and to walk slowly and deliberately, and her back all but twitched, as if some primitive sense were urging her to hurry, to run, to reach lights and people.

Here was the door. Closed and black and silent. By putting out her hand she could touch one of the cold panels. She could even enter——

There was a sound of paper rustling. It came from behind that blank closed door.

Katie's heart stopped and then pounded furiously.

Someone was in Charlotte's room. Someone, whispered a cold inner voice, or something. It would be like Charlotte to want things to be in order.

The sheer unreasoning horror of the thought forced Katie to open the door and prove its unreason. The latch clicked faintly under her hand, and she had an impression of movement within the room, and then she pushed the door open upon utter blackness.

"Who is it?" she said, her voice tight and small and strange.

Where was the light? Had there been a faint light that vanished just as she turned the door knob and the latch clicked? Why was there no sound? Where was the light switch? Her hand fumbled along the wall. She was in the room now, and it was silent and dark. But there could be only one of the family there—no need to be so terrified——

It was just then that, without any warning or sound, something flung itself upon her. She was pushed back against the wall and was struggling with a soft and shapeless thing that collapsed gently and slid away from her to the floor and still made no sound and no outcry and had no breath. After a long, horrible moment Katie's fingers found the light switch and snapped it.

Light flooded the room, and it was orderly and vacant, and on the floor, at her feet, was a crumpled bolster.

Hysteria caught at Katie's throat. She stifled it, both hands pressed to her mouth.

The door to the hall stood open. Whoever had been there had escaped into the darkness of the corridor beyond and was gone. It was only a step or two to the door. But the shadows of the corridor were blank and hid any movement down its length.

The room itself gave only one indication of anyone's presence. The large lower drawer of the writing desk was pulled out, and it was completely empty. Otherwise everything was in order. The doors, one leading to the bathroom adjoining and one leading to a small passage which gave in turn upon Mina's rooms, were both closed.

Katie took a long breath, snapped out the light, and turned into the corridor again, closing the door to Charlotte's room behind her. She went on toward the stairway; this time the feeling of being under observation was so strong that she ran, holding up her long skirt so she should not trip in her haste.

And yet whoever had been in Charlotte's room must have been one of the family. And a down-filled bolster is not a very dangerous weapon.

But what had been removed from that empty drawer—and why?

At the wide stairway there was a dim light.

She went down the stairs.

More light and a strong smell of cigarette smoke.

The lounge itself was in rather eerie twilight, with only a dismal wicker shape looming out of it here and there, and the winking black window panes reflecting tangled ferns against a blurred band of light which streamed from the passage that led toward the bookroom. The door to the bookroom was open and let warm light, clouded with blue smoke, into the passage, and there was the sound of men's voices.

At the lower step Katie sat down. She felt shaky and unnerved. The sound of those voices was for a moment reassuring.

Steven and Paul, talking it over.

Now that her heart had quieted and her breath came lightly again, she could even hear their words quite clearly, for the bookroom was just beside the lounge and the house was, otherwise, very still. And there was a third voice. A third voice, but a voice that was as familiar to that household as Mina's own, for it belonged to Chris Lorrel. He had heard the news, then, and had come to inquire. Good old Chris!

Chris Lorrel lived next door, and it was he who shared the entrance drive up from the public highway with Mina Petrie. He was also a family friend and had been the family lawyer ever since his father, Christopher Lorrel, senior, had died and passed on his clients as well as his estate to his stoutish, already middle-aged bachelor son. It was a double charge which Chris accepted with his customary equanimity. Accepted and discharged without any change in his comfortable ways, except that, with the years, he grew steadily pinker, larger, and scarcer as to hair until during the past year he had suddenly appeared with a neat, modest brown toupee, artfully threaded with silver. It was not, he had told Katie tranquilly, that he'd minded being bald; it was catching cold he'd hated. And then he had laughed and wheezed and wheezed and laughed until tears ran down his pink cheeks and Katie had had to pat his heaving, tightly coated back and Charlotte, disapprovingly, had rung for Jenks and a glass of water.

Charlotte.

Would there always be, at the thought of Charlotte, that cold clutch on her heart?

Chris was speaking. There was something different about his voice. Something that was no longer easy and good-natured.

"If we can just keep the police from discovering how things stood between Charlotte and Katie! But I'm afraid it's bound to come out," he was saying. There was a faint tinkle as of a glass being set on a silver tray.

"This business of the bonds didn't help matters any." That was Paul.

"What's that?" said Steven rather sharply. "What bonds?"

"Oh, didn't you know?" Paul somehow always knew. "Why, Charlotte gave Katie a largish order for some bonds. Katie bought them for her and they went up; Charlotte was tickled. Then they dropped to ten points below what she'd paid for them. Charlotte got on the telephone and ordered Katie to sell. So Katie sold. Then Charlotte simply reneged. Denied she'd ever bought them. Katie had to take the loss. Set her back some—how much, Chris?"

Katie listened over the sudden pounding of her pulses. Would Chris tell that she'd had to borrow it of him? And that she had no possible means of paying it back to him?

"Why, quite a sum, I believe," said Chris vaguely.

"You see, the trouble is that Charlotte, quite naturally, having injured Katie, hated her more than ever. I think you'll agree with me that hate is the only word for it. And the situation is rather bad. Mina dying, no will made yet, and Mina so markedly under Charlotte's influence. With Charlotte out of the picture, Katie may inherit a considerable sum. Otherwise, I doubt if she would have got a cent of Mina's money. I only hope," added Chris gravely, "that she'll enjoy it."

"Why, look here, Chris"—it was Steven's voice, quick and strained. "Do you mean they'll charge Katie with manslaughter?"

"Or worse," said Chris. "The police are not blind."

There was a sudden silence in the bookroom. I ought to move, thought Katie crazily. I ought to tell them I'm here.

But she didn't move. And she heard Chris's new, queerly cold voice saying:

"There'll be an adjourned inquest owing to reasonable doubt as to the cause of Charlotte's death."

"Reasonable doubt," said Steven, "That—why, that's when it's murder! Chris, you're out of your wits."

"No. You see, it's so obvious a point. Just how hard did Katie try *not* to kill Charlotte?"

CHAPTER VII

KATIE never remembered getting back through the silence and cold and darkness to her own room.

She did remember always, however, that night which was long and terrible and sleepless until gray dawn.

Morning came gray and cold and quiet. Ominously quiet.

Fog yet lay like a blanket over house and dripping park and still, dark lake. Katie, looking heavy-eyed from her window on the lake side of the house, could see through shifting gray wreaths only as far as the railing at the end of the lawn and that dimly. Beyond the railing all the world dropped away into thick gray space which had neither form nor meaning.

Her eyes were tired. There were faint purple smudges under them, and her face looked white, although Katie was actually not at all fragile. She was, instead, nicely tempered with steel. But the night just past had been one to try steel itself, and she was, that morning, incredibly tired. And there was the day to be met and faced.

She had killed Charlotte. And she was apt to be charged with manslaughter. With, perhaps, murder.

The world had changed for Katie in one dreadful moment below the bridge. She was immeasurably removed from the world in which she had lived only yesterday morning.

Yesterday morning—when she had stood before that very mirror, thinking of the concert, perhaps, and of Aunt Mina's offer of the car, and no doubt in the back of her mind of her own situation. Of money she had made and lost. Of bills, urgent, made before she, or anyone else, realized that things were going to be as bad as they had been. Of job-hunting when there were no jobs.

Of herself—the bright young business woman, she would have been thinking with a touch of scorn—with her money gone, her business gone, the amazing inner confidence in herself that had carried her so blithely over obstacles all but gone.

Everything had been so lavish: money, success, the thrills of independence, of spending money she had so easily earned, of cultivating more and more expensive tastes. It wasn't, she had discovered recently with a kind of shock, that those tastes were more fastidious; they were just more expensive. Something that everyone was buying. Something to order home, lavishly. To spend money on. But it didn't matter about spending, because there was always more money to spend. There would always be more.

But there hadn't been.

All that, however, belonged to yesterday, to the world Katie had lived in and known. Not to the queer, distorted place it had in one fearful moment become.

Pausing before the long mirror, she noted with mechanical approval the lines of the green, tweedish skirt and jacket she was wearing, the grace of the soft ivory blouse, the exactly right shade of the bit of crimson scarf. It was all very simple, but so expensively simple, the lines so subtly contrived. Yesterday she would have thought of the bill for it, still unpaid. To-day somehow it didn't matter.

The corridor was quiet. Quiet except for a blue-gray cloud that scudded over her feet, turned to flash a green, knowing glance at her, and vanished at the turn near the stairway, in the direction of Mina's rooms. It was Friquet, of course, suspicious as usual and very, very self-sufficient.

At the top of the stairway was Melissa, tall and silent. Even the breakfast tray she carried in her graceful brown hands was silent; not one piece of silver jostled against another, and not one cup tinkled against its saucer. The cream did not ripple even faintly in the silver jug.

"Good-morning, Melissa," said Katie, looking at the tray. It was easily identifiable. Many squat dishes, all covered but suggesting strong possibilities of oat-meal, eggs, toast, sausages perhaps—Katie sniffed and changed that item to bacon—fruit, and an extremely large silver pot of coffee. Mina's tray, of course. Queer that in spite of the long years of semi-invalid-ism and in spite of her present condition Mina had yet such a healthy and vigorous appetite.

"Good-morning, Miss Katie," Melissa was saying. She had a soft, velvety voice, high and negroid in qual-ity but never shrill. "If you please, Miz Petrie wants you to come to her room."

Katie's heart dropped. She was to be launched upon it at once, then.

"Very well, thank you, Melissa. Give me the tray and I'll take it to her."

"Yes, Miss Katie. Mr. Chris is there talking to her

now. She said not to wake you if you were still sleeping, but for you to come as soon as you were up."

Mina's own rooms—a large study, a small bedroom, and an ugly, shining bathroom—were as curiously blank and uncommunicative as Mina herself. There was practically nothing to which one might point and say: that object gives a clue to the personality of the owner. The room Katie entered was physically comfortable, esthetically distressing, not too crowded, however, for there were blank wall spaces which looked cold but were not. Mina's room was always sickeningly hot. And it always smelled earthy and moist from the plants that lined the window—an odor which mingled with a trace of coffee, of which Mina was inordinately fond. There was nothing of the delicate scent of perfume and powders and softly fragrant silks that usually characterizes a woman's rooms. Even the plants in the window never bore flowers; they were all thick-leaved plants with red and white veins and large, clumsy stems.

There was perhaps only one object in the room which was personal and significant, and that was an old photograph which hung just beside the heavy desk. It was a photograph of a man, bearded and dressed with a trace of dandyism after the fashion of a much earlier day, but still faintly familiar with its close-set eyes and high cheekbones and a curious, evanescent air of charm which survived even age and stiff portraiture. It was an air and a look that would have been familiar to Katie, even if she had not known, as she did know, that it was an old photograph of Paul's father, Claude Duchane—dead many years and, one might have thought, forgotten.

In all probability the photograph had actually been forgotten, or at least hidden away, for it was only during recent months that it had hung there on the wall. It was as if there had revived in Mina's faltering heart a kind of resurgence of that old love—a dying glow which in some mysterious way had rekindled itself. Her attitude, even, toward Paul had been perceptibly kinder, with a hint of lingering tenderness. It was an attitude that, vaguely, had irritated Katie, although, to do Paul justice, she was obliged to admit that he had not played upon Mina's sentiment. Not, at least, so far as she knew.

That morning Mina, wrapped in an old red flannel dressing gown but still thick and solid and rather awe-inspiring, sat in a tall armchair near the desk. Friquet was on her lap, a blue-gray shadow with inscrutable, gleaming green eyes. Chris Lorrel, who had opened the door, nodded briefly and said:

"Good-morning, Katie. Hope you slept. I'm sorry to hear about it."

No need to say what. Katie replied something, spoke to Mina and approached her with the tray. Mina looked quite as usual, but Chris was incredibly haggard, with his large face sagging into lines that were no longer easy and good-natured and his eyes looking small and wary as if they had retreated into the fat folds of flesh surrounding them. For so large a man Chris was unbelievably deft and silent in every motion; he crossed the room now toward the window with so light and swift a step that his unwieldy bulk seemed curiously elastic. Or pneumatic, thought Katie: a tethered balloon.

"Oh, there you are," Mina was saying. "And

you've brought my tray. That's a good girl. Bring it to me." She moved the cat to the back of the chair, where it lay composedly, and Katie adjusted the short green legs of the tray across the arms of the chair.

Mina's eyes were eager as she reached for the coffee pot. Chris and Katie both watched, Katie with a slight feeling of nausea, while Mina filled and drained two cups of strong black coffee. She looked up, then said in her flat voice: "Thank you, Katie. Sit down," and attacked the fruit. Even in the cold morning light her black eyes looked fierce and hot.

"I sent for you, Katie," went on Mina, "because I want you to tell me again, slowly, everything that happened last night. Chris tells me that the police are apt to make further inquiry."

The police.

"Tell it all just as it happened, Katie," said Chris. His voice, too, had changed. It was the voice Katie had heard coming from the bookroom the night before—cold and somehow detached.

Katie told it just as it happened. Briefly. But her palms were moist before she had more than begun, and her knees were unsteady, as if they no longer had substance.

Mina did not speak during the whole recital. Indeed, she scarcely looked at Katie, but instead, with her white face thrust forward and her shoulders hunched, ate steadily and methodically and enormously. Friquet from the top of the chair watched every bite, her green eyes catching strange lights and her great tail giving little impatient twitches as the bacon, piece by piece, disappeared.

Katie finished. Stopped. No one spoke.

Chris had turned at the window, so only his sagging, broad shoulders were outlined against the gray light.

Finally Mina ate the last muffin, poured some cream into a saucer and held it up toward Friquet. Friquet sniffed at it, refused it disdainfully to stare down at the plate that had held bacon, and Mina set the saucer back on the tray and at last looked at Katie. She asked no question. She made no comment. She said flatly:

"Thank you, Katie. That fool Clarence tangled things up last night until I scarcely knew just what had happened. You may go to your breakfast."

Chris stirred at that, walked lightly across the room, and opened the door again.

"Good girl," he said as she passed him, but she was conscious that he avoided fully meeting her eyes. She wondered fleetingly what impulse had kept her from bursting into the bookroom and telling them what she had overheard. Was it a curious kind of pride? Or was it, actually, terror?

Downstairs it was chilly and not too light. The lounge was deserted; the mirror over the desk reflected only ferns and black wicker and cold gray windows.

There was no one in the dining room and no one in the breakfast room beyond until Melissa came to ask if she wanted orange juice or grapefruit and how she liked her eggs.

"No eggs at all," said Katie. "What's happened to Hilda?"

Nothing, it developed, had happened to the cook. Something had, however, happened to the mirror in the cook's bedroom at the top of the house. It had fallen, said Melissa, and broken into a hundred pieces. No one had touched it. It just fell. Of its own accord.

But that wasn't all. While Hilda, phlegmatic by nature but shaken, was cooking breakfast she made the appalling discovery that the kitchen clock had stopped.

It had been wound all right, said Melissa softly, but it had stopped. And by stopping it added a finishing touch. Hilda's phlegmatic spirit shattered as thoroughly as the mirror and she had packed her bag, put a hat on her taffy-colored hair, heeded not the protestations of Jenks and Melissa but marched straight out of the house. She had paused, said Melissa, to turn off the gas under Mr. Siskinson's eggs, but that was all.

She had made one terse remark to Jenks to the effect that they could say all they pleased of accidents, but when mirrors broke themselves and clocks stopped themselves no money could keep her in their immediate vicinity. She had added cryptically that one sudden death was enough. And left.

"But where did she go?"

Melissa didn't know.

"But I can cook," said Melissa soothingly. "And Miz Petrie told me to he'p out till things get more settled. She says Miss Fanny will order meals."

"Aren't you afraid, too, Melissa?" asked Katie curiously.

A kind of dark ripple went over Melissa's face. She shook her head—that bright woolly head that ought to have been black.

"No'm," she said. "I ain't scared. I'll go make you some toast, Miss Katie."

The tall black figure moved on silent feet to the pantry door and disappeared as silently. For everyone else the pantry door squeaked.

And something was wrong. It wasn't right that a phlegmatic, Nordic cook should succumb to hysteria while a Negress remained bland and unperturbed in the face of smashing mirrors and clocks that stopped themselves. And sudden death.

Katie returned to her breakfast and wondered how long it would be until the police arrived. She hadn't, after that long night, any doubt but that they would arrive.

It was bad enough to have killed Charlotte. Bad enough to have been guiding that great remorseless car when it crushed out a life. Bad enough, all of it, but how infinitely worse was the thing that might be already on its way toward her!

At a sudden sound from the drive outside the windows, Katie looked up with a quick jerk of her head. It was, however, only a small truck labeled "Andrews, Cleaners," and she took a long, unsteady breath. Not the police then, yet.

She managed to eat some toast.

The lounge, when she came into it again, was still deserted. There might be time for a brief walk along the beach.

For an instant the mirror over the desk recorded a slender figure in green with a crimson knot at its throat and soft black hair. It caught just a flash of blue, troubled eyes. Then the door toward the lake had opened and Katie was descending a flag-stoned step to the lawn.

Still foggy. Still gray. Still cold, although the sleet

had gone and there was only fog and silence. Katie pulled the crimson knot closer and wondered how long the fog would last. Sometimes for as long as three or four days it had hung there, surrounding and making a dark, gloomy gray island of the house and strip of lawn and beach and untidy ravine and park. It stifled them; it pressed in at the doors and windows; it became now and then mysteriously impregnated with smoke and very black. Suffocating. Blinding.

Katie did not know that always, all her life thereafter, she was to fear fog. That it was always to recall to her certain things. Things that were weirdly unrelated. A wisp of black hair. A calendar. The faintest touch of a hand in the dark. The raucous yowl of a frantic cat.

She did not know that, then.

She crossed the lawn and reached the railing where lawn dropped precipitously away through mist-hung barberry bushes. She turned and followed the railing and reached, coming suddenly upon them in the heavy gray mist, the small flight of wooden steps which led steeply downward to the beach.

It was her favorite walk. Up and down that sandy strip of beach with only the lake and the sky and the sand. Chicago's towers away off toward the south, very remote and dreamlike and shimmering. And perhaps a few gulls peeping and swooping near. And sandpipers scooting like delicate wraiths across her way.

But today there were no distant towers, no gulls, no sandpipers. There were only gray lake and gray fog and the deep distant murmur of unseen waves breaking over hidden rocks.

She walked out close to the lake where the sand was packed and wet and saw at once that she was not alone on the beach. Her feet made sharp outlines that followed other outlines, and suddenly Steven loomed out of the fog ahead of her, took his pipe out of his mouth and said:

"Hello there, Katie."

He approached her. His quick eyes, eyes that were trained to see, scrutinized her face.

"Did you manage to rest?" he said in a casual way that did not match the intent look in his gray eyes.

"So-so," said Katie, lying.

"You look a bit fagged."

Katie touched her cheeks.

"An artist sees too much. I thought I'd been rather skillful this morning." She rubbed one cheek with her handkerchief and looked at the faint pink smudge on the white scrap of linen.

"I didn't mean rouge," said Steven. "I meant your eyes. Oh, they are nice enough eyes," he interpolated hastily. "But they look as if they hadn't slept much. And in Heaven's name don't use the word 'artist' in such a loose fashion. I'm a painter. A hard-working, worried, struggling son-of-a-gun of a painter."

"House?" inquired Katie, scrubbing at the other cheek with a vague notion of restoring balance.

"No, damn you," said Steven chivalrously. "Although as to that, I wish I were. Maybe I could support myself more adequately."

There was an undertone of truth in his last words. He looked out somberly into the mysterious gray reaches of lake and fog. Katie was moved by some obscure impulse to defend.

"Your pictures sold before the crash," she reminded him, taking care to keep any note of sympathy from her voice.

"So did your bonds," said Steven and laughed shortly. "Oh, well, so long as Aunt Mina is kind, I suppose we are lucky, you and I. If Aunt Mina had turned against us it would have been rather bad during these last months. See here, my dear," he turned suddenly to face her again. "There's something——" He broke off, as if he found words difficult.

"Something that's hard to tell me," said Katie quietly. It was coming now: he would warn her, tell her she was going to be charged with manslaughter. Or murder. One as bad as the other, thought Katie. Or was it?

"What's the difference," she said, "between manslaughter and murder? The technical difference, I mean."

Steven's eyes narrowed.

"Premeditation," he said shortly. "Why?"

"Oh, don't try to save my feelings, Steven," said Katie wearily. "I heard you talking in the bookroom last night. You and Chris and Paul. I couldn't have stopped listening if my life depended upon it." She stopped, struck by the phrase; perhaps her life would depend upon it. Her life.

She shivered suddenly and disconcertingly and without warning began to tremble.

It was a curiously humiliating experience. Her knees were unreliable, her back shivered and shivered, and something was wrong with her throat; she doubled up her fists and dug them deep into her pockets to hide their tremor, and she locked her teeth

together and tried to hold her whole body rigid so
that Steven should not see or sense the trembling. And
all the time she forced herself to meet his eyes without faltering.

But he knew it. He looked at her long and search-
ingly. He said:

"Why, Katie! Why, Katie darling—don't—— Why,
you poor little kid."

She tried to answer. To answer casually and flip-
pantly. She tried to remember that she was Katie
Warren, promising young business woman, successful
seller of bonds in those incredible, long-ago days of
careless gold.

But she couldn't talk, because her throat had
mysteriously shut up, and besides she must keep her
mouth firm and tight.

"Why, Katie!" said Steven again incredulously.
Then he put out his arms and pulled Katie up close to
him and fumbled into her pockets and pulled out her
doubled-up fists and held them warmly against his
face.

"Katie, don't—don't shake like that," he said.
"Don't, darling." He held her close and warm and
comfortingly, as if her emotion had touched him in
some strange, inscrutable way. As if he could not en-
dure that silent, defenseless trembling.

It would be the same with a bird that was frightened, thought Katie. Or a puppy. Anything helpless
and afraid.

It was warm in the hard circle of his arms. Warm
against his shoulder. Warm with his cheek suddenly
against her own. But something had changed.

There in the gray fog something had changed.

Katie stopped trembling. Steven was still, too. Did he know that something was different? Forever and forever different. His arms were holding her closer and closer. They were no longer tender and comforting but were instead urgent and strong. His cheek moved against hers, and he said jerkily:

"Where's your—mouth, Katie?" and found it.

From somewhere far away in a forgotten world came dull little thuds of sound. Steps on a wooden stairway, sounding dully through gray mist and across sand.

Steven finally lifted his head.

"There's someone," he said, and all at once Katie was standing apart from him. Her breath was unsteady, and she put her hands to her mouth as if his kisses must be visible, and then to her cheek. She knew that Steven was looking at her and that his eyes looked suddenly dark and luminous, as if there were lighted candles behind them. He was not smiling. He said in a breathless, inarticulate way:

"Katie—— Katie . . ."

She tried to breathe less unsteadily. Who was coming along the beach toward them? Had he seen? She must breathe more evenly. Steven, Steven, Steven. A figure was emerging from the mist.

Steven took a quick step nearer her.

"Katie . . ." he said again. There was in his husky voice and in his lighted eyes something very urgent, something that had to be said. But then Paul was at their side.

"The top of the morning to you," said Paul airily. "I thought you might like to know that the police are here. Making further inquiry about last night." He paused to look closely at Katie. "My God, you're looking handsome this morning, Katie. You looked like a half-drowned kitten last night. What's happened to you? Why, you're positively aflame. You——" He checked himself sharply; his dark eyes slid to Steven. There was a swiftly hidden flash of something like speculation in them. Then he said abruptly and with a rapid change from airiness to a kind of brusque impatience:

"They want us in the house. They're snooping all about the place. And there's a little brown man with them that looks like the devil incarnate. Better come along."

CHAPTER VIII

THE three walked along the beach, Katie between the two men, the cool gray fog touching her hot cheeks and mouth. She wondered how much Paul had seen. But it didn't matter. The police had come. They were waiting for her because she had killed Charlotte. Charlotte who had hated her.

Then they were going, single file, up the damp little wooden steps. At the top Steven stopped and put his hands on Katie's shoulders and looked deep into her eyes. Paul's veiled eyes watched, but Steven only said gravely:

"Don't be frightened, Katie. Just tell them what they want to know. Don't lose your head. Chris will be there. If you get tangled up, just leave things to him. He'll know what to say."

Paul smiled, and his white teeth flashed under his small black silk mustache.

"This advice to Katie! Our cool young captain of finance!" he said, laughing gently. "Don't you know, Steven, that Katie never loses her charming head?"

In the lounge the mirror was making fleeting reflections of blue uniforms and of Sergeant Caldwell's shrewd round face. Fanny was there, too, silent except for an occasional faint tinkle of beads and, somehow, resentful. There was Clarence, who looked tired and a bit blurred around the edges. Mina Petrie sat in an armchair, white and cold except for the fierce heat in her glowing dark eyes, and Friquet was a blue-gray cloud on Mina's black arm. Chris, a dark bulk unbelievably silent and lithe, was prowling in the background. There was a kind of latent ferocity in his shoulders and the strangely lithe swing of his thick body across the rugs and polished floor. He turned as the three entered, gave Katie a quick look, and moved over to say something in a low voice to Mina. And then Katie saw the man who had come with the police to question them. To question her, Katie Warren, with a view to discovering whether or not she had willfully murdered a woman who was her enemy.

He was a wiry little brown man, with thick leathery lips and eyes that shone like topazes and a cane which he hooked around his hard, leathery brown neck. His name was Crafft, and he got out eyeglasses with tortoise-shell rims and a wide black ribbon and peered through them at Katie, and Katie hated him at sight, and the mirror over the desk reflected coldly his smiling ugly brown face.

Katie hated him instinctively and was to fear him with sober reason. Sergeant Caldwell, however, respected him. So did the other police, and their feeling was at once evident and became increasingly pronounced.

He was an ugly, smart little man who looked quite capable of perpetrating the full catalogue of crimes himself alone and unaided. But he was, it developed, a detective. And he was, from sheer egotism if nothing else, impeccably honest in his profession. His colleagues knew that. Katie was to learn it. His private life was none of Katie's business.

"This," said Sergeant Caldwell coolly, in a way

which savored weirdly of an introduction and yet was not, "is the girl that killed her. I mean the girl that was driving the car."

"Ah," said Mr. Crafft. He held a small black notebook in his hand—Sergeant Caldwell's notebook, it appeared—and he glanced at it and then at Katie. "Miss Warren. H'm. Well—get the servants in here, too, Sergeant, and we'll get on with business."

"Sit down here, Katie," said Steven, and Katie sat on the divan, with Steven on one side of her and on the other Clarence, who looked up to nod briefly. His eyes were puffy, and he hurriedly returned his neat curly head to the support of well-manicured hands.

There was a curious, constrained moment of waiting. Katie felt cold and sick with suspense; actually sick, she thought vaguely, with that unpleasant sinking sensation in the pit of her stomach that one feels when an elevator drops seventeen stories or so in one reckless swoop. It was, she said to herself, only a matter of the solar plexus, but it was too bad that the solar plexus had been located with such careless juxtaposition to the place where food was digested. She began, crazily, to wonder where would be a better place.

And then Steven beside her moved so that very lightly his arm touched her and she felt all at once sane again and strong and more certain of herself. It would be difficult. But she had not meant to kill Charlotte. And so long as Steven remained there at her side she was a fortress within herself, made impregnable by the thing that had happened there on the beach and that she had not yet had time to look at and examine.

It was from that morning that Katie dated the feeling she was ever afterward to hold that the man, Crafft, was a kind of evil spirit, a being who was touched with another and a stranger world. He was a secretive, incalculable little brown man who knew too much. She was never to discover just how and where he learned all that he knew. He was like a djinn, very old in evil wisdom, very sly, diabolically crafty. Not for one instant, thought Katie, to be trusted. Yet, that morning, he was mild.

He stood there quiet, brown, and ugly, with his cane hooked around his wiry brown neck, his thick lips smiling gently, and his eyes looking rather like a hungry tiger's except that they were terribly knowing as well as avid in their topaz depths.

"A thoroughly disagreeable man," said Fanny afterward, with feeling. At the time she as well as the others was held by that gentle smile and those glowing eyes.

Near him were the police, who managed in their deference to look like so many gentlemen-in-waiting who made up in blue-clad brawn for what they might lack in courtliness and lace ruffles.

Owing to the darkness of the day, lights were on; the white dome light above threw all the faces in the room into a sharp relief which, Katie felt, must be gratifying to the detective. The lamp below the mirror made a small area of brighter light. The mirror itself silently registered the scene and added it perhaps as an incomplete commentary to the chapter called Charlotte Weinberg.

Gray fog pressed against the windows back of the ferns. Paul lit a cigarette, and the flame went up and down again sharply, and Chris ceased to prowl there back of the chair, and Mr. Crafft was speaking softly, swiftly, tersely.

He regretted that there was necessity to make further inquiry regarding the unfortunate accident of the previous day. They would understand that this inquiry was due to the fact that various circumstances had arisen which called for—er—further inquiry.

It was only a matter of routine, he assured them, purringly. They would realize that it would facilitate matters and make it easier all around if they would answer promptly and truthfully the inquiries it was his duty to make. In any case of violent death it was necessary to discover whether the death was due to accident or whether there was a chance of its being murder.

He paused there as if to give them a chance to grapple with that word. A word which he uttered calmly, matter-of-factly, purposefully.

Afterward Katie thought that they had all expected it; were, all of them, already armed and prepared for it.

For no one moved. No one showed surprise or consternation. All of them were prepared. Guarded.

Mr. Crafft, in one knowing glance, saw it too. His smile became more fixed. He went on, still purring.

Would Miss Katie Warren tell them, first, all she knew of the death of—he paused and adjusted his eyeglasses and referred to Sergeant Caldwell's notebook and said:

"Of Charlotte Weinberg."

There was a moment of silence.

Friquet on Mina's still black arm moved and stretched herself and yawned and showed sharp white teeth and a scarlet tongue.

Then Katie began.

It was not, however—yet—as she had expected. By this time the story more or less formulated itself and she could tell it with less fumbling. But there was still that cold clutch on her heart at the thought of Charlotte, and she could still feel the way the great car bumped and slid to a stop. Mr. Crafft listened, one hand caressing his cane, and then asked her no questions but turned instead to Paul.

Paul's story, too, had become set in certain lines. He told it calmly and easily and added gratuitously that Miss Warren could not possibly have stopped the car before it struck the woman moving before them.

"Thank you," said Mr. Crafft. "You say the sleet had frozen on the windshield?"

"Yes. Both wipers were stuck. It was impossible to see much."

"How about the headlights?"

Sergeant Caldwell bustled forward.

"It's there in the notebook, Mr. Crafft," he said. "They was both frosted with sleet."

Mr. Crafft said softly: "Thank you, Sergeant. I have your notebook at hand." But he shot a glance at Sergeant Caldwell which mysteriously impelled the latter to retire with expedition. It was mere accident that he walked clumsily backward to his position against the wall, but it heightened the effect he gave of being chief gentleman-in-waiting.

"What is your opinion, Mr. Duchane?" pursued

Mr. Crafft. "Do you think the headlights were heavily frosted?"

"I know they were. I tried to scrape off the sleet, but didn't succeed," said Paul. "We could see practically nothing ahead. And besides——" He stopped.

"Well?"

"I was only going to say that they must have been so heavily frosted as to obscure the light or Charlotte —that is, Miss Weinberg—would have seen them in time to avoid being—to avoid them."

Chris cleared his throat and wheezed and then said suavely that distances were very confusing in a fog.

"She may have seen the lights all right," he said, "but not realized that they were so near her. They may have looked to be some distance off."

"A good point," said Mr. Crafft pleasantly. "She may even have been waiting for a car and have assumed that this was the car and stepped forward to let her presence be known."

There was an instant's silence. Then Katie said steadily:

"She was not waiting for me."

"Ah," said Mr. Crafft. "That brings up another interesting point. Just what was it that took her out into the cold and fog? She was not dressed for the street, as you all know. No hat, no gloves, no pocketbook. Only a coat. She could not have been going far. If any one of you knows where she was going and why, it would save us all a great deal of time and trouble to tell us about it now."

He paused suggestively and pleasantly, but though the silence lengthened, no one made any effort to speak. Mr. Crafft, whose shining topaz eyes had not wavered in their steady, tiger-like stare, finally lifted his shoulders in the faintest possible shrug and resumed:

"I'm sorry none of you can help me. I trust it is not owing to unwillingness on your part." And before Fanny could utter more than a half-stifled squeak of indignation he went on: "There is another matter I'm extremely anxious to know something of. Shortly before her death Miss Weinberg wrote a communication of some kind with pen and ink. Can any one of you tell me just what that communication was?"

He paused again, waiting.

Mina stirred for the first time.

Her white face had sunk low on her black shoulders, and her white chin was thrust forward and her black eyes burned. She said flatly:

"What kind of communication, Mr. Crafft? A letter? Or what?"

The detective considered her slowly.

"I don't know," he said finally. "There were ink-stains on the middle finger of her right hand. I have every reason to believe that the stains were made very shortly before she died. It may be of some importance to discover exactly what she was writing. Do you know, Madame Petrie?"

The direct question did not at all discompose Mina's white face.

"I do not know," she answered as directly. "But I wish to tell you at this time, Mr. Crafft, that I and my family and household are only too ready to help you in any way possible. Miss Weinberg's death is, naturally, a very great shock and grief to me. And it is almost as great a shock to find that the police—that there is any necessity for further inquiry on the part of the police. It was an extremely sad and unfortunate accident. But it was accident—not murder. Why, there was no one—no one who would murder Charlotte."

It was perhaps one of the longest speeches Katie had ever heard Mina's habitually reticent lips utter. She thought, too, that it was sincere, although, owing possibly to Mina's characteristically flat voice, the thing itself sounded flat and unconvincing. The detective, however, had listened with the most flattering attention, and when she had finished he made a little bow.

"I thank you, Madame Petrie. I trust I need not assure you that we will do everything in our power to spare you any inconvenience or annoyance." He bowed again. Mina bent her head slowly forward. The preliminaries, thought Katie eerily; soon the battle would begin.

"And at the moment," went on Mr. Crafft, "I should like to make a few inquiries which only you can answer, if you will be so good, Madame Petrie." He glanced at the open notebook in his hand, caressed the cane with the other, appeared for a fraction of a second to commune with himself concerning something he found in the notebook, and then added suavely: "I shall try not to tire you." And Katie thought it likely that he'd read "Madame Petrie—dying" in Sergeant Caldwell's conscientious handwriting.

"Very well," said Mina, caressing the cat.

"You had known Miss Weinberg for some time?"

"Since girlhood. She was my cousin."

"Yes, of course. You knew her intimately?"

"We have shared the same house for some sixteen years," said Mina a bit grimly.

"Ah—yes. She was your companion, I understand?"

"That is right. She also ran the house for me. She was extremely efficient."

"That must have been a great relief to you?"

"Yes."

"A great relief, yes," said the little brown man blandly. "It will be very difficult for you to replace such a person in your household."

Fanny's long throat moved as if she'd swallowed convulsively, though her face remained tight and set. Mina did not blink.

"I have not thought of that yet," she said flatly. "And I grieve for a lost friend and cousin rather than for an efficient housekeeper."

"Certainly, certainly," said the detective soothingly, and it seemed to Katie that his half-smiling lips looked somehow pleased. "Miss Weinberg was an intelligent and sympathetic woman no doubt."

Mina hesitated then for the first time and finally did not reply at all.

"I said," repeated the detective, "that Miss Weinberg was an intelligent woman."

"Yes," repeated Mina, "I heard you say that, Mr. Crafft."

Clarence opened his eyes and looked up interestedly; at the quick motion of his head, however, an expression of acute pain crossed his face, and he closed his eyes tightly again.

Mr. Crafft remained blandly smiling.

"Madame Petrie, do you know of any enemy that Miss Weinberg might have had?"

"I know of no one who would have murdered Charlotte," said Mina immediately and very definitely.

Mr. Crafft blinked.

"Is there anything unusual that you know has happened in her life during recent months?"

"Nothing at all."

Clarence opened his eyes again.

"Oh, yes, there was, Mina," he said unexpectedly. "That thing last—" he paused, uttered a small groan and closed his eyes again—"that thing last summer," he concluded in a suffering voice.

"Clarence!" said Fanny seethingly and choked.

Mr. Crafft's yellow-green eyes were looking at Clarence. His hand caressed his cane gently.

"Yes, Mr. Siskinson?" he said softly.

Fanny made an impatient movement.

"Don't mind him, Mr.—er—Detective," she said. "He gets to talking like that. He's not," said Fanny viciously, "quite bright."

Clarence's eyes flew open, and he groaned and conquered it.

"Why, Fanny, how can you speak like that?" he said reproachfully. "You'll have the police thinking I'm not——" he screwed his eyes tight again suddenly and held his head on both sides, as if it threatened to split asunder, and said in a small limp voice: "—not responsible."

"Exactly," snapped Fanny. "What they ought to think." She looked at Mr. Crafft nervously. "Can't my husband be excused? He doesn't know anything about this affair."

"Well—not just at once, Mrs. Siskinson," said the detective, eyeing Clarence pleasantly and caressing his cane. "What was it you were about to tell us, Mr. Siskinson? Something," aided the detective gently, "about last summer. Something that happened to Miss Weinberg."

"Oh, that," said Clarence, without opening his eyes. "It was an accident. Just—accident."

Accident. A suddenly ominous word.

There was an alarmed silence. Katie knew that Chris had checked his silent prowl back of the chair and was looking—that they were all looking—at Clarence. It was as well Clarence's eyes were closed, for there was a quality in that combined gaze which would not have made him feel easier.

"But a very queer accident," said Clarence suddenly. "My God, hasn't anyone got any aspirin tablets?"

"An accident," said the detective softly. "What kind of accident, Mr. Siskinson?"

"Wings," said Clarence painfully, and leaned his head on his hand.

"It's noth——" observed Fanny and stopped as Mr. Crafft looked at her.

"Wings?" repeated the detective gently.

"Yes, of course," said Clarence. "And the point was, everybody knew she couldn't swim."

Sergeant Caldwell, looking addled, stepped forward. A brown cane jerked, and Sergeant Caldwell stepped backward again.

"Miss Weinberg couldn't swim, you mean?" said Mr. Crafft.

Clarence opened his eyes.

"Yes, of course. That's what I said. Have I," demanded Clarence in a wounded manner, "got to tell the whole story over again?"

"Ur-r-gh," remarked Sergeant Caldwell in a stifled way from the background.

"I think I know what he's trying to tell you about, Mr. Crafft," said Chris Lorrel suddenly.

"Yes, Mr. Lorrel? Then if you don't mind——"

"It's very simple," said Chris. "Miss Weinberg always wore these rubber affairs called water wings when she went bathing. She couldn't swim. And once last summer when she was out in fairly deep water the wings collapsed. I believe it was Jenks——" he glanced at Jenks who nodded—"yes, Jenks who heard her scream and got her to the beach. That's all."

The incident that, from Clarence's inadequate tongue, had seemed somehow to hold sinister meaning became, with Chris's telling, matter-of-fact, insignificant, merely an incident.

"I see," said Mr. Crafft. "You were here at the time, Mr. Lorrel?"

"Not just at the time it happened," said Chris. "I was here that night for dinner, however, and I remember there was some mention of it."

"Who was staying here at the house at the time?"

"I don't think I remember," said Chris slowly. "I believe we were all here to dinner. We often are."

"We were all here," said Paul. "I remember it. It was during one of those terribly hot week-ends in town, and Aunt Mina had asked me and Steven and Katie out here, where it was cooler."

"Do you remember that particular incident of the water wings?"

"Yes. Charlotte was very much annoyed."

"Scared," said Clarence.

"What's that, Mr. Siskinson?"

"I said Charlotte was scared. And she was. Thought some of us had punched holes in the wings. And," added Clarence reflectively, "I daresay someone did."

Fanny's face was red and taut, and her long hands clutched the arms of her chair suggestively. Otherwise no one moved for a long moment. Then Chris spoke:

"Charlotte was very much annoyed at the thought of having been sold wings that were no good. I really don't believe it occurred to her that someone might have been playing a practical joke. And I think myself that it was merely an accident." That alarming word again. Chris added, with a suggestion of haste: "I mean that I think it—well, just happened. Wasn't done for a joke."

"I didn't say anything about a joke," said Clarence dourly.

"Are you going so far as to state that you believe this affair was a deliberate attempt upon Miss Weinberg's life?" asked the detective, no longer bland and smiling.

Fanny coughed stridently, and Clarence glanced at his wife and looked all at once shriveled.

"I don't know anything about it," said Clarence, with acute uneasiness. "Except that it happened. And that it was queer. You see, she blew up the things herself with the bicycle pump down in the boathouse and didn't notice anything wrong with them. And they held up for a while—just about long enough for her to get out in deep water. And then——" Fanny coughed again and Clarence said hurriedly: "But that's all. Probably nothing. But very queer," he added stubbornly.

"I see," said the detective thoughtfully. They waited while he looked at Clarence and silently caressed his cane. There was a very palpable air of relief when, with his next question, it became apparent that he intended, at least for the moment, to drop the question of the mysteriously collapsing water wings. He turned, however, to Katie, and she felt a quick leap of her heart and was grateful again for Steven's presence there at her side.

"Now then, Miss Warren," said Mr. Crafft. "You mentioned a light in the summerhouse. Will you tell me that bit again?"

"It was only that—just as we got on the bridge, Paul said something about a light in the summerhouse. That's all."

"You didn't turn to look?"

"No," said Katie steadily. "I've thought of that. But I'm sure I didn't turn."

"Ah," said Mr. Crafft lingeringly. His eyes were half closed and avid, and his ugly brown head was tipped meditatively to one side and his cane still hooked around his neck. He looked at Paul.

"And *was* there a light in the summerhouse?" he said.

"Why, I——" Paul hesitated and then said frankly: "Actually I don't know. I thought I saw one. And I certainly saw a light of some kind. At the time I thought it was in the summerhouse, for it seemed to me I could see the square of a window, as if the light were back of it. But it was all so quick—I don't know, except that there *was* a light. It's possible that I just

thought of the summerhouse because I knew, of
course, that it was off in that direction. It was only
the briefest glimpse."

Mr. Crafft stroked the cane affectionately. There
was in his face a kind of latent ferocity. Like a sleepy
tiger, thought Katie, only he's not sleepy.

"The summerhouse is about twenty feet from the
bridge," murmured Mr. Crafft. "And the fog was extremely heavy. It must have been particularly bad
under all those trees and so near the lake. Are you
quite sure, Mr. Duchane, that you could have seen a
light in the summerhouse," said the little brown man
mildly, "when you couldn't see a woman who was
walking directly in the lights ahead of the car?"

A slow dull red crept into Paul's olive face.

"Not at all, Mr. Crafft. I told you I'm not sure
about it. But I did see a light of some kind in that
direction. I may have leaped to the conclusion that it
was in the summerhouse. But I know that I saw a
light."

"I see. By the way, Madame Petrie, I would like a
look at this summerhouse. I found this morning that it
was locked."

"It is always locked in the winter," said Mina
slowly.

"You have the key?"

"Yes."

"May I have it? Sometime during the day. Not
now."

"Certainly."

"Thank you. I suppose you had the key yesterday?"

"Why, yes, of course."

The cat stretched its neck and pushed a greedy head

against Mina's thick white hand until it resumed its slow, rhythmic caress.

"Now then." The detective glanced sharply around the room, singled out Jenks and addressed him. "You are Jenks?"

"Yes, sir. Adonijah Jenks."

"Adon——" The detective looked faintly startled. *"What?"*

"Adonijah," repeated Jenks with a touch of pride. "Accent on the *i*. It's quite simple, sir. Just try saying it. It only takes," he said encouragingly, "a time or two."

The detective ignored a curious rattling sound in Sergeant Caldwell's throat.

"Jenks will do quite nicely," Crafft said. "Will you tell me, Jenks, if any message came for Miss Weinberg yesterday?"

"You mean letters? There was one on the morning delivery. None in the afternoon."

"You don't happen to remember the letter—the looks of the envelope, for instance?"

Jenks looked a little embarrassed. He was a thin, small man, very sedate. He had—and cherished it in the place of family or hobby—a mysterious digestive disorder; he was honest, fairly conscientious, and occasionally pompous. His only vice so far as Katie knew was a scrapbook of clippings cut from the columns of medical advice in the newspapers, and he had managed for some ten years to get along with the other servants. He took, however, a lively, if decently restrained, interest in family affairs.

He cleared his throat now, nervously.

"Now that you mention it, sir, I believe I do remember the envelope," he said, nicely conveying the thought that it was not his habit to see envelopes. "This one had a return to a store on it. It may have been," said Jenks delicately, "a statement of her account."

"A bill?" said Mr. Crafft coarsely. "It will be in her desk, then. There were no other letters?"

"No, sir."

"None delivered by hand?"

"No, sir. I should have known."

"No telegrams?"

"Oh, no, sir."

"Well,"—Mr. Crafft smiled—"there's still the telephone."

Jenks's Adam's apple became agitated, but he said nothing.

"Was there a telephone message?" asked the detective directly.

"Well, you see, sir, I—er—had a toothache and had gone to my room in the afternoon. On the third floor."

"Well, I suppose there's an extension on the third floor?"

"Yes. Yes, sir, there is." Katie wondered why Jenks was suddenly so miserably ill at ease. Why he flashed a look at her that was so plainly frightened.

Mr. Crafft saw that frightened look.

"There was a telephone call," he said gently. "Do you know who called? You may as well tell the whole story, Jenks."

"There's not—much to tell, sir," Jenks gulped, shot another frightened look at Katie, and said rapidly: "I heard the telephone ring, and I got up and went to answer it. But somebody downstairs had already answered it and was talking. So I hung up and —went back to my own room."

"But not before you heard a scrap of conversation," purred the little brown man. "Come, Jenks, who was talking?"

"Miss—Charlotte," said Jenks desperately.

"And what did she say?"

"She said: 'Very well, then, at the bridge, but don't be late, Katie,' and then," concluded Jenks unhappily, "I hung up."

CHAPTER IX

KATIE realized that Steven had got to his feet. He was angry and white, and his eyebrows were straight and thunderous. And he was shouting at Chris furiously:

"Are you going to stand there and let Katie be dragged into this without a chance to defend herself? What kind of a lawyer do you think you are! Katie didn't have any appointment with Charlotte there at the bridge. She said so. Jenks is crazy."

"Now, Steven, you aren't making things any better," said Chris worriedly. He moved forward, a great, strangely lithe bulk. His eyes had retreated to dark slits in his huge face. "See here, Katie," he said, "you don't have to answer questions, you know, unless you like. Wouldn't it be better to wait until you've talked to someone? To me, if you wish?"

"Why, no," said Katie dazedly. "I don't mind answering questions. But I didn't telephone to Charlotte. I didn't have an appointment with her."

The room was very still. There was not even the faintest jingle of beads or bracelets from Fanny, who sat red and grim but who looked as if, under her quiet, all her muscles and nerves were gathered tense, like a cat ready for a spring. Mina's eyes smoldered. Clarence held his neat head and looked at Katie wearily. Melissa was just a dark part of the background as always. Paul smoked and looked through the smoke at Katie, and even Paul had a taut look about his eyes and mouth. And Mr. Crafft stood in the very center of them all, his brown head tipped, his eyes hungry and alight, and his leathery brown face frankly incredulous.

Incredulous! But they were all incredulous. Katie gave a queer little gasp. Her denial might as well not have been spoken.

For they all believed Jenks. His words had been so simple. So honest. So entirely convincing. Even the frightened way he had looked at her and the reluctance with which he had spoken were convincing. Steven himself must have believed it. Otherwise he would not have sprung so furiously to her defense.

Katie turned to Jenks.

"Why have you said all this?" she demanded. In spite of herself her voice wavered; she tried to steady it, and it only became jerky and husky, and there was all at once a great aching lump in her throat. "I did not talk to Charlotte."

Steven had reached for her hands and was holding them.

"Don't—don't be frightened. Jenks, what time was that call?"

"About tea time, sir. That would be around five o'clock. I'm sorry, Miss Katie."

"There, you see, Katie, that's all right. You were with Paul driving out here at that time. Jenks—misunderstood something he heard."

"How about it, Mr. Duchane?" said the detective quietly. "I suppose Miss Warren had no opportunities to telephone while she was driving from the Loop out here?"

Paul looked at his cigarette.

"None," he said promptly. "We were together every moment."

"Oh, but no, Paul——" Katie stopped abruptly. If Paul chose to lie to give her much-needed assistance in the face of Jenks's amazing story, why not permit it! But it was too late.

"Exactly where did you two meet?" asked the detective gently.

"About Washington, wasn't it, Katie?" said Paul.

Katie hesitated.

"No. Let me think. I had parked in a place on Monroe—I always park there. I had walked from Orchestra Hall to the parking station and then had driven back to Michigan as I always do, and it was at the first intersection that I met you. So that must have been Madison."

"I see," said the detective. "Now were you together all the time until you reached home? Or did you stop for something?"

"I stopped," said Katie, hating him. "Paul wanted some cigarettes."

"Where was that?"

She told him, and he recognized the number. He said:

"That's just across from your apartment, isn't it, Mr. Petrie?"

"Yes," said Steven, frowning. Katie felt a kind of chill; how much did the detective know about them all? Chris had said: "If we can just keep the police from discovering how things stood between Charlotte and Katie!"

"Did you wait in the car for Mr. Duchane, Miss Warren?" the little brown man was saying mildly.

"No," replied Katie desperately. "I crossed the street and rang the bell to Steven's apartment."

(Steven beside her had made no motion at all. But somehow she knew as clearly as if he had spoken that she had made some mistake—some blunder.)

"Did anyone answer?" went on the detective.

(Was that it? Was that her blunder? Then, where had Steven been? . . . She must reply.)

"No. No one answered the bell."

(Oh, Steven, forgive me if I've said the wrong thing.)

"Is there a telephone in the lobby?"

"Yes." The desk clerk. He knew her. Had he seen her drop the telephone? The police would question him, of course. And Steven hadn't wanted them to know that he was not in his apartment. Was ever anyone caught in such small and terrible meshes? She said, "I tried to telephone to Steven. But he didn't answer. And I put down the telephone just as the desk clerk came in." And she knew that it sounded like an afterthought.

"Did the desk clerk recognize you?"

"Yes."

"Did you ask him where Mr. Petrie was?"

"Yes," said Katie.

"Did he know?"

"No."

"Then what did you do?"

"I went back to the car and waited for Mr. Duchane. It was only a moment or two."

"I see. Well, Mr. Petrie, where were you yesterday afternoon? Between," said the detective in a leisurely way, "between, say, four and six o'clock? I suppose you can readily tell us."

"I'm not sure that I can," said Steven. His voice was very cool and undisturbed. Yet Katie sat rigid and almost breathless, as if any motion on her part might distract him from some very difficult and dangerous task. You might hold your breath so, watching a surgeon.

"Let me see—I went over to town just after Paul left. I wanted to put in an order for some new palette knives. The fog was over everything and—if it's an alibi you want, I'm afraid I haven't one, for I got interested in the fog and light effects and just wandered about for—oh, I don't know how long. Finally I got my car and drove out here. It was very slow going. I left the car just outside the gate——"

"What time did you leave it there, Mr. Petrie?"

"Why—around six-thirty or so, I imagine. The ambulance was just leaving with Char—it was just leaving when I reached the house."

"Why did you leave your car outside the gate, then, Mr. Petrie?"

"I wanted to walk up to the house. Besides, it was dangerous—the drive to the house, I mean."

"You didn't know what had happened?"

"No."

"You knew nothing of it?"

"No."

"Then," said the detective slowly, "why did you telephone urgently for the doctor at about half-past five?"

Even the ferns were listening—listening.

"Because I wanted to see him," said Steven coolly. "I suppose the office girl told you I wanted to see him?"

"It doesn't really matter how I know, does it, Mr. Petrie?" said the detective, smiling. "However, she did relay your calls—several of them—and Dr. Mannsen told me when I interviewed him earlier this morning. Do you mind telling us why you wanted to see him? There was a certain urgency which impressed the office girl——"

"Not at all," said Steven. "Although I should prefer speaking to you alone. However, it's no secret—I was very anxious about my aunt's health, and I wanted to know if Dr. Mannsen thought she had improved. It seemed to me," said Steven, speaking with an unaccustomed emphasis and a detailed explanation of motives which was unlike him—"it seemed to me that Aunt Mina had been distinctly better for several weeks, and I wanted the doctor's opinion. Charlotte did not see the same improvement that I saw."

"Oh, no," burst out Fanny. "Charlotte thought that Mina was about to——" She checked herself with a horrified glance at Mina. "That is," she went on hurriedly, making it worse, "Charlotte feared the worst."

Paul said smoothly: "Charlotte's affection for Aunt Mina took that form. You are really much stronger, aren't you, Aunt Mina?" Mina's white face did not move, and her black eyes burned steadily, and the detective said:

"Now if you'll just explain why your inquiries were so extremely urgent, Mr. Petrie——"

"I don't believe they were any more urgent than their reason justifies," said Steven in a stiff manner which was, to Katie's ears, only, probably, a shade too stiff.

"M'm'm," murmured the detective and sheered suddenly to Paul.

"Did you use the telephone in the shop where you stopped for cigarettes?"

"No," said Paul. "But there was a telephone booth there, and I could have used it. And I don't suppose I can prove I didn't use it. But I didn't call Charlotte, if that's what you're getting at."

Mr. Crafft looked at Jenks.

"Did you get the impression, when you overheard that bit of conversation, that Miss Weinberg was speaking *to* Miss Warren or *of* Miss Warren? I mean, did you feel that she was addressing——"

"Oh, I understand you perfectly, sir," said Jenks, "and I really can't say. I just heard those words—that's all. But it's a nice point—I can quite see that it's a nice point, sir. My impression, naturally, was that Miss Katie was speaking to her. But I might have been mistaken. For, as you imply, I didn't hear Miss Katie's voice. No, no, I assure you I didn't hear Miss Katie's voice." His assurance, thought Katie sadly, was a little too eager to carry much weight.

"How are the house telephones arranged?" asked Mr. Crafft suddenly. "Are all the telephones in the house on one wire?"

No one replied for a moment, and then Jenks and Chris and Fanny all started at once. Fanny won.

"There are three telephones," she said definitely. "One in the kitchen, and one in Madame Petrie's

rooms. The third is the general house telephone—
there it is on the desk beside you—which has two
extensions, one on each floor."

"Thank you," said the detective, looking at the
telephone. "And by the way, how many latchkeys are
there to the house? I suppose you have a key, Miss
Warren?"

"Why, yes, of course," said Katie.

"And you, Mr. Petrie?"

"Certainly."

Mina stirred.

"There are a number of latchkeys in existence, Mr.
Crafft," she said flatly. "My nephew is here a great
deal. Also Katie and Paul. They have keys, naturally.
And since Mrs. Siskinson and her husband have been
here, they've had keys, of course."

"Mr. Lorrel?" inquired the detective, looking at
the ribbon on his eyeglasses.

"Yes," said Chris in a voice like a growl. "This
place is like home to me. Has been for years."

"Ah—I quite understand. Oh, Mr. Lorrel—while
we are on the subject of alibis, will you be good enough
to tell me where you were yesterday afternoon? Between four o'clock and six."

Chris's eyes retreated further. He looked angry.

"I don't mind telling you at all, Mr. Crafft," he
said. "But I'm afraid I have no alibi. I had to see a
client out in Riverside. I drove out, failed to see the
client, and returned. It's away west, as you know, and
as I drove slowly on my return trip, it took some time."

"But I suppose you inquired of someone for your—
client," said Mr. Crafft softly. "It's only a matter of
form, you know, Mr. Lorrel."

"I know," said Chris. "But as a matter of fact I didn't inquire for him. I went direct to his office, which was closed. His name's Frank Ellin, if you want to know."

"Thank you, Mr. Lorrel. And you, Mr. Siskinson, were on the beach walking until you came in about five?"

"Eh?" said Clarence, lifting his head in a startled fashion.

"According to what your wife told Sergeant Caldwell," repeated the detective, "you and Mrs. Siskinson were walking on the beach until you came in the house at five o'clock."

"Did Fanny say that?" said Clarence wearily. "Oh, well, then it's all right. If she says so."

"Do you mean you were on the beach?" said the detective with softly menacing deliberation.

"Didn't I tell you——" Clarence opened his eyes and met the detective's glance and said hurriedly: "Oh, yes. Yes, yes. Dear me, yes."

"And you came in at five o'clock?"

"If Fanny—that is, yes."

"Did you see Miss Weinberg?"

Clarence's eyes traveled helplessly to Fanny and back to the detective.

"No," he said limply.

"Do you know anything of her death that you've not told?" demanded the detective, suddenly very stern and grim.

"No. No, no—dear me, no," volleyed Clarence agitatedly. He paused, looked at the detective, and then added unexpectedly, "Except that I think it's damn queer."

"You do?" said the detective softly.

"Yes, of course. Damn queer. You see, if Charlotte saw a car coming at her, she'd hop out of the way. Nippy. That was Charlotte. Always on the trigger. I could understand it," said Clarence largely, "if she had been drinking a bit. One gets a bit confused, you know," he said reflectively, "not quite one's self. Things a bit blurry—not real sure what you're doing——"

"Clarence," said Fanny tersely, "will you please check your drunken reminiscences!"

"Now, Fanny, I was only saying that Charlotte wasn't drunk. Charlotte never drank. Charlotte was, in fact," said Clarence, with a note of painful recollection in his voice, "a complete teetotaler. And expected everyone else to be. So I don't see why under heaven she just stood there and let Katie kill her."

"An interesting view," purred the detective. And Katie knew that Sergeant Caldwell had suddenly all but pricked up his ears. The little brown djinn had turned to her again.

"I suppose you have not yet recalled telephoning to Miss Weinberg——" he was saying suavely, smiling at her.

Steven leaned forward, starting to speak, but Katie forestalled him.

"I assure you, Mr. Crafft," she said furiously and clearly, "that I shall not recall telephoning to Charlotte. I did not do so. And furthermore, she——" Katie caught her breath, and her hands clung to each other, and the words came rapidly: "Oh, this is all unnecessary. Charlotte wasn't murdered. She couldn't have been murdered. Don't you understand! She was moving. I saw her. Moving! There in front of the car. There was no one with her. She was struck by— by the car. It wasn't murder!"

Again, to her horror, she felt incredulity in the silence into which her words fell. Not, she thought swiftly, from Mina. Not from Steven, although there was still something strange and unfathomable in his face. But there it was, stony and blank in the faces of the police. In the bland brown face of the detective which still held its small fixed smile.

"I only wish, Miss Warren," said the detective smoothly, "that your assurance were sufficient. Unfortunately, I fear it is not impartial."

"Oh——" Katie shrank back and Steven said angrily: "Chris, is this sort of thing permissible?"

Chris Lorrel looked silently at the detective for a moment. The little brown man met his gaze with assurance. It seemed to Katie that there was a kind of unspoken communication between them. Then Chris said reluctantly, as if it hurt him:

"I'm afraid it is, Steve. The thing is out of our hands. In God's name," said Chris, turning suddenly savage and swinging around upon them like a great angry bear—"in God's name what's been going on here?"

Fanny bristled. Mina did not move, except that her eyes burned and probed Chris's angry face. His rage was sudden, unexpected, and to Katie inexplicable. It was as if Chris had been struck with a blow for which he had been unprepared. Something, too, that was unfair, that caught him unaware, and that had been aimed directly at him, Chris Lorrel.

Clarence mumbled something, and Fanny, still bristling, shot him a nervous glance and addressed Chris, seethingly.

"I don't know what you mean, I'm sure, Chris Lorrel, to speak to us in such a fashion. Nothing's been 'going on here,' as you put it. I don't know why you should suddenly side with the police and look at us like we were all criminals. Charlotte was killed accidentally and——"

"That hair," said Clarence distinctly. "Don't forget that——"

"You be quiet, Clarence Siskinson," said Fanny sharply, deflected. She hurled Clarence a tensely admonishing cobalt glance which was charged with increasing nervousness and returned to Chris. "You know as much about this family as anybody, Chris. You are as much a part of it as anybody. If something —I don't know what dreadful thing you are hinting at, I'm sure—has been going on here, you should know as much as anyone else about it." Her voice had risen louder, shriller, to cover a curious steady mumbling on Clarence's part. As she paused for very lack of furious breath, the mumbling became words:

". . . black," mumbled Clarence. "And woolly. That's what it was. And I said murder all along. Murder. I knew it from the beginning. Black. And woolly."

Exasperation struggled with rage in Fanny's strong florid face and glittering blue eyes. She took a long breath preparatory to a flood of speech, but Mr. Crafft's cane jerked suggestively, and she fell into baffled, raging silence.

Clarence, at the unexpected silence, opened his eyes, perceived belatedly that he was again in the unenviable position of being, literally, the object of all eyes, including the tigerish and lighted eyes of Mr. Crafft, and closed his own eyes again with a faint groan.

"And what," said the detective softly, "is all this?"

Clarence's neat legs rippled gracefully; in anyone else it would have been a wriggle.

"Only," said Clarence in a goaded voice, "a little bit of hair."

"Go on. What about it?"

"Nothing. Nothing at all. Only," added Clarence with his fatal passion for truth, "only that it was black. And woolly."

Sergeant Caldwell, looking apoplectic, surged from the background and then back again like a restless blue wave with a pink top.

"And exactly why did you think it was murder?" said the detective. His mellow, gentle voice became occasionally very thin and sharp and cruel.

"Oh—h——" Clarence opened his eyes helplessly. "If you must know, it was in Charlotte's hand. And I found it."

"S-g-g-le," observed Sergeant Caldwell, in a stifled manner.

It took perhaps five laborious moments to extract from Clarence an account of the wisp of black hair, at the end of which Sergeant Caldwell, a silent but not at all an impassive participant, was frankly panting. And it was then that Mina Petrie furnished them all with an unexpected moment of drama.

For she had, she said flatly, lost the hair.

For just an instant Mr. Crafft's thick brown nostrils quivered.

"But Madame Petrie," said Mr. Crafft in soft expostulation, "it's an extraordinary thing to lose."

"An extraordinary thing to find," said Mina flatly. "Not, however, an extraordinary thing to lose."

Chris's eyes opened, and Mr. Crafft himself looked for an instant a bit taken aback. Then Mina went on flatly and entirely without double meaning:

"It was very small, you know. Just a wisp of hair. I wrapped it in a handkerchief, and when I reached my own rooms I think I put it on the dressing table in my bathroom. But this morning it was not there. We looked, Melissa and I, all over the room. But we could not find it."

"Did you find the handkerchief in which it was wrapped?"

"No."

"Does that bathroom open directly upon your own room, Madame Petrie?"

"No. You may go upstairs and look at it if you wish. It enters upon a short passage, a kind of hall, which connects my rooms with Charlotte—with the room Miss Weinberg occupied."

"That room was, I suppose, unoccupied last night?"

Thin white lids dropped suddenly over Mina's eyes. "Yes," she said. "Certainly."

Mr. Crafft rubbed a brown palm caressingly up and down his cane.

"If the person who took that bit of hair will tell us about it now, it will save us quite a lot of time and energy," he said softly, looking at no one.

Katie thought of that midnight caller in Charlotte's room; of that empty drawer and the absurd bolster. Should she tell of it? It meant probably only a bit of secret ferreting on Fanny's account; somehow the whole incident savored of Fanny. But it would prove that she, Katie, had been in Charlotte's room and within easy proximity of that vanishing bit of hair. Better not to tell of it. They would only look incredulous and avoid her eyes when she explained her presence there. Chris was wheezing and saying something in a rather hoarse, breathless voice:

". . . not just an inquiry into accident. That's clear. You as good as told me——" He stopped, and Mr. Crafft purred.

"What did I tell you?"

"Well, you didn't say it in so many words," said Chris. "But you gave me to understand——"

"You are an astute man, Mr. Lorrel," said the little brown man, sighing. "And you are quite right. This is, definitely, an inquiry into murder."

CHAPTER X

FOR a long moment the mirror over the desk was the only thing in that room which seemed to be alive and sentient. And that was only because, while everything else in the room stopped, the mirror went right on adding to its own secret record. It caught and held Mina's feverish eyes and Katie's white teeth catching for a second her crimson lower lip. It held Paul's veiled dark eyes and high, olive cheekbones and a blue wisp of smoke.

It caught, from one angle or another, all of them and held them, and dominating the whole was a leathery little brown djinn who ought rightly to have come out of a bottle.

Then Chris, mysteriously angry again, wheezed and said huskily:

"How do you know Charlotte was murdered?"

There was a faint motion over them; the mirror recorded that small ripple. It was as if each had repeated after Chris: "How do you know Charlotte was murdered?"

Then Fanny leaned forward. Her bracelets tinkled, and her strong face was pale mauve, and her nostrils looked pinched.

"Were there—injuries?" she asked hoarsely.

"There were no injuries that were not, probably, made by the car," said Mr. Crafft. "It was, however, murder."

"But why?" insisted Chris. "Why——"

"Miss Weinberg was murdered," said the detective tersely. "It is my business to fix the guilt. I must do it in my own way. Miss Warren——"

Katie suddenly came to life.

"She couldn't have been murdered. I tell you I saw her moving. Walking. I know I killed her. But I didn't mean to kill Charlotte. Murder—that means premeditation. But I didn't plan to kill Charlotte."

She would, perhaps, goaded by a mad feeling that she must somehow convince them, have kept on repeating it. But there was again that blank wall of silence and incredulity and deafness. No one seemed to hear her. So Katie stopped talking. It was exactly like one of those horribly futile dreams, when you keep ascending the same ladder over and over again and never reach the top.

Mr. Crafft looked up suddenly from Sergeant Caldwell's black notebook.

"Jenks," he said directly, "did you serve tea yesterday afternoon?"

"No, sir. As I said, I had a toothache and had retired to my room with a hot-water bottle."

"Then who served tea?"

Jenks looked doubtful but murmured:

"Melissa, sir, I suppose."

"Melissa?" It was an inquiry. Melissa stepped respectfully forward. Her dark face was quiet and her tall body tranquil and not unbeautiful.

"I was cleaning the linen cupboards upstairs, sir," she said in a velvet soft voice. "Maybe it was Hilda who made tea."

"Hilda?" snapped the detective, suddenly less amiable. "Who's she?"

Fanny tinkled and leaned forward.

"She is the cook," she said. "Or, more accurately, *was* the cook. She left this morning, owing, I believe, to a mirror having smashed itself and the kitchen clock having stopped. No one knows where she went," continued Fanny, purring a bit herself as Mr. Crafft's brown leather face became touched with a faintly human look of exasperation. "But her name is Hilda Hansen. I daresay you can readily discover her."

Mr. Crafft shot one lighted glance toward Sergeant Caldwell.

"Find her."

"Find—Hilda Hansen?" inquired Sergeant Caldwell, looking worried.

"Certainly."

"But—this Hilda Hansen——"

"Well?"

"It's only that there's quite a few Hansens——"

"She is probably in Chicago," said Mr. Crafft, with the effect of giving street and number. "Find her at once."

"Yes. Certainly. By all means." Sergeant Caldwell looked uneasily around him, discovered one of the lesser gentlemen-in-waiting, and his face cleared. "Find Hilda Hansen," he said magnificently.

Mr. Crafft relented.

"Where did she come from? How long has she been with you? What do you know about her?"

Mina Petrie replied:

"She has been with me some seven or eight years. I know nothing about her. Jenks!"

"Yes, madame."

"Will you tell the police anything they wish to know?"

The gentleman-in-waiting jerked his head toward the vestibule, whither Jenks followed him. But Jenks must have known little, for he returned very shortly, and the policeman departed. He looked, however, fully capable of finding a dozen Hilda Hansens. Which was, indeed, a not improbable development.

Mr. Crafft was holding his eyeglasses poised in one hand and the notebook in the other.

"It's a rather interesting point," he said softly, "that the tea tray was so obviously untouched. Well, well——" The notebook went suddenly into his own pocket. His eyeglasses vanished, and there was all at once a note of finality in his voice.

"I thank you, Madame Petrie," he said, suddenly, affable once more and purring. "You have been very patient. Of course, you understand this is, unfortunately, only a beginning. I'm afraid that Sergeant Caldwell and I will find it our duty to interview all of you, separately—perhaps many times. I might add, though I regret the necessity for it, that while you may, of course, go on about your affairs as usual, still I must ask you to hold yourselves at the disposition of the police. Not, in other words, to deviate from your usual ways," he added, smiling.

Neither the smile nor the implication was pleasant.

Mina was rising. The cat made a swift, blue-gray arc to the floor. Mina said with an effect of great dignity:

"You may be assured, Mr. Crafft, that we shall endeavor to give you every possible assistance. This terrible thing you have told us adds to our shock and grief. I shall be most grateful if you will keep me informed of the progress of your—inquiry. Please feel free to employ my house and my domestic staff in any way that may facilitate matters. My affairs are in the hands of my lawyer, Mr. Lorrel, who will act for me at all times. It is all," concluded Mina, "very distressing."

She said it with all the passion with which she might have asked for a glass of water or more salt. And yet a fire burned somewhere back of these fierce, seeking eyes. It was, Katie thought, as if Mina were dying not from any physical weakness but from some inward furnace that consumed its own ashes back of her dead-white face. As if her mortal enemy were not bodily illness but instead that gluttonous flame.

Then Mina turned and laid her thick white hand upon Melissa's tranquil black arm and began to mount the stairway. And all at once she was only a stolid Dutch house-frau with her black hair in a tight bun on top of her head, and her shoulders hunched from working, and a sharp eye out for any undusted corners or unpolished mahogany. And a woman who had need, poor soul, to set her house in order.

Pity fled, though, and a dizzy, sick sense of fear shook Katie again. For Chris was suddenly at her elbow. That older Chris—worried and haggard-looking and mysteriously angry.

"Crafft says will we wait for him in the bookroom. He wants to question you more at length, Katie. He's got Jenks and the chauffeur in the dining room now. God knows what they'll say——"

At the door of the passage Katie paused and looked

back. Steven and Paul and Sergeant Caldwell were among the little group of men standing in the center of the room, held together apparently by Sergeant Caldwell, who was speaking—asking questions, Katie supposed, for he had, this time, a red-backed notebook in his hand. Clarence and Fanny were sitting somewhat nervously on the edges of their chairs, waiting, and through the wide door into the dining room Katie could see William's thin, anxious face and the way his hands twisted his cap while he replied to some questions from the detective.

Steven's blond head shone under the light, and he turned and gave her a long look over Sergeant Caldwell's conscientiously bent head. It was a long, darkly shining look which held something so strong and so glowing that Katie felt suddenly warm and glowing herself, as if he had kissed her again.

Queer.

She followed Chris rather dazedly into the bookroom. Was it possible that in the midst of that seething dark kaleidoscope that had caught her she had managed to fall in love? That, besides everything else! It was a gorgeous feeling, tumultuous, terribly sweet—yet somehow tempered with sadness, as though now you were vulnerable. Now fate could reach you.

She had killed Charlotte. And somehow it had been murder.

The bookroom was perhaps the only beautiful room in Mina Petrie's house. It was a rather small, octagonal room with gleaming oak panels which alternated with book-laden shelves that went to the ceiling. There was the soft, worn beauty of old rugs, and the satin patina of one or two old and lovely pieces of furniture. There was the comfort of deeply cushioned chairs and divans and well-adjusted reading lamps. Usually the leaded casement windows lit the room softly with a faintly amber light. That morning, however, even after Chris had turned on the light in a table lamp, the room remained dark and shadowy. The fireplace was dead and, owing, probably, to the excitement of the morning, Jenks had not dusted the room, and there was still the desolation of ashes and many cigarette ends in the ashtrays, a crumpled newspaper or two, chairs out of place, and a tray with empty, sticky-looking glasses on it.

Chris went lightly across the rugs, pulled open one of the casement windows, and the cold, damp air drifted reluctantly into the room.

"Chris, what am I going to do?" said Katie desperately. "Charlotte wasn't murdered. She was alive, walking in front of the car. I didn't purposely strike her. Oh, I didn't, Chris!"

Chris closed the window, lightly and deftly and without a sound, as his wide fingers always somehow managed to do. Then he began to walk, still lightly, up and down the rug. He was between the little area of light, cast by the table lamp, and the bookshelves, so that his shadow, huge and bulky and scarcely more silent than Chris, followed him up and down, up and down, against the rows of books.

"Look here, Katie," he said uneasily. "Just how did you feel toward Charlotte?"

Katie pushed her hands wearily across her forehead and sat down on the divan. How *had* she felt toward the dead woman? The dead woman who had hated her; who had been, wherever possible, her enemy.

"I mean," said Chris, "did you and Charlotte have any well—scenes? Out-and-out words, you know. Anything, I mean, that the servants might quote."

"Oh, that," said Katie. "No. Never."

"Not even about the bonds?"

"No. She just insisted she'd never ordered them. I had taken the order over the telephone, you know—hadn't her written signature. Because it was Charlotte. Oh, there was no use making a scene with her about it.—I don't know how I'm going to pay you what I owe you, Chris. My note is worth at the moment just about one dime."

"Don't worry about that, Katie. Now that Charlotte's dead, Mina will put you in her will. There's not much doubt of that. Charlotte always feared you, Katie; I suppose she was actually afraid you'd get too close to Mina. Push her out. But it's queer—that you were driving the car."

"Don't, Chris. I—that's brutal. I didn't mean to kill her."

"I know. But it's a brutal business, Katie."

"You sound frightened."

She wanted to add: "And angry. Why are you angry, Chris?" But she did not.

He flashed a quick look at her and passed his huge hand over his neat brown hair. His large face looked moist, and his eyes had retreated into the pendulous folds of flesh until they were very small and dark.

"I am frightened, Katie. I don't understand what's been going on. There's something—something underneath—that scares me. Murder——" He checked himself. "Here's Crafft—I'll try to help you with him," he promised, and sat down opposite Katie, sink-

ing far down into the cushions and yet looking as if he
might as easily untether himself and float bulkily upward.

There was, that morning, little opportunity for
Chris's aid. For Mr. Crafft knew exactly what he
wanted to ask, knew so exactly that he left no loop-
holes.

He already knew, he told Katie, briefly, that Miss
Weinberg had stood in the way of Katie's legal adop-
tion by Madame Petrie. He also knew, somehow,
about the bonds. He knew, after a skillful question or
two directed at Chris, that Mina Petrie was dying and
had not yet made her will. He disposed of all that
with an ease that left Katie feeling uncertain and
singularly exposed to attack. And it came.

"Did you recognize Miss Weinberg when she
stepped in front of the car?"

"No. I only saw a moving figure."

"But it *was moving?* Walking, would you say?
Running? Trying to avoid the car?"

"I don't know. I only know it was moving."

"I see. When did you realize it was Miss Weinberg?"

"After I had got the car stopped. Paul got out and
ran back along the road, and I followed him. He said
he thought it was Charlotte."

"Now when you saw this moving figure you put
your foot on the brake?"

"Yes, of course. And the other foot on the clutch."

"Immediately?"

"Yes."

"Would you say within three seconds? Two?"

"As quickly as I could act, Mr. Crafft. I did it instinctively."

"And did the car respond immediately?"

"No. We were on a down grade, and it was slippery, as I said."

"But I should think the car would diminish in speed or skid at once. You surely noticed that it did."

"N—no," said Katie hesitating. "I don't remember that it swerved, either. But it is all very confused."

"But the car did go slower at once?"

"N—no. Not at once."

"It didn't by any chance seem to go faster?"

"Wait, Katie," interrupted Chris. "Don't answer."

"Now, now, Mr. Lorrel, are you going to make our task more difficult?" said Mr. Crafft smiling. "Miss Warren, don't you think it possible that—your foot was on the gas throttle instead of the brake?"

"No—*no—no*——"

"Katie!" It was Chris, warning. Katie caught herself.

"No. I am sure that my foot was on the brake," she said. So that was what they would say! But she could still feel that helpless, futile pressure. "I'm positive I actually stood on the brake and clutch. You can't mistake the gas throttle for the brake."

"I didn't say mistake," said Mr. Crafft gently.

Chris rumbled, and Mr. Crafft went quickly on:

"You knew that Madame Petrie's will was not made, Miss Warren?"

"I believe I did," said Katie, her voice husky with anger that dared not, somehow, become articulate.

"You believe you did. And you know that Miss Weinberg was not friendly to your interests?"

"I knew that Charlotte was not friendly to me."

"You knew that her influence with Madame Petrie would be exerted against you?"

"Katie, you need not answer that." It was Chris again, warning and angry.

"There are plenty of ways to prove that, Mr. Lorrel," said the detective pleasantly. "There's no evading the fact that Miss Weinberg's death at just this time was a most fortunate turn for Miss Warren. And it is, certainly, a rather curious coincidence that it was Miss Warren herself who killed Miss Weinberg."

"That isn't proof," said Chris.

"Proof of murder, you mean?"

"You said you had evidence of murder."

"I'm afraid we have, Mr. Lorrel. I'm afraid——"

A blue bulk materialized in the doorway. It was Sergeant Caldwell, and he managed to convey without speech an earnest and even pressing need to speak to Mr. Crafft. The detective waved his cane apologetically but at the same time authoritatively and went like a quick brown shadow to the doorway and into the passage outside.

The small passage, wood-paneled and hollow, was almost perfectly acoustic.

"They've identified the car," began Sergeant Caldwell eagerly. "The one that was parked outside the grounds so long yesterday afternoon and the bus driver saw and reported to us."

"Well?"

"It belongs to this nephew. Steven Petrie. The artist fellow."

"He was here, then, at the time of the murder. Anything else?"

"Yes—this letter: the man searching the Weinberg

room found it in her desk. It's dated yesterday. I guess it's the one you're after. It's——"

The detective said something quick and low and indistinguishable except in its tone of warning, and Sergeant Caldwell's voice promptly lowered.

Katie was leaning forward, striving to hear what they were saying. And what had they said? She remembered with rather terrible clarity the dark silent windows of Steven's apartment. Herself ringing the bell. Loud enough, she thought, to wake the dead.

She listened with every nerve strained. Chris was listening, too, although he did not turn his head. What letter had they found? But the only word she could distinguish from that suddenly hushed murmur of voices was the word "summerhouse."

It was, however, a significant word.

And she must warn Steven. She must warn him at once.

Then Sergeant Caldwell's voice lifted clearer as he turned hurriedly away.

"I'll get him," he promised. "He just left a few minutes ago. He's probably at his studio. We'll have him sewed up before he knows we're after him."

Then Mr. Crafft returned.

He was smiling, his thick nostrils quivering a bit. He had a letter in one brown hand, and it seemed to give him great satisfaction.

"Well," he said smilingly to Chris, "I believe we've found the letter Miss Weinberg was writing just before she died. It was in an envelope, addressed and ready to send." He held the letter and read slowly. He seemed to be looking only at the letter, yet Katie felt quite sure somehow that he was conscious of every fleeting expression in her face or in Chris's.

It was an extraordinary letter. It began without salutation and was very short:

" 'You cannot further deny this despicable masquerade. I have proof of the cruel advantage you are taking of Mina's affection. I have proof and will show it to you. It is true that she believes, but she knows her destiny too well to be swerved by shadows. She is influenced toward you, yes; it wasn't difficult for me to discover the means you took. I can at any moment expose you. But there is no need for us to quarrel. I suggest a truce, until, say, after the twenty-sixth. My terms are clear: a part of your share in her will for my silence now. You promised to arrange a meeting with me. I am writing this so it will be ready to post if you refuse to meet me.' "

Mr. Crafft looked at them slowly.

"It is signed Charlotte Weinberg. And it is addressed to Steven Petrie.

"As she signed her name, something startled her and her pen jabbed into the paper. She was arranging to meet Steven Petrie. We must ask Mr. Petrie regarding this 'despicable masquerade.' "

He paused. Katie sat as if stunned. "There's a mistake—a mistake—some terrible mistake." She thought she was speaking aloud but couldn't have been, for neither Chris nor the detective looked at her.

"But Miss Weinberg was quite willing to let it continue providing she herself could get in on the swag. . . . I think I must know," said the little brown man, "just what scheme Miss Weinberg was engaged upon herself. Just why the twenty-sixth was suggested with such an elaborately casual manner. Oh, altogether a very interesting letter," he purred.

His knowing eyes seemed to comprehend that Katie could tell him no more and that Chris at the moment was stubbornly angry, like a great tormented bear. "I'll see you both later," said Mr. Crafft, with dubious promise.

He was all at once gone. And Chris without a word or a look was gone, too. And she must find Steven.

The lounge was again empty of policemen. With a feeling of incredulity Katie caught a glimpse of Mr. Crafft driving away in an automobile with the blue shoulders of a policeman beside him.

An ugly little brown djinn driving away in an automobile.

It would have been more in character had he turned into brown smoke and poured himself into a bottle.

"And I wish I had the cork," thought Katie viciously.

Clarence emerged, ruffled and rather bruised-looking, from the dining room, gave her a harassed glance, replied, to her question, that Paul and Steven had both gone, he thought to town, apparently without let or hindrance from the police. He added that lunch was served in the dining room, if she cared to have any, and went wearily upstairs, as if he had found the morning and Mr. Crafft somewhat trying.

Fanny, too, had vanished. She was having lunch with Madame Petrie, said Jenks, who also looked rather exhausted.

"Did Mr. Steven say where he was going?" Katie asked Jenks.

"No, ma'am."

There was only one possible way to reach Steven at once, and that was by telephone to his studio.

But no one answered. She tried again and again; still there was no answer.

She ate something and tried not to think of Charlotte and hated the big, silent house, and tried again to telephone to Steven and again without result.

It was a long, strange afternoon. Quiet and dark and lonely, with the fog growing heavier.

Katie tried to rest, she tried to read. She finally gave herself up to thinking of Charlotte's death, of her own danger. Of murder. Murder in that somber house.

It wasn't sensible. It wasn't even conceivable.

But Charlotte was dead.

And she had killed her. Yet she hadn't killed Charlotte, because Charlotte was murdered, and she hadn't murdered her.

It was a vicious, terrible circle, and there wasn't any sense to any of it. And she felt sick and frightened, and the house was chilly and silent, with fog pushing at the windows.

At intervals she tried to telephone to Steven. If she only, she thought frantically, knew what the police were doing! Where and when they would strike.

There wasn't, perhaps, much use in continuing her attempt to reach him by telephone. The telephone drew her, however.

How quiet it had grown in the house! And how dark the amber windows there in the little bookroom had become! It was, she thought, and shuddered, growing dark out there under the trees, on that slippery road around the ravine. Dark and foggy. There was, however, no sleet tonight.

She rose, afraid of her own thoughts, and went through the little passage to the lounge.

It was silent and empty. The lights had been turned off in the dining room beyond, and it was a dark twilight cavern, ghostly. The small Lowestoft table lamp was lighted, and the light struggled passively with the gray twilight. Katie crossed to the windows, but there was only gray black fog beyond.

The house was so still.

She turned, shivering a little, back to the desk and sat down, and the little area of light made a silhouette of her figure and threw her face into brightness. As she sat down, Friquet rose, a silent blue-gray shadow there on the desk, and Katie's heart leaped before she realized it was only the cat. Friquet stretched slowly and sat down again, great shining eyes watching Katie. It was, thought Katie, an ominous name. The cat was probably the mausoleum of many sparrows. And she didn't like the way the cat stared up toward the stairway or out toward the dark windows.

Katie put out her hand toward the telephone and stopped. Why *had* Steven's car been parked outside the tangled, fog-masked park at exactly the hour when Charlotte had undertaken her mysterious journey? What *did* that letter mean?

Katie never knew how long she sat there at the desk, staring at the blotter, trying to answer questions that had no answers.

Presently she roused herself. It had grown darker. The little area of light in which she sat looked bright and exposed against the darkness of the room. There were heavy shadows along the stairway and in the corners, and the door to the dining room was black.

The cat was asleep again, smug and complacent. Katie glanced up and at the mirror. It reflected her own face, white against the crowding shadows of the lounge. A fern picked itself out and then fell into shadow. A black wicker chair caught a shining high-light. She could see the wide doorway into the dining room, but the great room itself was an empty well of blackness.

It must be very near five o'clock.

Her fingers reached out idly and picked up a pen and she looked at it. What had the detective said about Charlotte's fingers? That they were inkstained. That she had been writing something. Perhaps she had sat at that desk. With her small elaborately coifed black head bent over, writing. Perhaps the mirror had reflected her small powdered face with its wrinkled eyelids and calculative black eyes.

The cat moved. In one single, silent motion it was on its feet, listening.

Its eyes were staring beyond Katie into the black-ness of the dining room. Its eyes were staring and moved fixedly as if following some moving object, and the end of its tail was suddenly twitching in short, sharp little jerks.

And Katie was listening too. Her body was numb and cold and rigid, all but her heart, and she could not turn, and the mirror showed only black depths.

Then there was a small sound from somewhere in the dining room. A faint tinkling sound. It was like a cup rattling against the saucer.

It would be Jenks, bringing a tea tray.

But the cat's eyes shone, and it opened its red mouth and drew its lips back over sharp teeth in a long sound-less snarl.

It was just then that the telephone rang. Rang sharply, insistently, shattering and piercing the silence.

CHAPTER XI

THE telephone rang again.

The cat did not move, but Katie finally put out a hand and took up the telephone without looking at it and held it to her ear.

She did not speak. Her mouth moved, but no sound came from it. Her eyes were riveted on the mirror. Curious there was no light in all that black depth. That no motion could be seen, where there must be motion.

Then she realized that at the other end of the wire someone was waiting for her voice. She could feel that presence vividly, and she knew suddenly that whoever waited for her voice did so with excitement.

She tried and tried again and finally said, "Hello. Hello."

Still the cat did not move, and still there was no motion in the mirrored blackness behind her.

A hurried low voice answered:

"Katie. Katie, is that you?"

"Steven!"

"Katie—I've got to talk to you—it's terribly important. Listen——"

"Wait. There's someone in the dining room. Wait——"

His voice had succeeded in rousing her so that she could shake off the paralysis of terror that had gripped her. She rose from the desk and turned and saw no one. With the telephone lying there on the blotter and Steven waiting, she knew exactly what to do. She walked to the nearest light switch and snapped it, and light flooded the lounge and entered the dining room in a wide path. And she followed it, and reached for the dining-room light switch, and that blackness fled and that room was full of light. No one was there. But there was no tea tray on the table or long buffet, either.

Katie stood looking at the door to the butler's pantry. It was quiet. It did not move. Singular that she should feel so definitely that it had only stopped moving. That perhaps its wooden panels were still vibrating.

But Steven was waiting.

She turned swiftly back to the desk. As she snatched the telephone, she saw that Friquet was sitting, now, with her tail wrapped quietly around her paws and was no longer snarling. Her wide eyes, though, still watched the dining room with rather chilling vigilance.

Katie sat on the edge of the desk, so that she, too, faced that lighted blank dining room.

"Steven, I've been trying since noon to find you. Steven——"

"Hush, Katie. Talk low. Tell me quickly. Are you all right? Has anything happened? Your voice doesn't sound right."

"Nothing. Nothing." Her voice was almost a whisper. "Only, Steven, they are going to arrest you."

"Arrest me!"

"Yes. Oh, it's Charlotte's letter. A terrible letter. And your car, you know. They've identified it."

There was a brief silence at the other end of the wire. Then Steven's voice again:

"Tell me, Katie. Hurry."

"They say—they say your car was parked outside the grounds late yesterday afternoon. At about the time Charlotte was—was out there. And then Charlotte wrote a letter to you. Threatening you and as if you had been threatening her and——"

"Katie, you are incoherent. Talk slowly. What on earth do you mean?"

"A note." Katie was almost sobbing in her haste and anxiety. "It went like this . . ." She told him as best she could recall exactly what Charlotte had said. "What *did* she mean, Steven? What masquerade? What are you doing? Oh, I know it is some terrible mistake, but you must tell me, Steven."

"Katie——" There was a kind of groan in his voice. "If I could only see you. Katie, you must believe me. Will you?"

"Oh, Steven, don't be silly. You know I believe you. You—you needn't ask."

"I know. Katie—little Katie—— But I don't know what the letter means. I don't *know*. But I'd better tell you, Katie, that it was my car. And that I was there. In the grounds. That much is true. But I don't know about the letter."

"Oh——"

"What do you mean by that? If I could only see you——"

"*Why? Why* were you here, Steven? You didn't come into the house until——"

"Hush—someone might hear you. Until long enough afterward to be safe. I can't tell you why,

Katie. I can't tell you. Look here———" He paused, and Katie felt he was looking at a watch. "I've got to hurry. I've only got a moment. And, my dear— listen as you never listened in your life before. I've got to tell you something without—well, without telling you."

"Yes. Yes." (The letter, Steven: I believe you. But that letter that Charlotte wrote—oh, Steven, tell me.)

"Katie—Oh, Lord, I hope I'm doing the best thing!"

"What is it?"

"See here. Don't trust anybody. Not *anybody*, do you understand, Katie? No matter who it is. Don't take any chances."

"What do you mean?" There was something that throbbed and fluttered wildly in her throat.

"I suppose I'm scaring the life out of you. But I've got to, Katie. There isn't anything else———" He stopped abruptly, took a long breath, and said more briskly, "Brace up, my child, and do as I tell you. It may sound absolutely wild, but do it. Now listen. In the bookroom, in the lower right-hand drawer of Uncle Petrie's old desk, there ought to be a revolver. Take it and—and hide it. In the back drawing room there's a couple of old swords crossed over the mantel. Remember?"

"Yes—but good heavens———"

"Hide them, too. Get rid of everything that anybody might—that might hurt anybody."

"I—you———" Katie's knees felt weak. Her voice shook and stopped.

"Now, Katie, don't get scared. It's just a notion of

mine. I'm an artist and a man of temperament and nerves. I've a right to my whims."

"You aren't making things better by laughing about it."

"Was I laughing? I'm sorry. But put it down to nerves. Only——" the attempted lightness left his voice, and he concluded grimly—"only do as I say. Will you, Katie?"

"Yes—yes—but Steven, what are you——"

"And another thing: Do exactly as Aunt Mina tells you to do. Don't cross her in the smallest· thing. Please her every way you can."

"I—why, yes, Steven. But you must explain. You have frightened me. I don't understand. I don't——"

"Katie, perhaps I'd better tell you I didn't kill Charlotte. *But I knew, you see, that it was going to happen.* I——" His voice stopped. The silence lengthened.

"Steven!" whispered Katie desperately. *"What do you mean?* You must tell me more." She stopped sharply. Had the telephone clicked at the other end? "Steven! Steven! *Where are you!"*

There was another faint click. Then a bored voice sang:

"Number, please."

"You—you cut me off, operator. Connect me again."

"What number, please."

"The number I was talking to! I've got to have it. I——"

"You'll have to give me the number, please," sang the voice.

"I don't know the number. You—cut me off——"

"Excuse it, please," chortled the voice musically, and the telephone clicked again.

Slowly Katie's hand started downward with the telephone.

Presently she sat down again in the desk chair.

So Steven had been there on the grounds, out in the dark, fog-enshrouded park with its twisting paths and ghostly shrubbery and slippery, slippery road, at the very hour when Charlotte was killed. Had he come to meet Charlotte? Was that the meeting that Charlotte's letter referred to?

And he had not come into the house until later. Much later. And he had known—*could* he have said that?

But he *had* said it. Inconceivable. *He had known it was going to happen.*

She remembered the moment she had stood in the entrance of the apartment house, ringing, ringing the bell labeled "Steven Petrie."

And she remembered what Paul had said. He had left Steven's apartment, and Steven was there. It would have taken Paul perhaps fifteen minutes, if he had not stopped on the way, to reach the safety island where she had seen him and offered him a lift homeward. It had taken, owing to the slow-moving traffic and the block at the bridge, at least twenty minutes to reach Steven's apartment again; longer, at any rate, than it would have taken to walk the same distance with no delay.

In that thirty or forty minutes, Steven had turned out his friends, left his apartment and driven to the estate. Allowing for their delay while Paul bought cigarettes and her own very slow and careful driving,

Steven might have reached the Petrie grounds as much as an hour before their own arrival and its tragic dénouement.

But Steven had parked his car somewhere outside the grounds.

Why? There was unfortunately only one reason, and that was that Steven did not want his presence known. Well, that had been apparent from the first, thought Katie impatiently. Of course he hadn't wanted it known that he was at the house or in the grounds that afternoon. Otherwise he would have told of it immediately upon his arrival at the house later in the evening.

But he did not mention it. He only asked—what had he said? Oh, yes. He had hurried across the vestibule and said, "What's happened? Is it Aunt Mina?" And then he had looked at them, and his face had become all at once guarded and strange, and he had said in a different voice: "Why are these policemen here?" And there was that letter Charlotte had written. And Steven had known it was going to happen. He hadn't killed Charlotte, he'd said, but he had known she was going to be killed.

Then why had he let it happen? Why had he let Katie kill Charlotte?

And where was Steven?

Katie shook her head impatiently again and pressed slim fingers to her temples.

Curious how persistent was the nagging consciousness of that little wisp of black hair that had been in Charlotte's palm. How *had* it got there? And how strangely sinister the knowledge of it was! How strongly and yet how inexplicably it suggested some nameless evil. Its disappearance quite obviously confirmed its significance. Found in Charlotte's hand, it might have meant anything or nothing. Vanishing from Mina's dressing table, it meant decidedly a clue.

But a clue to what?

Friquet, moved by one of those incalculable impulses with which cats are beset, dropped lightly off the desk and took a few stealthy steps toward the dining room and paused to stare fixedly at, so far as Katie could see, nothing at all. But the cat's great shining eyes seemed to see on through the three-dimensional world to some other unplumbed dimension. She went on then, strolling with an air of nonchalance except that her back legs were very stiff and cautious and high. Katie watched the cat until she reached the swinging door to the pantry, where Friquet paused and held her red-brown nose, which looked exactly like an eraser on a pencil top, down close to the floor.

She sniffed and she sniffed, delicately but with growing intensity. Katie watched the cat with a kind of uneasy fascination. She sniffed all around the floor and up and down the crack under the pantry door. Then quite suddenly became rigid and still.

The pantry door opened, and Melissa, carrying a tea tray, entered the dining room.

She did not look at the floor, and was engaged in balancing the tray in her deft brown hands and could not have seen the cat. But she avoided Friquet gracefully as if by instinct and came through the bright white light toward the lounge. She was very neat in her afternoon apron and cap, and very decorous, with her red hair smooth and tight, and she was intent only upon getting the tray to the table without spilling the cream.

"Melissa," said Katie, "who was in the dining room just now? Was it you?"

Melissa set the tray down anxiously and turned.

"No, ma'am."

Katie looked at her doubtfully.

"But there was someone there," she insisted. "And I thought it must be you."

Melissa's velvet eyes were soft and warm, always with that faint red glow.

"I was upstairs, Miss Katie. I came down the back stairway just now."

"Who is in the kitchen?"

"Nobody, Miss Katie. Nobody at all."

"Well, where's Jenks, then?"

"I don't know, Miss Katie. Miss Katie, ma'am——" She hesitated, all at once less tranquil.

Katie's nerves tightened.

"Yes, Melissa."

"It's dinner—Miss Fanny wrote out a menu and she's got something on it she calls crêpes suzette. And I don't know how to make them crêpes."

"Oh." Katie relaxed and walked to the table and poured herself a cup of tea. Conscious then of Melissa's waiting presence, she said succinctly: "Pancakes. Eggs, water, flour: very thin, with no shortening. Spread them with—oh, anything sweet and fruity and roll them up. I'll show you."

"Never mind, Miss Katie. Thank you, ma'am."

Melissa very silently disappeared. Katie, feeling

rather silly, applied herself to hot toast and tea. But, after all, there had been someone in that darkened room.

"Don't trust anybody," Steven had said. And he had repeated: "Not *anybody*. . . . Don't take any chances."

And there was something else he had asked her to do.

She had better do it before the police returned. Once they came back to that house, there was no telling what might happen. She might not again be free. Free from observation, amended Katie with a kind of inward gasp.

The house was yet very quiet.

Uncle Petrie's worn and rather lovely old desk was in the bookroom. Katie turned on lights in the passage and lights in the dark bookroom before she entered it. Somehow the bright whiteness only emphasized the emptiness and silence of the place.

She put her hand on the drawer—the lower right-hand drawer, Steven had said—and glanced over her shoulder at the doorway before she opened it. It was an entirely instinctive gesture, that quick glance. There was no one near, there could be no one.

Under a stack of old account books she found the revolver. An old, battered-looking thing with a long barrel and a curved wooden handle. Katie had the barest speaking acquaintance with revolvers, but she did know enough to look, with rather uneasy caution, in the chamber. It was fully loaded, which did not tend to relieve Katie's growing feeling of unease, for she wasn't just sure how to go about unloading it. She put it, carefully pointed toward the wall, down upon the desk and regarded it dubiously. There it was, as Steven had said, but what could she do with it?

She thought rather approvingly of all of Lake Michigan's mysterious gray depths at her elbow—or more exactly at the edge of the lawn. Afterward she remembered that moment with a kind of appalled incredulity, for it was only a disinclination toward going out alone through the black fog that kept her from going down to the beach and throwing the gun as far as she could send it into that irretrievable black depth beyond the fog. But she didn't. After some thought she took the gun to the small coatroom that opened off the vestibule. She turned on more lights as she went and saw no one.

In the coatroom—a bare little room, with a scattering of overshoes on a shelf, an umbrella stand, a small blank window, and a row of hooks and empty hangers along the wall—she went straight to the umbrella stand. It was a rather ghastly thing in bronze, with a dreadful bronze cherub holding out lumpy arms and legs. It had, however, a false bottom, made for the entirely practical purpose of holding water that might drip from the upper chamber which held, theoretically, wet umbrellas.

Katie glanced again at the door, reached down into the bronze cylinder, pulled up the bottom of it, which was not bronze but some kind of light metal with holes in it, and explored with her hand below. There was plenty of room for the revolver she carried, and in less than a moment it was at the bottom of the umbrella stand, the false bottom was tightly in place, and Katie straightened up and gave the smiling bronze cherub the first look of approval she had ever accorded it.

And remembered suddenly a bright summer day in her childhood when the bronze cherub stood proudly in the vestibule. There was sunlight slanting on it, and Charlotte was somewhere near, vivacious, with a high, black, curly pompadour and a tiny waist and sweeping full skirt that fitted padded hips, carrying something in her hand. Charlotte, younger, of course, but always wiry, always terribly energetic, always at Mina's elbow. And always keeping herself between Mina and the slender child with long slim legs and big, sober eyes; the child that, curiously, was Katie. And yet could be remembered as a separate person, distinct from the Katie Warren who bent over that bronze cherub to hide a revolver. The Katie Warren who had killed Charlotte.

She couldn't remember anything of that particular day; it was just an unexpected, illusive sunlit scene that was there in her memory and then was gone. But, she thought, suppose Charlotte could have looked ahead —could have known what that child would sometime bring upon her.

And there was suddenly almost a feeling of Charlotte's presence. Katie had a queer conviction that, when she walked out of the little coatroom and through the open vestibule, Charlotte would be sitting at the small desk in the lounge, with her powdered eyelids lowered perhaps and her curled elaborate hair reflected in the mirror above.

Charlotte was not there, of course. But Fanny was sitting on one of the wicker chairs in a curiously strained attitude suggesting suddenly checked motion.

She was looking steadily toward the windows, black now and shining. She did not turn as Katie entered the lounge, and did not speak. But as Katie turned toward the passage, it gave her a queer feeling of shock to note that Fanny's glittering blue eyes were watching, through the ferns, Katie's own moving reflection in the winking black window panes.

It was only Fanny, she told herself. And she couldn't have seen her hide the revolver, for the door to the coatroom was around the angle of stairs and vestibule and its interior visible only from the vestibule, or window. And anyway, she told herself again, it was only Fanny. Katie went on toward the crowded old drawing rooms, two of them, opening widely into each other.

The old swords were difficult to detach. Katie had to crawl up on a rather shaky table to do it, and she felt convinced that every winking black window pane held an unseen face watching her as she unfastened the swords and took them down. Silly and clumsy-looking as decorations, they proved to be unexpectedly light and vibrant in her hands, almost as if they were alive.

She hid the swords—rather helplessly and for lack of a better place, for a sword is an extraordinarily difficult thing to hide—in the fireplace. There was a heavy bronze fire screen which, when replaced, completely concealed the whole grate. She felt extremely silly and ashamed when she paused at the door, leaving, and looked up at the vacant place on the wall. But Steven's words and his voice were suddenly too clear in her mind, and she no longer felt ridiculous and melodramatic. And she went back into the long,

cold drawing room with its thick rugs and strangely
mingled chairs and tables and picked up a small ornamental dagger with an onyx handle, and after another
uneasy glance toward the black windows, hid it, too,
behind the fire screen.

And went upstairs to her own room. When she
went through the lounge, Fanny had disappeared.

Dinner time came, and there were still no sounds
in the somber, shadowy house.

Clarence looked up from a newspaper as Katie
came slowly down the stairs.

"Fanny," said Clarence, "isn't coming down. She's
going to eat with Mina. And since neither Paul nor
Steven has turned up, I propose that we don't wait
for them."

Katie was aware that he was trying, not very successfully, to stuff the newspaper inside his neat coat
without her being aware of his possession of it.

"Very well," she said. "Let me see that paper, if
you please, Clarence."

"Oh, now, Katie, you don't want to look at it."

"Is it that bad?"

"Oh—no," said Clarence judiciously. "It's not—
there's a picture of Charlotte and a picture of you."

"Give it to me," said Katie again.

It wasn't actually as bad as she had feared. But
then, during that dreadful day and night there was
little that her imagination had not encompassed in the
way of ugliness.

They ate without much conversation. The dining
room was too large, too bright, too empty; the crystal-
hung chandelier overhead too brittle and gay.

Katie kept listening for the sound of a car on the

drive outside, for the door opening, for Steven's footsteps crossing the lounge. But he did not come.

Jenks, assisting Melissa, came and went silently. There was about him a distinct air of apology, and he served Katie with a kind of sorrowful solicitude.

She must question Jenks herself, thought Katie, about that telephone call. She watched him speculatively. He had seemed honest, that was the curious part of it. Honest and sincerely regretful.

Where was Steven?

And what were the police doing?

Clarence was fidgety.

He passed his neat hand over his chin again and leaned forward suddenly, confidentially:

"Katie," he said, "the funniest thing has happened."

Katie looked at him. Clarence, probably for the first time in his life, looked vaguely untidy. There was something unnatural about him, something wrong. Something very trivial, yet singularly inconsistent.

"Katie,"—Clarence glanced quickly toward the pantry door to be sure Jenks was safely behind it and leaned forward to whisper across the expanse of glowing white damask and silver and china—"Katie," he whispered, "my razor's gone."

CHAPTER XII

THE revolver was in the umbrella stand guarded by a dreadful bronze cherub; the swords and an onyx-handled dagger were hidden. Clarence hadn't shaved, and his nice chin was faintly dusky below violet-scented powder, and he looked vaguely untidy. And Steven had said—Katie did not need to remind herself of what Steven had said.

She put out her hand and took up a goblet and held it to her lips, keeping her eyes steadily upon Clarence. She was conscious of the cold water against her lips. Then she took care to set the goblet down again very steadily, and she said:

"You've mislaid it."

"No, I haven't, Katie. I've had that razor for years. A good old-fashioned straight edge. They don't make them any sharper."

A faint chill crept up Katie's back and along her elbows.

She repeated: "You've just mislaid it."

"But I tell you I haven't mislaid it," protested Clarence peevishly. "I never mislay it. I don't lose things. Now if I'd been trusted to keep that little bit of hair last night," he said in an injured fashion, "I'd have had it all ready for the police to look at. You mark my words, Katie, that little bit of woolly hair would have led to the discovery of Charlotte's murderer."

There was a small tinkling from the doorway. Fanny, floating in green chiffon and beads, was advancing toward them.

"What's that about Charlotte's murderer?" she said. "No, no, don't get up, Clarence. I'm just going to sit down and have some dessert with you. Mina didn't care for any."

She sat down as she spoke.

Fanny was in an extremely good humor. That was at once evident. Her cobalt eyes glittered; there was a kind of satisfied yet eager look about her face. Her white hair was violently askew.

"I've been," she said with just a touch of importance in her manner, "with Mina all afternoon. Reading aloud to her. It seems that Charlotte never read aloud to her. Did Melissa get the crêpes suzette made all right?"

There was a distinct air of self-congratulation about her. However the rest felt about Charlotte's death, Fanny was almost frankly jubilant. There was a tinge even of the proprietorial in her voice as she spoke of Melissa, as if Fanny already saw herself managing the house, managing Mina.

"Melissa was rather troubled about dinner," said Katie a bit crisply. "She's not really used to doing much cooking, you know, Fanny."

Fanny shot her a bright glance which held a sudden spark of fire.

"My dear Katie," she said, "I was managing a house and servants before you were born. Or thought of," she added to clinch it. Her voice had an edge that made Clarence look at her rather apprehensively. "Where," went on Fanny, "is Paul? And I thought

Steven was going to stay out here for a few days. At least until after the funeral and this terrible inquiry. Isn't it terrible, Katie? I feel so sorry for you, my dear."

"Oh, Katie will be all right," said Clarence easily. "Don't worry about her." His fingers were toying delicately with the stem of the goblet at his plate. It was a goblet filled with water, but the gesture was suggestive, as was also the look he cast at the buffet and then, baffled, at Fanny. He sighed. "The police haven't been back here again. Wonder what they are doing?"

"Plenty, in all probability." Fanny's eyes were sharply inquisitive. "Katie, why *did* you telephone to Charlotte and ask her to meet you at the bridge?"

Katie took a long breath before she answered.

"I didn't telephone," she said.

"But, my dear," said Fanny, "wouldn't it be better to—well, not to persist in that denial? Wouldn't it be better to tell the truth about it and say just what happened? It might not be so———"

"I have told the truth, Fanny," said Katie dangerously.

"Of course she has," murmured Clarence in a detached way, patently preoccupied with various concerns of his own. "Why don't we all go into the lounge? Or the bookroom. Sit and talk there. Much more comfortable."

Fanny's bright, hard glance all but punctured him.

"And leave you alone in the dining room?" she said and returned to Katie.

"Katie, you are pursuing a very dangerous course. The police should know everything. Everything." She

paused to give point to her words, and Katie, harassed, said:

"Does that include bolster-throwing, Fanny?"

Katie could not tell whether Fanny's suddenly blank
look was actually uncomprehending or whether it held
a secret. After all, she hadn't known that it was Fanny
in Charlotte's room the previous night. She had only
suspected it.

"I don't know what you mean," said Fanny definitely. There was a commotion in the lounge, and she
turned quickly to look. "Ah, there's Chris. And Paul.
Now we shall know something of what's going on."

But they didn't, though they sat for what seemed
to Katie hours in a small group in the bookroom, talking in a curiously desultory way. There was, after the
first few eager questions Fanny asked, a kind of reluctance to talk of the matter. Chris sank down into
a chair, filling it to overflowing, and smoked a very
long cigar steadily, his eyes half closed and his expression not one to invite further questions. Paul smoked,
too, and was less unwilling to talk but could tell them
little. Clarence was preoccupied, moving restlessly
about the room, but not, under Fanny's eye, getting
farther than the door.

The police, it seemed, were engaged in their own
mysterious activities. Chris only knew that they were
trying to find Steven (he glanced at Katie as he said
that). And he knew that so far they had not succeeded.

"I wonder where he is," said Paul. "I tried to telephone to him a couple of times and stopped at his
studio on my way out from town. But it was dark,
and no one answered the bell. There were, however,"

Paul added amusedly, "a couple of plain-clothes men making themselves prominently unobtrusive about the entrance."

Chris glowered at Paul over his cigar.

"There's nothing to smile at about it," he said. "God knows, Paul, if you had seen what I've seen of murder inquiries and murder trials, you wouldn't be so amused. And as for detectives, it may interest you to know that one has followed you all day."

"I don't doubt it," said Paul pleasantly. "And if so, he's had an edifying day. I sat in the office all afternoon hoping someone would be suddenly possessed of a desire to buy a country estate. Nobody was. But why should one follow me?"

"Why should one follow any of us?" growled Chris. "That's one of the pleasures of an inquiry into murder."

"Really, Chris," said Fanny stridently, "I think they have been most considerate. They haven't been near the house all afternoon."

"That's just it," said Chris. He spoke with a kind of sharp impatience. "It's a carefully worked out system. You haven't any notion of the persistence and force and tenacity that's back of it all. Oh, well—no use talking about it." He rose, a great, black bulk which threw an enormous shadow against the books. "How's Mina standing all this?"

"With surprising fortitude," said Fanny. "She looks really stronger than I have seen her look since we came. Don't you think so, Katie?"

"I don't know. I haven't seen her since noon. Chris, what can we expect of the police?"

Chris spread his huge hands in a helpless gesture.

"Katie, I don't have the faintest notion. There is, however, to be an inquest tomorrow at one o'clock. You'll all have to go."

The heavy, somber house, surrounded by black fog, was as silent as it had been all that long afternoon. There were now lights and a few people, but the lights emphasized the emptiness and the people were too few, too negligible to offset that emptiness. It was as if it listened. Listened and waited. And outside black fog pressed against the black windows, and it waited and listened, too.

They were all carefully not looking at Katie. So carefully avoiding her with their eyes that she couldn't have felt more prominently under observation. She lifted her chin a bit and forced Chris to look at her directly. She wished he were not so anxious, so sympathetic.

"I'm afraid I don't know much about an inquest, Chris," she said. She made her voice steady and cool, and could feel Fanny's quick, sharply astonished glance. "What do we do?"

"I think this will be only a formality," said Chris. "Nothing to worry about. Of course, I can't say. They'll probably just adjourn. But you'll all have to go. I'll tell William to have the big car ready and where to go. I'll go up now and see Mina. That is, if she'll see me. Has the doctor been here today, Fanny?"

Fanny, floating in green chiffon, disappeared toward the stairway with him. Clarence, like a puppy let off a leash, quivering with eagerness, vanished toward the dining room, and Paul lounged over toward Katie.

"Have a cigarette? Don't worry about this inquest, Katie." He sat down beside her. The light touched his high olive cheekbones and gleamed on his smooth black hair. He was smiling, with a flash of white teeth under his silky black mustache. The same charming smile that, probably, long ago had won Mina's heart. For he looked, thought Katie, remarkably like the picture of his father which adorned the wall in Mina's room. No wonder Mina had been so tenderly inclined toward him of late.

His smile had gone.

"What's the matter?" he said abruptly. "You're looking at me as if I were some kind of insect you were about to—dismember and classify." He smiled, turning on his charm warmly. "Come on, Katie, cheer up. Your eyes are like—I don't know what. Blue—tragic—— After all, my dear, you couldn't help killing Charlotte. See here, have you been outdoors today?"

"Not since morning." Morning. Tomorrow morning would bring an inquest. An inquest into the murder of Charlotte Weinberg, and she, Katie, would be the principal witness. The suspect. Unless—where *was* Steven?

Paul uttered an irritated exclamation and rose impatiently.

"You look as stern and sober as any of your Puritan ancestors," he said. "In fact, I've often noted with regret a decided strain of the Puritan in you, Katie. There's no use being so desperately intense and stern about things. What do you say to a walk in the fog? Not very pleasant weather, but it will do you good to get away from the house."

"Very well. Paul——" She paused, struck by the thought. "Look here, you go and ask Aunt Mina for a key to the summerhouse while I get a wrap."

"The summerhouse!"

"Yes, of course. I don't believe the police have been inside it yet."

"But why do you——"

"I want to look inside it myself. I don't *know* why. So don't ask me. I'll be down again in a minute or two."

He did not, apparently, fancy the errand, but when Katie met him again on the stairs, a long cape with a scarlet-lined hood which fell over her shoulders pulled around her, he had got the key. But the police, he told her, had already examined the summerhouse.

"They've still got a key to it," he said, opening the wide front door and letting in a damp cold breath of air. "But Aunt Mina had two keys. This is the other one."

Katie pulled the hood up over her head. The cape swirled around her, and the monkish hood shadowed her face.

They walked across the steps and under the dim entrance light. Beyond the pale little circle were wavering, impenetrable fog wreaths that made a gray black wall. Just for an instant Katie hesitated. A silly errand, useless since the police had already been there. Yet she must see for herself the summerhouse.

Their feet on the graveled drive before the door made little crisps of sound. The radiance over the door grew fainter and fainter and then vanished entirely and they were walking in soft damp blackness. It was not, however, difficult to keep to the road. As

Katie's eyes became adjusted to the darkness, she could see Paul, a dim shape, moving beside her. They left the gravel and started over the winding old part of the drive and began to descend rapidly toward the ravine and bridge. They said little, and their feet on the road made small impacts of sound, weird in that bewildering blackness.

For blackness had suddenly swallowed them. Katie realized all at once how remote they were from the house and from people. It was like being suspended in an unknown and somehow threatening world. Steven had said: Don't trust *anybody.*

Anybody. That included Paul.

"What's the matter, Katie?" said Paul's voice eerily out of the blackness near her.

"N-nothing," said Katie, keeping tight hold on herself. "Why?"

"I thought you said something. It's as black as the ace of spades out here."

He checked himself suddenly and stopped and put one hand out and touched her arm. Katie stopped, too, and was somehow aware that Paul was listening.

She listened also. But there was nothing to hear. Paul laughed shortly.

"All right. Let's go on. Thought I heard somebody following us."

Katie's heart gave a kind of leap into her throat.

"Fog is queer," she managed to say very steadily. "Does all kinds of queer things to one's ears."

"I know," said Paul's voice.

"Even one's voice," went on Katie, feeling that she must talk. "Comes out of the fog in a queer muffled way. Paul, what on earth is grape hair?"

"Grape *hair!*"

"Yes. And glocks?"

"Sh——"

He stopped again and Katie stopped, too, and strained her ears to hear any sound. Far away and blunted by the intervening blankets of fog and the wide black stretch of park was the murmurous vague sound of traffic. It was so far away, so vague that it only emphasized their distance and their remoteness from the world they knew.

Surrounding them was nothing but mysterious, silent darkness.

"H'm," said Paul's voice presently. He spoke in a low tone, as if he might be, in that black remoteness, overheard. "Curious. I could have sworn I heard a footstep. And quite near, too. Well—let's go on. The bridge ought to be about here somewhere. What were you saying about hair?"

"I said what is grape hair?" said Katie. Briefly she told him of the scrap of conversation. Was someone there in the fog with them? Why? Unconsciously, to cover her inward uneasiness, she had lifted her voice a little. She repeated: "So, what is grape hair?"

"I don't know, I'm sure," said Paul shortly. "Or apricot hair either. Look out—here's a railing somewhere here. Ah—over this way, Katie."

Across the bridge where a great car had slithered and slipped and finally turned. Then off the road and into thicker blackness, and up a little slope that was slippery with dead wet leaves, and very black.

Paul stumbled. Katie heard a quick breath and a kind of scramble.

"Curses!" he said. "I forgot that damn concrete

step. Here we are, Katie. Wait a minute and I'll have the door open. Here, hold my lighter so I can find the padlock."

The little flame made a queer weird point of light. Then the door creaked and was deeper blackness, and the musty, damp smell of all summerhouses rose to Katie's nostrils.

There was an electric light in the place, as they both knew, and Paul reached through the black open space and fumbled for the switch, and the interior of the summerhouse sprang into view.

It was bare and cold and damp and singularly unprepossessing. There were a few cobwebs on the ceiling, and a long rustic table under the window, and a few garden chairs leaned inhospitably against the wall.

And, as Katie was forced presently to admit, there was nothing that even faintly resembled a clue.

It was only a cold, bare summerhouse. Blank and uncommunicative. It gave no evidence of anyone's presence then or ever.

But then, thought Katie wearily, what could she have expected to discover?

"Well, there's nothing of much interest here," said Paul, turning from contemplating the black window pane. "I hope you are satisfied, Katie. I could have sworn I saw a light in here last night. Curious what a strong impression it was. And yet—I suppose I didn't. Let's go back to the house."

"I suppose we may as well," said Katie reluctantly.

Paul put his hand on the door and dropped the key.

It clattered somewhere and perversely vanished. And it was owing to having bent to look under the rustic table, while Paul groped in the shadow back of the open door, that Katie found what she found. What she found and was to wish that she had not found.

For it was the broken end of a palette knife. Snapped off and wedged somehow under the leg of the the rustic table.

A palette knife. And it was new and bright and shining. Even the broken edge was unrusted.

"Here's the key," said Paul, rising.

What had Steven told the police? Something about palette knives.

Katie closed her pink palm around the bit of sharp steel and rose too. Paul hadn't seen. She felt sure of that.

But how had a broken palette knife got there, inside the summerhouse? What had broken it? If it had lain there since sometime during the summer, when Steven might conceivably have been painting there, the broken edge would have rusted. The rest of it was stainless steel and might not—Katie wasn't sure— have rusted for some time. But the broken edge wouldn't have remained bright and new.

Had Steven, then, been in the summerhouse during his mysterious visit in the park just before Charlotte's death? Why hadn't he told of it? Why had he brought a palette knife with him? Why had it broken?

She must see Steven. She must see him at once. Perhaps even now he was at the house waiting.

"Well," said Paul, "what are you staring at? Ready?"

"Yes. Yes, I——" Katie stopped. She was facing that glittering black window pane, else she would not have seen suddenly a flicker of motion behind it. Something glimmered palely and moved and vanished.

The shining black window pane winked evilly at her.

She must have made some sound, for Paul wheeled. *"What is it?"*

"There," whispered Katie. "At the window, something——"

Paul was outside. She heard his step on the concrete platform. Then he was back at the open door, smiling.

"Nonsense, Katie," he said. "There's nothing here. Come along before you take to seeing ghosts."

It was not, thought Katie vaguely, a fortunate choice of words. If there were ever any spirit that would be driven to revisit and hold to and harry its earthly sphere, it would be Charlotte's. She held the small lighter again for Paul while he replaced the padlock and snapped it shut.

The sharp bit of steel bit into her palm.

"Let's go back through the park," she said. "It's much shorter."

"All right," said Paul. "If we can find our way. Don't slip."

They were, however, scarcely into the park before Katie regretted her suggestion. For the black park was not, that night, a pleasant place. It was still and yet not still. It was black and mysterious, and branches reached suddenly out of it to slap their faces, and moisture dripped now and then from the crowding trees, and it was very dark and blind.

"Better let me go ahead, Katie. Can you see me clear enough to follow?"

"Oh, yes," said Katie.

"Righto. I'll find the way. You follow me."

She could dimly see him, a dark shape looming ahead, and she followed.

She did not know exactly how or when she became so definitely possessed of a feeling of a presence somewhere in the park near them. There may have been the subdued echo of a footstep somewhere. Or a rustle in the trees.

At any rate she knew it all at once, and she stopped to listen. But there was nothing—nothing at all. Paul going on ahead. Moisture in the air and dripping from wet and sodden shrubbery, and nothing but damp, murmurous darkness. Nothing there.

Paul had got a little ahead, and she hurried a bit until she could again see that dim outline of his shoulders. She wondered if one could get so used to the dark that he could see in the dark as a cat sees. She'd read stories of men who were put in prison, in solitary confinement and in the dark, getting so they could see. And so that light blinded them. As she, Katie, was blinded by the fog. Blinded and very nearly suffocated and—— *What was that?*

And where was she?

They were not on the path at all.

She could feel wet leaves and twigs and all the dead litter of the untidy park under her feet. Where was the path? Paul had again got ahead. There were his shoulders, dimly black, moving ahead of her. She hurried, running, slipping. Then she knew that the black shape moving ahead of her was no longer moving. It was still, suddenly motionless, waiting for her silently.

And just then away off in the blackness and fog behind her she heard Paul's voice:

"Katie—Katie!"

For one terrible instant Katie could not move. She could not even think.

Then, muffled and eerie, came Paul's voice again, calling her. It was away back somewhere in the fog—and it called: "Katie—where are you?"

The dim shape ahead was still motionless. Or was it? Had it moved? Had it turned? Had it vanished in the blackness?

Then Katie had turned and was running—brushing through shrubbery and sheering blindly around trees and avoiding things that reached out of the blackness and clutched at her swirling cape and touched her shoulders ghostily and pulled her hood from her head.

The path must be somewhere near. How had she got away from it? How had she followed that dim moving shape that was not Paul?

"Katie—where on earth——" Paul's voice was near—to the right—her feet were on the turf path.

"Paul!" she cried breathlessly, and then he was there before her; she could see the dim black outline of his shoulders, a blur that was his face.

"Where on earth were you, Katie?" he said irritably.

"I was—lost," Katie choked. "Paul, there's someone else. In the park."

"Nonsense. Come along. We are nearly at the house."

The house. And perhaps Steven.

"No, no, Paul, there *was* someone. I got confused

somehow—I don't know how—I followed someone else—it wasn't you——"

"Katie, Katie, pull yourself together, darling. You're not rational. You're all upset. See, there's the light over the door."

There was that faint radiant area. It was suddenly all that mattered to Katie. Light and safety and perhaps Steven. There was the crisp sound of gravel under their feet. They crossed the space, and Paul got out his latchkey.

Then they were inside the house, the great door between them and the dripping black mystery of the park. The park where someone padded stealthily along on furtive feet through dead wet leaves.

Katie hurried to the lounge—to the bookroom. Jenks was there, folding the evening papers decorously with not a suggestion of having been reading them when the door opened.

"Has Mr. Steven come yet?" said Katie anxiously.

"No, Miss Katie."

Katie's heart sank. Quite literally it did just that as if it had suddenly grown heavy.

"And he's not telephoned?"

Jenks shook his head, implying the right shade of impersonal regret.

"No, Miss Katie."

Katie turned and went slowly back to the lounge. Paul had got out of his coat and was standing before the mirror over the desk, smoothing his shining black hair. Katie, approaching the desk, sat down, and the mirror reflected brightly the vivid patch of scarlet that was the lining of her hood, fallen back over her shoulders. It reflected Katie's arrogant little nose and her crimson mouth and the long sweep of dark eye-lashes that lay on her cheek and covered the vivid sword-blue of her eyes. It reflected the little silver beads of moisture caught in her soft dark hair. And above her it reflected Paul's olive face and black silk mustache.

"He's not there," said Katie, returning the telephone to its cradle.

"Who, Steven?"

"Yes." Katie sat still, looking soberly at the silent telephone. How sharp that tiny shaft of steel was in her hand!

"Why do you want to talk to Steven, Katie?" asked Paul softly. "Is it to ask him about the thing you found in the summerhouse?"

Katie turned slowly in her chair to stare upward into Paul's half-veiled dark eyes. The long blue cape fell from her slender shoulders to the floor; the mirror caught the clear reflection of her upturned blue gaze and the sweep of her chin. Paul smiled and was his most charming self.

"Do tell me, Katie darling, what it was. You've got it there in your pretty hand, you know. Won't you let me see?"

CHAPTER XIII

SOMEONE was moving down the stairway. It was Chris, big and black and lithe. He looked over the railing at the two before the desk. Katie rose, gripping the thing in her hand as if Paul might suddenly wrench it from her grasp, and Paul's warm smile became less warm. He said with a kind of malicious amusement:

"Katie's got a clue, Chris. And she's scared to death. Has people prowling in the park—all sorts of nonsense."

Chris reached the lowest step and came lightly across toward them. He looked terribly tired. There were lines Katie had not before seen around his eyes. If he heard Paul's comment he paid no attention to it.

"I'm going home," he said wearily. "I'm tired. I wish the inquest tomorrow were over—safely over. There's no telling——" He broke off suddenly. "But don't worry, Katie. They'll likely just meet and adjourn without asking any of you to talk. Better stop and speak to Mina before you go to bed, Katie."

"How is Aunt Mina?" asked Paul.

Chris's tired, narrow eyes went to Paul.

"I don't know how she feels," he said slowly. "And she said the doctor hadn't been here today. But I must say—I haven't seen her looking so well in—I don't know how long. Months. It's—amazing."

"Nerves, I suppose," suggested Paul watching Chris.

"Nerves?" Chris considered it slowly and then shrugged in a vast but somehow suave and doubtful fashion. "I don't know. It strikes me as something deeper than surface stimulation. She looks—relaxed, somehow. Stronger. I don't know." He paused for a thoughtful moment. "It's something I don't understand," he said finally. "Well—I'm going."

He paused, hesitated, touched Katie with those tired, half-hidden eyes, and then said abruptly:

"By the way, Paul—I'm in rather a hole. Temporarily. Need some cash. Can you loan me, say, a few thousand for ninety days? I'll have plenty then. It's just a temporary affair."

Katie started forward.

"Chris, do you need what I borr——"

Chris checked her peremptorily.

"How about it, Paul?"

Paul's eyes were veiled.

"Gosh, Chris, I'm sorry," he said gracefully. "But the fact is—well, I've got everything in that real estate development. It's all tied up, you know. There's nobody I'd rather oblige than you, Chris. But I just don't have it. Terribly sorry, you know."

Chris's eyes had retreated.

"Oh, that's all right," he said in a rather strained way. "I'll get along." He changed the subject abruptly.

"You're staying here, of course, Paul. Steven hasn't turned up, has he? Wonder where he is. Mina asked him to stay out here for a while. Well, I'm going." He coughed and wheezed. "Rotten weather," he said. "Good-night, Katie. Don't worry. Things'll be all right, I hope."

"Good-night," said Katie and added "Good-night, Paul." She went to the stairway hurriedly before he could question her again. She was conscious of his dark eyes faintly mocking her haste. Then he strolled toward the door with Chris, and Katie rounded the turn of the stairs.

But she did not stop to say good-night to Mina. They had all, she thought, paid their court that day. Their court to Mina. Mina who was rich. Mina whose days were measured. Mina who was dying. Mina who had not yet made her will.

Something that was obscurely a wish to defend Mina against something else that was almost equally obscure kept Katie from visiting Mina that night. She went on straight through silent halls to her own room. Melissa had been there; the counterpane was neatly folded away, the bed turned down, and the light glowing on the bedside table.

Katie locked the door. She unclenched her palm and walked to the light and looked at the small bit of steel. After a long time she hid the thing in a small blue vanity case, under the powder compact.

The box of capsules the doctor had left was on the table, and Katie took two of them. Her sleep was long and dreamless, though once she roused, feeling that someone had called her and had tried to open the door. She was not, however, sufficiently roused for the occurrence, if occurrence it was and not a dream, to make a vivid impression upon her.

She slept late and, drugged, heavily. And rose to another gray, dark day. It was Thursday, February twenty-fourth. Once during the morning she stopped to look at the calendar which hung just below the mirror in the lounge and to wonder what significance the twenty-sixth had for Charlotte. The twenty-sixth. But Charlotte was dead.

It was a day, too, that in Katie's life was to be remembered for three things.

The first was, perhaps, the worst. And it became, with the inquest, somehow official, and that was that Steven had disappeared.

He had talked to Katie over the telephone—that strange conversation, terrible and sinister in the light of his disappearance—had broken off without a word of farewell or conclusion—and, so far as anyone knew or could discover, had vanished from the haunts of man.

The police had searched. Chris, even, and Paul took a hand in the search during the morning. Steven was not in his studio. He was not to be found at his one club. No one had seen him. No one knew anything about him, and the late morning papers carried the story in headlines—WELL-KNOWN ARTIST DISAPPEARS—and his pictures, and still no one knew what had happened to him.

Well-known artist, read Katie. He was not well-known. And he hated being called an artist. But he had certainly and terribly disappeared. And it was, as the smaller headlines went on to tell: "Following North Shore Murder. Inquest to Reveal Crime."

There was her picture, too. Touched up and unrecognizable, which made it a little easier. And the account of it all was kinder somehow than she'd feared; it said that mystery surrounded Charlotte's death, and there was a long story about Mina Petrie which sounded suspiciously like an obituary and which

Katie thought possibly had been already prepared, though less voluminously. It mentioned her gifts to public institutions, her quiet and secluded life, and the late Horace Petrie. There wasn't much to say—not much, in fact, that anyone could say—beyond a mention of her various donations and one scholarship, but it was fully embroidered.

Then there was the inquest, which, however, did not reveal crime. Did not, in fact, reveal anything. It was very brief, amazingly short, and was, as Chris had predicted, immediately adjourned. Mr. Crafft was there, brown and smiling and gesticulating shortly with his eyeglasses.

In the hall, after the inquest was over, he drew Katie aside. Mina had been excused and had remained with Melissa in her somber house.

"How is Madame Petrie? Not the worse for all this, I hope?"

"No," said Katie honestly. "In fact, she's——" She stopped.

"She's what?" said the detective quickly, his topaz eyes shining.

Katie pulled on her gloves.

"I was only going to say that Chris—that is, Mr. Lorrel, you know—thinks she is actually better."

"Better? How?"

"Why, I—I don't just know," said Katie reluctantly. She wished she had said nothing.

"Nonsense," said Mr. Crafft pleasantly. "What did he say?"

"He only said," replied Katie helplessly, "that Aunt Mina seemed somehow stronger. As if—well—he said, as if she were relaxed."

Mr. Crafft stared at Katie unwinkingly for a moment. Then he said abruptly:

"Another thing, Miss Warren. Do you know of anything that has been taken away from the house since the—murder? Think now. Anything at all?"

"N-no," said Katie slowly. "Unless—I saw a cleaner's truck leaving the house yesterday morning. But I don't know anything about it."

The detective's eyes flickered once.

"Did you see the name on it?" he asked softly.

"Andrews," said Katie. "But——"

"Thank you," said the detective. "Good-morning."

And then Fanny and Katie and Clarence were in the car again, driving homeward through heavy fog, with William silent and careful in the front seat at the wheel and Jenks's thin neck decorous beside him. Chris and Paul were following in Chris's coupé.

The whole thing was unreal. The drive through the fog, the gradually increasing traffic, the lights and the fog of the Loop, and the inquest, so evidently to the men there—judge, policemen, reporters—merely a casual part of the day's work. They were going back to Mina Petrie's somber house, and it was still unreal.

The drive was masked in fog. The tires swished over wet pavements. Lights loomed dimly out of fog and passed them or waited for their own passage. Then the traffic grew thinner gradually, their speed increased, Fanny coughed and talked about the smoke in the air, Clarence was restless and watched what he could see of the road ahead. And finally they were driving along the narrow road beyond the gates, were crossing again that narrow bridge above a ravine, were going around the curve.

"It must have happened right here," said Fanny with ghoulish eagerness. "Is that right, Katie?"

"Yes. No. I don't know," said Katie.

Fanny's bright eyes sought out Katie's profile in the semidusk of the car. Clarence sighed and leaned both gloved hands on his cane and peered ahead. Around them was the silent park again. And Katie realized that their excursion out into the world of normality and familiarity was not really an excursion at all. For they had carried their own world with them. The fog had surrounded them, had held them. That new strange world had accompanied them all the time. There hadn't been any change at all.

And what had happened to Steven? Queer the detective hadn't asked her that. But perhaps he knew it was no use asking her.

Behind them, as they alighted, Chris's car drew up with a spattering of gravel.

Melissa opened the door for them. Madame Petrie wished to see Mr. Lorrel, she said, surveying them with tranquil eyes. And, no, Mr. Steven had not returned and had not telephoned.

"But two policemen were here," said Melissa.

"Two policemen!" Fanny, who was halfway up the stairs, whirled. "What did they do?"

"I don't know, Miss Fanny," said Melissa submissively. "Except, I guess they were looking for something."

"Well," said Fanny after a moment, "did they find anything?"

Melissa shook her bright head.

"I don't know, ma'am."

Katie lingered in the lounge until they had all gone

upstairs—Chris to tell Mina about the inquest, of course, and the others to surround Mina with attention. Mina who was at last, with Charlotte's death, unguarded and exposed. Mina who was rich. Mina who was dying. Mina who had not yet made her will.

And she must make it soon.

When Melissa, too, had gone and Jenks was lighting a fire in the bookroom, Katie went quietly to the little coatroom, off the vestibule.

The gun was still under the care of the jovial, leering bronze cherub. And her blue vanity case, guarding the broken bit of steel, was in her bag.

But where was Steven?

Perhaps she ought to have told the detective of her conversation with Steven. But she had not dared lest, under the detective's questions, she tell too much. Steven had made such damning admissions; she could hear the detective: Ah, so he admitted being on the grounds. Why? But he didn't know about the letter? Dear me! And he knew it was going to happen. How very interesting!

No, she must not tell it.

But where had Steven gone and why?

She knew that, naturally, the general belief was that Steven had gone voluntarily. She knew, too, that the police called it escape; though the newspapers, so far, had been cautious, it was the obvious conclusion. And it was, she thought, a conclusion which was almost, to the family, unavoidable. They said, however, very little, although Chris was nervous, and Fanny had a tendency to jump when the telephone rang, and Paul watched her with veiled dark eyes. But no one said openly: Did Steven murder Charlotte?

No one, that is, of the family, and in Katie's hearing.

But Steven hadn't murdered Charlotte.

How could anyone have murdered Charlotte when Katie had seen her? Had seen her moving before the car.

Katie's cape was before her on the coat rack. With a swift motion of decision she threw it around her shoulders and pulled the scarlet-lined hood over her head.

It was only at dusk that the park and dark ravine became so curiously threatening. She let herself quietly out the front door.

The fog was faintly lighter, mysteriously for the moment free of pall of smoke, and it felt clean and cool. She could see for some distance—the black curve of the old road, the bare, wet brown branches of trees, the nebulous, looming shapes of shrubbery.

Katie walked briskly along the road. She reached the curve below the bridge and examined the road and the shrubs on either side long and thoroughly. She was not at all nervous. The park was no longer hidden in darkness and fog, and she was entirely free from the unpleasant feeling of being under observation by hidden, furtive eyes, which, strangely, she had begun to feel almost continually in the great, silent house. It was not a nice sensation; she would be standing perhaps at a window or would be pretending to read, when, impelled by a distinct impression that eyes somewhere were watching her, the fine hair at the nape of her neck would feel, actually, as if it had stirred gently, and she would turn quickly to look. But there was never anything there.

She found the deep rut that the heavy car had plowed up at the side of the road, and the place where she had finally stopped. She walked back to, as near as she could determine, the place where Charlotte's body had lain and forced herself to examine that spot, too. She went to the trees and shrubbery on either side of the road parallel to the place where Charlotte had stood when the car struck her.

The trees were low so near the ravine. She looked up, measuring the thickness and height of the branches that arched over the road. A grisly thought had struck her that Charlotte might have been dead before the car struck her and that her body might possibly have been suspended somehow in the path of the car. A rope over this branch—or that one—tied somehow to Charlotte's body and holding it suspended, would give it a ghastly semblance of motion.

And that was all, strive though she might to resurrect the scene, that she could remember. There was just a black shape wavering out of blackness and moving just before the dim headlights. She was only sure that it had moved.

The branches above were brown and wet, and she could not tell whether or not any of them showed a worn spot where a rope or wire had rubbed. Standing there, straining her eyes upward in a futile effort to discover a rubbed white spot on the brown branch, Katie heard quite suddenly a small sound of footsteps somewhere. She whirled about as if she were on a pivot.

A small man, plump and a bit shabby, gray-haired and gray-bearded, with the high pink cheeks of the

Bavarian and the round eye hollows, stood there looking at her.

He held a newspaper in one hand, and after looking at her half timidly, half assertively for a moment, he came slowly forward.

He wasn't a detective, that was certain. And it was equally certain that he was bursting with some knowledge that must be communicated.

He came closer, peering from under bushy gray eyebrows.

"Is this vere—these beoble live?" he asked. He spoke with a strong rolling German accent; his *s*'s hissed, his *p*'s were all *b*'s, and his *w*'s, like *v*'s. Katie glanced at the newspaper he held toward her. He held it so that headlines and the picture of Charlotte were uppermost. His hand grasping the newspaper was smooth and strong, with the fingers of a man who uses them finely and delicately.

"Yes," said Katie.

"Iss Mr. Steven Bedrie here?" he asked.

"No; not now."

He hesitated. "Who are you?" he asked finally.

"I'm Miss Warren."

He came a step nearer her. His eyes were a clear Bavarian blue. He looked puzzled and a little apprehensive beneath his bold front.

"The girl that the automobile vas driving?"

"Yes."

He looked at her closely and then nodded. He tapped the newspaper with his other hand and said:

"This woman. This Charlotte Veinberg. I have seen her. To my shop she game. I—I——" He paused, faint bewilderment in his clear blue eyes. "I do nod know vot to do."

"Do you mean that you knew Charlotte Weinberg?"

He nodded uncertainly.

Katie's heart leaped. Was it possible that this shabby, troubled little man held any clue at all to the secret that was Charlotte?

"I am Katie Warren who was driving the car," she said steadily. "And I didn't mean to kill her, but I have been—they think I murdered her. Is there anything you know that you can tell me?"

His clear blue eyes recognized truth. She felt a sudden conviction that it was duty—plain, abstract duty and nothing else—that had brought him there.

He nodded again as if communing with himself.

"Vell," he said, "id iss nod easy to say. I read about the inqvest and I think perhaps I, Herman Schmidt, know something of this woman. Something her own family do nod know. I fear—I have a gread wrong done."

He stood there peering at her. He was anxious and honestly troubled and bursting with some knowledge. Katie knew she must be patient and deft. He must not be frightened away.

"What have you done that you think was a great wrong?" she asked gently.

"I thoughd only a joke it vas," he said anxiously. "I did nod know. Until in my shop this woman inquire——" He broke off abruptly, his pale blue eyes traveling on past Katie's shoulder. They were standing at the side of the road, and his gaze went on through bare but concealing shrubbery to a curve above them. Katie turned.

Chris and Paul were walking slowly along, both looking downward absently, both talking. The little German's face was no longer rosy. It was instead gray. And without a word he whirled and scurried into the shrubbery and was gone like a rabbit before Katie realized, even, that he had such an intention.

She told herself he was a crank. Murder trials always brought them out.

But his clear blue eyes were unforgettable. She found the path through the park and thus avoided Chris and Paul.

It was a queer, slow day. That day, the twenty-fourth, to Katie was characterized chiefly by three things, Steven's disappearance, the adjourned inquest, and finally the curious, interrupted interview with the anxious little German, whose clear blue eyes haunted her. She kept hoping that he would return. But he did not come, and Steven did not come, and the telephone did not ring. It was at last dinner time, and Mina and Fanny and everyone but Clarence had vanished, and Clarence was taciturn and fussy about the soup.

"Did you find your razor?" she asked once.

He did not look at her.

"No," he said. "I borrowed a safety of Paul."

Katie went straight to her room after dinner. She knew that Paul and Chris had returned and that they were all gathered in the bookroom talking, but she had no wish to join them.

She felt tired—inexpressibly weary.

But it was impossible to sleep. She turned and twisted for hours, trying to piece together some explanation, some answer to the questions that would not let her rest.

Gradually the house grew silent and dark and slumbrous and Katie was still awake. Finally she turned on the light and reached for the little box of capsules the doctor had left her. They were not in the drawer where she'd placed them and where her hand fumbled in search of them. She blinked in the light, and then saw that the box was there on the bedside table, invitingly near her hand.

She opened it and hesitated over the gray-white capsules and then in sheer self-exasperation closed the box without taking one and returned the box to the drawer.

She did finally grow drowsy. Her window was on the lake side and was open. Just as she fell asleep there came through the fog and darkness a muffled, far-away throb. It was distant, faint, but steady, like a pulse beating mysteriously away out somewhere in the lake, hidden by the fog.

"A launch," thought Katie drowsily. "Queer night to take out a launch."

CHAPTER XIV

IT WAS also, perhaps, owing to her window being on the lake side of the house that she did not hear echoes of the commotion that early morning brought. No faint sounds of the tremor of excitement reached her until Melissa knocked at the door of her room.

"It's the police again, Miss Katie," she called to Katie's drowsy inquiry. "They want to see you. Right away, please, ma'am."

"Why, Melissa! What's happened?" cried Katie. But Melissa had gone, for there was no reply. There had been some queer suggestion of strangled shock and terror in that velvet voice. Katie's fingers flew and yet, curiously, at the head of the stairway a few moments later she paused, dreading the descent.

In the lounge were several policemen, standing about very gravely and importantly. Clarence was there on a chair, looking ruffled and harassed. Paul and Chris were there, too, both very sober, and Fanny was pacing the floor and jingling as she walked and all but wringing her long strong hands.

They all looked up as Katie came slowly down the stairway and Chris came forward to meet her.

"Hello, Katie," he said. The light from above fell directly on his face, and it looked tired and old and haggard, with his eyes retreating in folds of flesh. "They want you in the bookroom. Crafft's in there."

"Good-morning, Miss Warren." It was the detective himself. He was standing in the passage beyond the lounge. "In here, if you please."

The bookroom was cold and vaguely untidy. The day was dark again, though less foggy, and the table lamp was lighted.

The detective closed the door and advanced smoothly.

"Sit down, Miss Warren," he said. He was no longer purring. Katie sat down. It had come, then: she wondered why he didn't just arrest her at once and have done with it. But he began to question her, directly and as if time pressed. His line of inquiry, however, was unexpected.

"See here, Miss Warren, all of you seem to think that Miss Weinberg had tremendous influence with Madame Petrie. Now then—I shan't mince matters. You are a sensible young woman. I want to know exactly why you feel that."

"Why, I—it was quite apparent, Mr. Crafft."

"That's exactly what I want to know. Just *how* was it apparent?"

Katie hesitated.

"In practically everything. I don't believe Aunt Mina would have taken any decisive step without consulting Charlotte."

"Madame Petrie, then, asked Miss Weinberg's advice continually?"

"Oh, always. That is, she talked of things to Charlotte. Depended upon her."

"You think she would not have gone contrary to Miss Weinberg's advice?"

It was, Katie supposed helplessly, a trap.

"I don't believe so, no."

"I suppose Madame Petrie was very much attached to Miss Weinberg?"

"I—don't know," said Katie doubtfully.

"Hasn't she grieved since Miss Weinberg's death?" The topaz eyes were very luminous; his voice very gentle and easy.

"I don't know," said Katie. "I wouldn't know. Aunt Mina is not an ordinary person."

"But your impressions, Miss Warren. What are your impressions of it all? Did Madame Petrie admire Miss Weinberg? Did she love her? Did she respect her business acumen? Her social gifts? Just why was Miss Weinberg so firmly entrenched in the house here?" He paused while Katie stared into his eyes.

"I don't know," she said again. "None of those suggestions seem quite to cover it."

Mr. Crafft permitted himself a faint sigh that was like a little puff of smoke. He looked at his watch and reached for his cane which had been disposed across the table top. He hooked the cane expertly around his little brown neck.

"Very well. Now then, perhaps you can tell me this. Was Miss Weinberg a nervous woman?"

"N-no. She always seemed very certain of herself."

"H'm. Didn't jump at sudden noises? Scream when —er—when a door banged, for instance?"

"No."

"Wasn't nervous or apprehensive about a possible accident?"

"No." Katie's mouth twisted a little. "Quite the contrary. Charlotte was always very cool-headed.

Always knew exactly what to do. If you are trying to make out, Mr. Crafft, that Charlotte lived in terror of—of anything at all, you are wrong. I don't think Charlotte was ever afraid of anything in her life. Or anyone."

"Not even Madame Petrie?"

"No."

"But was Madame Petrie," said Mr. Crafft very gently, "afraid of Charlotte?"

His thick mouth had closed tightly. His thick, blunt nostrils were flared a little, hungrily. His eyes bored avidly into Katie's.

"I don't know," she confessed finally, with honesty. "I don't think it was fear. Exactly."

"Well," said Mr. Crafft, "what was it? Exactly."

"Aunt Mina gave Charlotte almost her complete confidence. I think Aunt Mina would have done anything Charlotte advised her to do. And I feel sure that Aunt Mina would not have willingly injured Charlotte. Or angered her. But why don't you ask Aunt Mina these questions?"

"I have," said Mr. Crafft grimly. There was a marked absence of purring in his tone, which was rather gratifying. "But your aunt—that is, Madame Petrie—did not fear Miss Weinberg?"

"N-no," said Katie. "It wasn't that. But it's very near it."

"In other words you all feel that Miss Weinberg had some hold upon Madame Petrie?"

"No, no," cried Katie. "I said nothing of the kind. I only know that Charlotte actually ruled things. And if that sounds disloyal to Aunt Mina, it isn't. Aunt Mina has been an invalid for a long time. And Aunt

Mina has always been very kind to me, in spite of Charlotte's dislike for me."

"So Miss Weinberg permitted Madame Petrie to go so far with her kindness and generosity but no farther?"

"You are making me say things that I didn't say," said Katie, thoroughly angry. "I had no reason to expect Aunt Mina's kindness and generosity. And certainly Charlotte didn't interfere with—things like that."

"No," said Mr. Crafft softly. "She reserved her strength for the important matters. Such as who should inherit after Madame Petrie's death."

"I didn't say that, either!"

"It's a curious thing," said Mr. Crafft, "that you all, even Mr. Lorrel, admit that Miss Weinberg could twist your aunt around her little finger if she chose. But none of you knows—or else you pretend not to know—the source of Miss Weinberg's influence with Madame Petrie. Really, Miss Warren, don't you realize that you are in a very dangerous situation? If you are innocent, as you say, wouldn't it be better to help us discover who is guilty?"

"I realize it perfectly," said Katie gravely. "And I realize that I killed Charlotte. But I don't understand why you haven't arrested me and charged me with murder."

She tried without success to plumb the yellow-green eyes of the detective. He said, after an instant's pause:

"Perhaps there is no immediate need for that, Miss Warren. When did you last see Steven Petrie?"

The abrupt switch was disconcerting—almost as

disconcerting as the definite threat that, to Katie, his words held.

"Day before yesterday. That's the twenty-third. In the morning."

"You've not seen him since?"

He hadn't said talked to him since, thought Katie.

"No," she said, feeling justified in the evasion.

"Do you know where he is?"

"No."

"Do you know why he has gone?"

"No, Mr. Crafft—if you think I—deliberately killed Charlotte, why are you trying to find Steven?"

He looked at her blandly and smiled.

"Perhaps we need two suspects, Miss Warren," he said. "Or perhaps we merely need a witness. However, I don't mind telling you that things point, according to my notion, to there being more than one person involved. If my theory is correct——" He did not pursue that line of thought further, but swerved:

"Do you know, Miss Warren, if Mr. Lorrel has a power-of-attorney for Madame Petrie's affairs?"

"I believe he has," said Katie slowly.

"Another question: did anyone know, the afternoon Miss Weinberg was killed, that you would be coming home by just the way, I meant the route, you followed?"

"Why—I—they all knew, I suppose, that I'd gone to a concert. And I usually go straight to Michigan from the parking station and then straight home."

She could discover nothing from his look, and he went on, with, so far as she could see, no logic at all, to another question:

"Miss Weinberg had what amounts to a habit of tea-drinking in the afternoon, hadn't she?"

"Yes."

"Do you happen to know whether or not she liked sugar in her tea?"

"Quantities of it," said Katie definitely. "But the teapot that afternoon was full, Mr. Crafft. The cups were clean, and nothing had been touched."

"Yes, I know. Which convinces me it had been used. If you can tell me who refilled the teapot and washed one cup I can tell you—well, not everything, perhaps, but something.

"Now, Miss Warren, this will be more difficult, but try to recall exactly what happened when you stopped the car to permit Paul Duchane to open and close the gates: had you any impression at all of someone being about or near the car?"

"No. But it was dark, and I could scarcely see through the glass, you know. And the doors were closed—I only heard the motor running."

"When Mr. Duchane closed the gate and tried to wipe off the headlights, you are sure you saw no one else?"

"Positive that I saw no one," said Katie carefully. "But I suppose someone might have been quite near."

"But there was no jar of the car, for instance? As if someone had stood on the running board of the car?"

"No," said Katie sharply. "What—who—I don't understand you. There was only Paul and me. I'm sure."

"But you aren't sure of anything outside the car?"

"No," said Katie, curiously reluctant.

"So I thought. By the way, Miss Warren, were you

quite positive that the name on that cleaner's truck yesterday was Andrews?"

"Quite."

"Very well." His face changed. All blandness vanished. "Will you put on a wrap, Miss Warren, and come with me? I have something to show you."

The throb of restrained terror in Melissa's velvet voice—the anxious, sober faces in the lounge—the threat of the hovering police—the tremor of excitement that made itself felt somehow through the whole somber house. . . .

"What is it?" said Katie, suddenly husky. "Not—Steven——"

"No," said Mr. Crafft. "Try taking a long breath, Miss Warren."

She did so and was less limp, and her heart began to beat again. The little brown man was eyeing her meditatively.

"So that's the way of it," he said. "H'm—well. Come along, Miss Warren, if you please."

He opened the door for her.

It was silent in the lounge, all of them watching as Katie took a wrap from the coat rack in the vestibule.

The mirror over the desk caught a flash of Katie's scarlet-lined hood and of a brown, ugly face.

"Sergeant Caldwell," said Mr. Crafft as they reached the door that led upon the lawn, and the chief gentleman-in-waiting, very pink, his blue chest laboring with suppressed excitement, followed them.

They went straight across the lawn. The fog had lifted considerably, although the day was still and gray. The lawn and house and strip of beach were, however, clear, though away out beyond a stretch of gray water the fog lingered, and as they descended the little wooden steps to the beach, Katie saw that a misty gray curtain yet shut off the shore line and the city.

The sand was wet, and it was heavy going. Suddenly Mr. Crafft stopped.

Some men were clustering about something that was on the beach. Katie had only a vague impression of dark figures, something that looked like a camera and was, and a blue-coated policeman or two.

What was Mina's camel's-hair autorobe doing there on the beach?

Then Mr. Crafft bent and with a quick jerk pulled aside the robe.

"Do you know this man?" he said. "Look at him."

Katie looked. The gray mists over the lake advanced and advanced and became black and very nearly engulfed her. Would have quite engulfed her had she not fought them back.

Yet it was only the little German. Little Herman Schmidt. Lying there with his Bavarian blue eyes open and looking wonderingly and perplexedly at the gray silent sky. Lying there with a hole in his heart and the waves lapping lazily at his feet. And somewhere near a gull was swooping and cheeping.

"You've seen him before," said Mr. Crafft. "Who is he?"

"Herman—Schmidt," said Katie with enormous difficulty.

"And who is he?"

"I—don't know."

"Where have you seen him?"

"Here—in the drive——"

"When?"

"Yesterday."

"Why did he come? What did he want?"

Mr. Crafft's voice was no longer bland and purring; it was sharp and thin and cruel. The men were all staring, watching Mr. Crafft, watching Katie, looking at the dead man at her feet. The man at the camera was chewing gum vigorously, and Sergeant Caldwell was breathing heavily with excitement. Around them was gray-brown sand, and gray waves were lapping quietly beside them. The sky was gray, too, and far away, and the air very fresh and clear.

What had he wanted? Why, of course—it was Steven he had asked for. Steven.

"He wanted——" Katie caught herself barely in time to bite back Steven's name. "He had a picture. The newspaper picture of Charlotte."

She must conceal Steven's name; Steven was in danger, Steven had vanished, the man at her feet had quite evidently been murdered, and he had known Steven. Her experience thus far with Mr. Crafft and the police had not been of a nature to impress her with their perspicacity. After all, she knew that she hadn't murdered Charlotte, and they leaned strongly to the belief that she had. If they knew that the murdered man had inquired for Steven, they might make of the knowledge anything and everything.

"So he had Miss Weinberg's photograph," the detective was saying. "Won't you tell me, Miss Warren, exactly what he said and what his purpose was?"

"He said he knew Charlotte. That she had come to his shop. And then he said something about a joke and that he feared he had done a great wrong. That's all I know."

"Didn't you ask him to explain? How did he

happen to talk to you? Are you sure that is all he said?"

"That's all. We were standing there in the drive, and he looked up and saw Chris Lorrel and Paul walking down from the house. He slipped away before I could stop him and was gone."

"See here, Miss Warren, suppose you tell me as much as you can remember of the conversation."

"I've told you. However, I'll try to go over it exactly. He asked first if this was the place where 'these people' lived. He was carrying the newspaper and pushed it out so I could see. He asked me who I was. He seemed very hesitant and undecided. He spoke with a strong German accent, and he looked honest"—Katie choked, and her eyes went irresistibly to the perplexed blue eyes there on the sand. She looked away again quickly and out toward the lake, as she told, as nearly as she could recall it, the brief bit of dialogue. She omitted only the little German's first inquiry.

"Did he seem frightened when he—ran away?"

"I scarcely know. It seemed so to me."

"Then you feel that he knew either Mr. Lorrel or Paul Duchane? Or both?"

"I don't know." Had there been recognition as well as fright in his clear eyes? She shook her head impatiently. "I don't know.—Don't you think it would be better to—to cover him?"

"In a moment, Miss Warren. There's something else I want you to see. McQuade!"

"Here it is, sir." One of the silent men stepped forward.

"Have you ever seen this gun before, Miss Warren?"

She looked at the revolver the man called Mc-Quade was holding before her eyes. It was long and old, with a curved wooden handle.

"Yes," she said helplessly. "I think so."

"Where?"

"It belonged to Uncle Petrie," said Katie, feeling sick. "I don't know anything more—I—feel——"

"Come now, there's no use your going to pieces, Miss Warren. You've held up admirably so far. Hysterics won't help you at all. Now tell us why your fingerprints are on this gun."

"Because I—I had it—I——"

"Hey," cried Sergeant Caldwell. "If you're going to confess, somebody better write this down. Anything you say may be used against——"

"That's enough." Mr. Crafft's soft words were exactly like a very thin whip swishing venomously through the air. Sergeant Caldwell grew scarlet.

Katie took a long breath and flung up her chin.

"I don't believe I am obliged to answer that question, Mr. Crafft. However, I'm perfectly willing to do so. I found that gun in a drawer of Uncle Petrie's desk. I felt nervous about having a loaded revolver about, and I hid it in the bottom of an old bronze umbrella stand. It's in the coatroom, if you want to look at it. And I hid two swords and a dagger up the chimney in one of the drawing rooms."

"Why? Were you—nervous about them, too?"

"Yes."

"Any particular reason for your nervousness?"

"No," said Katie, because there was nothing else to say.

"Could anyone have seen you hide this revolver?"

"No—— That is, yes," said Katie. "There was the window. And when I came out, Mrs. Siskinson was in the lounge. And that's all I know. Except that I am certainly not confessing to murder. Now or ever."

The man at the camera thoughtfully took out a package of gum, opened and added by slow degrees another stick of gum to the one he was already chewing. Otherwise no one moved for the long moment during which Katie forced herself to meet Mr. Crafft's shining yellow-green eyes.

A gull flashed near with a lovely swoop of white wings and a glimpse of pink feet. Little Herman Schmidt, lying so terribly still, no longer worried, no longer trying to do his duty. His clear blue eyes looking upward could not see that flash of white and pink and gray against the far-away gray sky. Mr. Crafft said:

"Who do you think might use the revolver? Or the swords?"

"No one in particular."

"I see," he said silkily. "You were nervous. Just nervous. It looks as though your attack of nervousness was singularly well founded."

His cane jerked, and his manner changed, becoming brisk and businesslike.

• "Sergeant Caldwell, will you take Miss Warren back to the house? I had better tell you now, Miss Warren, that we request you to make no effort to leave."

There was an unpleasant emphasis on the word "request." Katie, however, refused to let him see that she caught the emphasis and its significance. She said coolly: "Good-morning," and turned away.

The honors, if there were any, which was doubtful, were on her side.

But Sergeant Caldwell was striding there beside her, floundering a bit owing to the loose sand, and very big and solid and not to be overlooked. And presently they passed the spot where she'd stood with Steven.

How long ago it seemed! And yet she could almost feel his lips again, warm and urgent, and his arms holding her and binding her against him away from the world that had so suddenly grown strange and terrifying.

She hastened her footsteps, which were lighter and more accustomed to sand, and Sergeant Caldwell became crimson again and short of breath.

On the little wooden steps she stopped and turned with her hand resting on the damp railing. Sergeant Caldwell had been kind to her that dreadful hour after Charlotte had been killed, she remembered; and she remembered how he'd looked, just for an instant, as if he felt sorry for her.

"Sergeant Caldwell," she said directly, "why don't they arrest me?"

He checked himself so abruptly that he was obliged to grasp the railing to keep his balance, a bit of enforced agility which did not tend to soothe his already riled temper.

"Young woman," he said, gripping the railing, "you're as good as arrested right now."

"But why do they wait?" she insisted. "Is it because

there's something they know—you know—that makes
you think I didn't do it? What is it?"

She caught a faint look of surprise in his eyes before he spoke:

"You'll hear enough about it when we get hold of
young Petrie," he said evasively. "There might've
been the two of you in on the deal, you know. It's
called," added Sergeant Caldwell, "an accessory before the fact. Will you please get on, miss?"

Katie got on.

Melissa was waiting just inside the lounge, with the
message that Madame Petrie wanted Katie to come
to her room at once. Melissa, thought Katie, looked,
for the first time in her knowledge, troubled and no
longer calm. There was nothing definite, only a feeling of something about the tall woman that was less
tranquil, less still. It was as if something had stirred
the bottom of a very deep pool, so deep that on the
top there was only the faintest ripple to indicate that
deep turbulence.

"In a moment, Melissa," said Katie and went to the
coatroom. It was true, then. The gun was gone.

Who, then, had taken it? Who had used it for murder?

A queer kind of chill went up Katie's back. There
were not many people who had access to that dreadful bronze cherub. And there was no doubt at all
about its being murder.

Steven had said to hide the things. Steven had said
not to trust anybody. What, then, did Steven know?

He had also said not to cross Mina in any way.
And she was keeping Mina waiting then.

Katie replaced the false bottom. The bronze cherub

was mute and ugly, and again Katie's memory flashed back to a little girl with long legs and serious eyes; and Charlotte pompadoured and small-waisted and alert. This time, in that swift memory, Charlotte had a book in her hand—a slim blue book, powdered with gold. It was, Katie realized, some familiar book —familiar to the household and familiar to the child. Then the memory was gone again, and Katie was in the present.

Melissa walked up the stairs just behind Katie, very near her, and Katie wondered if Melissa was growing frightened. She hoped not, parenthetically, for, after all, meals had to be prepared, and she couldn't quite see Jenks, for all his air of efficiency, cooking and serving a meal. And the next upon whom logically would fall the task would be Katie herself. Unless Aunt Mina could be stirred to quicker action in the matter of discovering a new cook, and Aunt Mina was notoriously slow. Jenks had been there ten years at least. William perhaps seven.

"How long have you been here, Melissa?" asked Katie without turning.

"A little over a year, ma'am," said Melissa softly. How silently she moved! Had it not been for that velvet voice behind her, Katie wouldn't actually have known that Melissa was there following her so closely on that padded silent stairway.

Katie went on around the landing.

"I've forgotten how you happened to come."

"Miss Charlotte hired me, ma'am," explained Melissa gently.

"But what happened to the other girl, the one before you? I've forgotten."

There was an instant or two before Melissa replied. Then she said:

"It was about the spoons, Miss Katie."

"About the—oh, yes. I remember."

They had reached the top of the stairs and turned toward the wing where Mina's rooms were located. Melissa was still close and silent behind Katie. The spoons, of course. Some silver spoons had vanished, and Charlotte attributed the disappearance to the, then, second girl, with the immediate result that the girl vanished and Melissa arrived. Charlotte at the helm was much swifter than Mina.

At the intersection in the hall they met Jenks. He was carrying a vacuum cleaner and looked pale and worried.

Katie stopped.

"I want you to tell me again about that telephone call," she said. "Exactly what was it you heard?"

He set down the vacuum cleaner and looked a bit paler, his Adam's apple moving up and down anxiously.

"I'm sorry about that, Miss Katie," he said. "I didn't mean to tell it. He—the ugly brown man got it out of me before I knew what I was doing."

"But you see, Jenks," said Katie soberly, "I didn't telephone."

He looked at her pityingly.

"No, Miss Katie," he said soothingly.

Anger swept Katie. She longed to reach out and take the slender little man by his white shoulders and shake him till his Adam's apple traveled up and down in good earnest. He took a backward step nervously.

"I only told what I heard, Miss Katie. And I'm

sorry I ever went to the telephone. If I'd ever guessed what it was going to get me into, I'd never have gone to it. Never in the world!"

"You are positive it was Miss Charlotte talking?"

"Oh, positive. I couldn't be mistaken about that."

"Now tell me again exactly what you heard her say."

"It was just as I said, Miss Katie. She said, 'Very well, then, at the bridge, but don't be late, Katie.' That was all I heard."

"Think now, Jenks, how she said it. Was it like this: 'Don't be late, Katie,' as if she were addressing me? Or was it: 'Don't be late. Katie——' as if she had started a new sentence and you only heard the first word of it?"

Jenks listened anxiously, judiciously, with his head tipped on one side and his eyes on Katie's.

"No, Miss Katie," he said regretfully. "I'm sorry, but it sounded like she was talking to you. There was a kind of pause after she said 'Katie,' as if that was all. And then I hung up."

"So you didn't actually hear anything that was said after that?"

"No."

"And the conversation could have continued indefinitely so far as you know?"

"Yes," admitted Jenks, with an expression that doubted it.

"Then Miss Charlotte could have said: 'Katie will be home soon' or 'Katie is coming along the drive' or anything of the kind without your knowing it?"

"I suppose so," said Jenks, still with an exasperating blend of doubt and regret. "But that's what I heard, Miss Katie. And I had to tell it."

"Oh, yes, you had to tell it," said Katie, feeling savage. "But don't forget, Jenks, that you didn't actually hear any word after she said 'Katie' and that she might have said anything."

"Oh, yes, I'll remember," he promised hopefully. "It'll probably come up in the trial.

"No doubt," said Katie crisply. "If you are present. That's all, Jenks. Except that I hope you choke." The latter observation was uttered only in Katie's mind, and Jenks moved away righteously and unperturbed. Katie turned to the Negro maid. "Melissa," she said, "I've not had any breakfast. Will you fix something for me, please? Bring it up here."

It seemed to Katie that there was the barest shade of reluctance in Melissa's manner as she turned again toward the stairs. A few more days, thought Katie, and they'd all be gibbering idiots, afraid of the dark, afraid of every shadow, afraid of one another.

And with good reason. Who had taken the revolver?

Katie walked hurriedly toward her own room. Mina could wait.

The passage was somehow more shadowy than Katie remembered it. Curious how empty and dark and silent the house was in spite of the people that lived in it.

The little brown detective had said that her nervousness had been singularly well founded. Katie gave her room a quick searching glance before she entered it.

There was, of course, no one there, although someone had been there, for the room was already aired and dusted and the bed neat and smooth in its daytime dress. Melissa was combining her duties in the most praiseworthy fashion.

The little blue powder box was still snug in Katie's black suède handbag. And it was untouched, and the broken end of the palette knife was still there, hidden.

Accessory before the fact. It was not a pleasant thought. That was a kind of conspiracy. Evidently, then, the police had got some bit of evidence that led them to think that there were at least two people involved in Charlotte's death. That one person alone could not have accomplished it.

No, it was not a pleasant thought.

And on the beach lay little Herman Schmidt with his blue Bavarian eyes open and staring at the gray sky.

She was looking absently at the small bedside table. It was dusted and neat and tidy. Tidy except for a box of capsules placed invitingly near for a groping, drowsy hand.

She had put that box away in the drawer, she thought, still absently. Queer that Melissa had so carefully extracted it and placed it there on top of the table. Exactly where Katie's hand could reach for it. So invitingly near.

She ceased being absent and only half aware and was all at once alert. She crossed to the table and picked up the box and opened it and looked scrutinizingly at the capsules.

They were just capsules, opaque, grayish white, shining as she tipped the box. There were five of them left.

CHAPTER XV

KATIE never knew how or why she was so immediately and terribly certain that the capsules had been tampered with. But her conviction could not have been firmer had she actually seen someone changing the capsules. Or, more definitely, the powder in the capsules.

She didn't know exactly what the capsules the doctor had given her contained but thought it was probably some harmless and mild opiate. And she was suddenly as certain as she was ever certain of anything in her whole life that the present powder the capsules contained was anything but harmless.

She remembered with cold clearness how she had hesitated over that box only the night before. How near she had come to taking one then.

When had the capsules been changed? It must have been some time during the previous day, for there would scarcely have been time and opportunity since she had left her room that morning. Moreover, Melissa must have been in and out of the room during her own absence, for as she had already noted the room was made neat for the day. Perhaps Melissa herself had changed the capsules.

She would give the box to Mr. Crafft.

The mirror over the dressing table winked and seemed to move, and Katie glanced quickly.

The door was still open, and someone was moving just out of sight in the passage outside.

She closed the box quickly and, holding it clutched in her hand, went swiftly to the door. But it was only Clarence, neat and graceful, moving with the ease and lightness of a dancer.

He did not hear her and did not turn, but Katie stood watching him thoughtfully.

What did she, or any of them for that matter, know of Clarence beyond the facts that he was Fanny's husband, neat, graceful, and pleasant-mannered, had never, so far as anyone knew, done a stroke of work in his life and had lived, so far as anyone knew, on bequests and occasional gifts from various relatives. He also drank a bit too often and a bit too much. Did any of them know the real Clarence Siskinson? Or was there one?

And after all, it had been Clarence who had found the bit of woolly black hair in Charlotte's dead hand. Or had it been? Had he actually found it?

It was certain that he had called their own attention to it, that he wouldn't let it rest, that he had insisted on telling the police of it. He had also been the first to talk of murder.

On the surface, it sounded like honest bewilderment. But it might equally well have been the act of a guilty man, striving to appear innocent, throwing in the bit of woolly black hair in order to confuse them, and talking of it in order to emphasize it. It might even have been Clarence who took the bit of hair from Mina's room. But it might have been any other of that household, too. Even Chris Lorrel was as much a part of the family and was as much at home in the house as any of them.

And the razor Clarence had lost—Katie caught her breath suddenly. Had he really lost it?

She must give the capsules to Mr. Crafft. She must discover what the police were doing. She must hurry to see Mina.

Ahead of her down the hall she could see Clarence's figure outlined. Clarence, too, was nervous. For when he reached the passage which went to Mina's room, he looked with quick little jerks of his curly head up and down the passage before he entered it. She followed him, hastening, so that just as he knocked at the door she came up beside him. At the little breath of motion from her skirts and her footsteps he whirled and looked for an instant faintly green. There was real alarm in his eyes before he laughed rather thinly and said: "Oh, it's you, Katie. You gave me quite a start."

All marks of a man honestly frightened.

Yet perhaps a man in fear of the police might start when approached without warning.

"Come in," said Fanny's voice. It was strident with irritation.

Clarence opened the door, and Katie preceded him into the bare, earthy-smelling, hot room.

They entered upon a tableau, and Katie knew at once why Fanny's voice had carried such irritation. It was because they had interrupted something that Fanny did not want interrupted.

Mina was sitting, an erect, thick, black column, in one of the tall chairs. Chris was sitting opposite her, with his chair drawn up to a table, and he was writing hastily on a pad of paper, and Fanny was hovering indomitably over Mina.

Chris's pen poised itself above the paper as the two entered the room. Mina's white face moved slowly toward them, and her eyes burned into Katie's inquiringly, and Fanny, fluttering in some kind of dark silk with great purple flowers sprawling across it, came toward them. Her eyes were shining, and her bracelets jingled.

She gave Clarence a look of extreme annoyance and did not look at Katie at all.

She said rather savagely: "Sit down and be quiet. Mina is very busy."

Clarence looked inquisitively at Mina and then at Chris.

"What's he doing?" he asked Fanny and then raised his voice to repeat the question. "What are you writing, Chris?"

"It's business affairs for Mina," said Fanny hurriedly. "Don't interrupt."

Clarence ambled past her, evaded rather neatly her outstretched long hand as if he hadn't seen its clutch, and approached Mina.

"How are you feeling this morning, Mina?" he asked pleasantly. "Has the doctor been here yet?"

His eyes slid past Mina's white face to the table and the pad of paper before Chris.

"Quite well, thank you, Clarence. As well as I shall ever be, perhaps." She spoke flatly, as was her custom, without interest, as if what she said were merely a passive flow of words that had no immediate connection or concern with her. At the same time, that morning, there was a kind of throbbing undertone of vigor.

She gave the strangest impression of possessing within herself some secret spring that had long been dormant and was only beginning to stir.

It was an extraordinary and unaccountable impression, unaccountable because there was nothing tangible, nothing definite and physical, upon which to base it. Yet there it was, as if some deep-flowing stream had been dammed up and were suddenly released. Or as if Mina had suddenly been relieved of a weight that had paralyzed her, and gradually strength were flowing back into her nerves and muscles.

Perhaps Charlotte had been that weight. Of all that Katie knew of the long association of the two women, only one definite fact emerged, and that was that Mina completely, if inexplicably, depended upon Charlotte's judgment and decision in matters of importance. And in matters of no importance. Kitty remembered suddenly, from some distant past, Mina's voice saying: "What would you think of a ride along the lake today, Charlotte? It's nice and sunny." And Charlotte's voice: "No. It's not a good day for a ride." And Mina's immediate acceptance.

Queer.

And now all at once Charlotte was murdered and Mina was stronger.

Then Katie realized that Chris was speaking to her. He had also, she noted, quite casually extended his hands and wrists so that they shielded the paper from Clarence's straying eyes.

"Did Crafft question you, Katie?" he was asking.

"Yes." . . . Little Herman Schmidt, with his troubled blue eyes.

"Katie," said Mina, "what about your uncle's gun? I recognized it at once, of course. They say it was used to—to murder this man. But I don't understand how that could be."

"Oh, yes," said Katie helplessly. "It's Uncle Petrie's gun."

Chris glanced at Katie sharply.

"The police say there were fingerprints on it," he said slowly. "And from the way they talked I gathered the fingerprints belonged to someone here in the household."

"The way they've been blowing yellow powder and taking pictures all over the place," snapped Fanny, "it would be no great wonder if they discovered somebody's fingerprints somewhere. They act as if one of us had murdered him."

"As if——" said Mina and stopped, for once aware of her own words. She sat there looking at Fanny. No one moved, and no one seemed to breathe, while Mina's white chin sank lower on her black bosom and her eyes burned into Fanny's suddenly frightened face. As if one of us had murdered him, Fanny had said swiftly and impatiently.

Presently Chris cleared his throat heavily.

"Now, Fanny, you don't want to go around saying things like that." His words were mild, yet he was suddenly and inexplicably angry again. "Shall we go on with this, Mina?" he asked, indicating the paper before him with one of his huge, deft hands.

For a long moment she seemed to ponder some question back of those feverish eyes. "Today's the twenty-fifth," she said slowly. "Tomorrow is the twenty-sixth. But—no." There was an air of having come to some very grave and somehow dangerous decision. It was actually as if the short struggle to make that decision had tired her, for she turned to

Katie and said in a suddenly weary voice: "I'm making my will. Come here to me, Katie."

There was the barest suggestion of warmth in her weary tone. Katie had always had the feeling that away back somewhere Mina had, and usually concealed, a kind of fondness for her. Now, as she moved across the hot bare room, Katie was conscious of that affection, problematical though it was in many respects. And she was also conscious of Chris and Clarence and Fanny all falling suddenly silent and motionless to watch her.

Mina reached out one of her thick white hands and took Katie's hand. She lifted her face a bit, so that her dark hot eyes could search Katie's face.

"Your eyes," she said presently in her usual flat and blank voice, "are like your mother's eyes. Clear and blue and deep as water." She released Katie's hand suddenly and turned to Chris. "I've changed my mind," she said. "I'll not make my will today. What have I said there?"

Fanny's bracelets tinkled agitatedly.

"Shall I read it?"

Katie was aware of a kind of eagerness in Clarence's face which in the clear morning light was uncertain and pink and puffy, its neat lines a bit blurred. Clarence needed footlights, make-up, the glamour of distance. Cold morning light was devastating.

"Shall I read it?" said Chris again, slowly and somehow reluctantly, and at the same moment some-one knocked at the door and immediately opened it. It was Paul.

"May I come in?"

"Yes, of course, Paul," said Mina, smiling.

"How are you, Aunt dear?" he asked, leaning over

her solicitously. From the wall above his sleek head his own eyes watched and smiled charmingly. Mina's eyes plunged upward to those pictured eyes and lingered there. And Friquet, on her lap, gave Paul a green glance of disapproval and yawned and leaped to the floor, and Fanny sniffed audibly and jingled her bracelets.

"Well enough," said Mina, her voice faintly warm and fond.

"Good," said Paul. "I was afraid this horrible business down on the beach——" He stopped expressively. "I telephoned the doctor he'd better come along to see you this morning; after all, it must have been a shock to you, Aunt Mina. Even if you didn't know who the man was."

"The shock," said Mina unexpectedly, "was your uncle's gun being used."

The sudden tense awareness of their common thought filled the hushed, hot room.

Fanny's swiftly impatient words they had evaded. As they were to evade, from then on, any open acknowledgment of that thing that lay between them. But just for an instant it walked, cat-like, among them.

Katie thought: I'm becoming hysterical. I'm not myself. I'm standing here afraid to meet other eyes because there is live knowledge like a presence in this room. We all know—we all suspect—we all think: is it Chris, is it Paul, is it Clarence—is it Fanny? And they think: is it Katie? They think: she killed Charlotte. They think—or Chris thinks, if he knows: her fingerprints were on the gun that killed Herman Schmidt.

She put her hands in the pockets of her brief little

coat, and her fingers encountered a flat pasteboard box.

But I know that, she thought swiftly. I know that if I had taken capsules last night I would not be standing here alive this morning.

Then she was aware that Chris was again evading, refusing to meet the knowledge that they shared.

"Shall I read what we've written here?" he was asking Mina again.

Paul's dark eyes slid quickly to the paper under Chris's hands. His slender silken eyebrows went upward delicately.

"Am I interrupting?" he said pleasantly.

"No, no, Paul. It's as much your business as anyone's. I'm making my will. But I've changed my mind. I thought I knew what was wisest to do, but I—— No, no, tear it up, Chris."

"But Mina," said Fanny quickly, "wouldn't it be a good plan to just sign it and forget about it, now you have done so much? Then it will be off your mind."

"No—no," said Mina. "Tear it all up, Chris."

"Oh, you mustn't waste all that energy and thought," cooed Fanny. Her voice was blandishing, yet her face held sharp anxiety. "Don't tear it up, Chris."

"No—no," repeated Mina. "I'm not sure that's the way I wanted it. You deserve it, Fanny. You are good to me. And tomorrow——" She checked herself, and her hot eyes plunged again upon the calendar. She said: "Maybe it isn't fair to leave so much to you, Fanny, anyway. Tear it up, Chris."

It was indecent to stand there and watch that slow shocking wave of purple that surged up in Fanny's strong face. It was not endurable. Somebody ought to move—somebody ought to say something. Somebody——

Clarence was suddenly galvanized into incredible action. He ran his small hands through his hair with one amazing gesture of frenzy and sprang toward Fanny, his neat little legs making a convulsive leap.

"To you!" he cried in a high voice. "Is she leaving everything to *you*? Oh, my God!"

And before anyone could speak or move, Melissa knocked at the door and opened it, and said quietly: "The doctor, ma'am."

"Ask him to come in," said Mina.

He came in, brisk, alert, blandly professional, and hurried.

"Good-morning. Good-morning," he said. "Dear me, Madame Petrie! What's going on here?—Policemen all over the place and somebody taken for a ride on your very doorstep, beach steps anyway. Ha, Ha! —thank you."

It was Paul who had brought forward a chair.

The doctor sat down, and at the same moment Chris rose, and there was a sound of paper tearing.

"I'll burn these," said Chris. "If you want me, Mina, I shall probably be here in the house most of the day."

"And I shall be here also," said Paul. "Stop on your way out, Doctor, and tell us how she is."

Fanny had had a moment to find herself. She shot a look that was choked with fury at Clarence and said with incongruous sweetness of voice: "Do you want me to stay, Mina?"

"If you like," said Mina indifferently, and Fanny's

eyes were bright with triumph as the others left her alone with Mina and the doctor. She was the confidential friend, after all, her eyes said. Stepping smoothly into Charlotte's place.

Katie glanced thoughtfully at Clarence. He was red, and there was a curiously ugly look of brooding in his narrowed eyes. If they hadn't interrupted, she and Clarence, Mina would have finished making a will that must have been largely in Fanny's favor.

Katie didn't envy Clarence when once Fanny's fury could unleash itself upon him. And yet—there had been something terrible, something ugly and desperate and shocking, in Clarence's sudden outburst.

He looked at her sidewise as they went down the stairway.

"It's a funny thing," he said unexpectedly, "what's happened to my razor."

At the foot of the stairs Melissa, who had preceded them, was waiting.

"Your breakfast, Miss Katie," she said.

"Later," said Katie. "Is the detective here?"

"The little ugly man?" asked Melissa. "He's in the bookroom, Miss Katie."

In the bookroom Mr. Crafft was questioning William and Jenks, both of them pale and more than a little ill at ease.

As Katie, her hand still in her pocket clutching that little pasteboard box, hesitated in the doorway, he looked up, saw her, and jerked his cane in what was an invitation to enter.

"Want to see me?" he said. "Sit down. That's about all now. You found the body early this morning and came to the house and told Jenks and he telephoned the precinct station. You're sure you touched nothing?"

"Nothing," said William earnestly. "Nothing." He was a lean, awkward man, with washed-out gray eyes and a long, horsy face. He looked, now, frightened and probably was.

Mr. Crafft turned suddenly toward Katie as if her presence had put him in mind of a question he had been intending to ask her for some time.

"Miss Warren, you have told me that on the night Charlotte Weinberg was killed you distinctly remember putting your foot on the brake in an effort to stop the car. I believe you said you stood on the footbrake and clutch?"

"Yes."

"And you are entirely sure you didn't touch the gas throttle?"

"Yes. And anyway, if I had released the clutch, as I did at once instinctively, it would have made no difference in the speed of the car if I *had* pressed the gas throttle instead of the brake."

"True," said Mr. Crafft gently. He smiled slowly as if, after all, Katie might prove to be fairer game than he had supposed and said blandly: "Unless your right foot touched the gas throttle a fraction of a second earlier than your left foot released the clutch. That fractional second would be quite sufficient to let through enough gas to give the car impetus. It would, in such a case, give a kind of leap ahead before the clutch could possibly disengage the engine. Then, if your foot continued to press the gas throttle instead of the brake, the engine would race, and the car would coast rapidly owing to the last impetus to its speed."

He turned to William, who had been listening anxiously, his pale eyes wide.

"Sergeant Caldwell tells me the brake was in perfect order."

"Oh, yes, sir," said William eagerly, although with a rather regretful glance at Katie. "I looked just after we brought Miss Charlotte to the house. I thought maybe something had gone wrong with the car. Miss Katie is a good driver," added William earnestly, trying to help Katie. "Never loses her head. Does just what she intends to do."

"M'm—yes. That was my impression," said the detective dryly. "But you say there was nothing wrong with the brakes?"

"No, sir," said the chauffeur.

"When did you test them?"

"Oh, right away, sir. It was me that took the car around to the garage right after the police had left. They worked fine."

"I see. Very well. You may go, both of you. But remain here at home until further—er—notice. Thank you both."

In the doorway William's pale, horsy face turned over his shoulder.

"I'm sorry about them brakes, Miss Katie," he said sadly.

Mr. Crafft's hard brown hand reached upward caressingly toward his cane. He unhooked it and drew it around him and looked at it lovingly.

"Do you think, Miss Warren," he said pleasantly, "that Paul Duchane could have touched the gas throttle with his foot before you managed to release the clutch?"

CHAPTER XVI

"Paul!" said Katie. "Paul!"

"Paul," said the detective, looking at her disapprovingly. "Certainly, Paul. Who else was with you?"

"P—Paul," said Katie again with a kind of gasp. "I never thought of it."

"Apparently not," said Mr. Crafft testily. "But try thinking of it."

"You mean he—he did it on purpose? So the car would strike Charlotte? But that would be murder."

"Dear me, yes," said the little brown man with a kind of snap. "What do you think I'm investigating? A charge of speeding?"

He paused, and as Katie still did not speak, he said impatiently:

"Come, come, Miss Warren. It can't be such a shock to you as all that. I should think you would jump at the chance to shift the responsibility for Miss Weinberg's death."

"It's just," said Katie, "that it makes it seem—real. I—it's been rather nightmarish to me—it——" She stopped. "Mr. Crafft—why do you say Charlotte was murdered? We've got to know. It's not fair to go on like this keeping it secret."

Again there was a little flicker of interest in the brown ugly face. Even tigers, Katie supposed, might like a fair chance; there was no sport in game that ran straight into their claws.

"Why, yes, I'll tell you," he agreed readily. "It's just been three days, however, and we felt——" He did not finish his sentence but went on swiftly: "Madame Petrie requested that Miss Weinberg's—er —remains be cremated."

"Yes," said Katie, vaguely remembering.

"There was some doubt in Sergeant Caldwell's mind regarding the accident when he discovered that you, who drove the car, were apt to profit so largely by Miss Weinberg's death. It seemed, to Sergeant Caldwell's simple and forthright mind, a too fortuitous accident to let pass without investigation. So he ordered an autopsy."

"Well——" Katie was leaning forward.

"And the autopsy," said Mr. Crafft gently—"the autopsy showed that Miss Weinberg had taken an extremely large quantity of a hypnotic drug. Had taken it—or been given it—only a short time previous to her death."

"A hypnotic drug," said Katie slowly. "But that——"

"The commercial name for the particular drug that was found is sodium pyratol. It is founded on a barbituric acid, and there are a number of preparations similar to it. It is used to induce sleep, or quiet, and is simply a hypnotic. The immediate results," said Mr. Crafft slowly, watching Katie, "are a kind of numbness. Dizziness. It is possible to walk and move and talk, but there is a feeling of great drowsiness and confusion. A kind of lack of coördination of muscles. One does eventually go to sleep. I'm explaining it stripped of the medical phrases with which our medical examiner told it to me. But I trust I am making my meaning sufficiently clear."

"Oh, yes," said Katie in a small voice. "Quite. You mean that Charlotte was unable to move quickly. Would have been confused and uncertain. That it would have been a simple matter for one so minded to strike her with the car, for she was so hypnotized with—what is it?—sodium pyratol—that she could not have moved quickly to escape it. This—drug—simply insured her inability to escape."

"You're doing very well," said the detective. "Go on."

"That would mean that it was all carefully planned," said Katie, again with a breathless little gasp.

"Very carefully planned," said Mr. Crafft softly. "Oh, very carefully planned."

"And you don't see," rushed on Katie, "how I could possibly have given Charlotte—or somehow induced her to take—the sodium—what's its name?—and yet have gone to a concert and driven out from the Loop and struck her with the car there in the road. And that's why you haven't actually and formally charged me with murder."

"I see," said the detective, "how you could have telephoned her to meet you there at the bridge, and could have been prepared and ready to strike her, seemingly as an accident."

"But I didn't telephone," protested Katie.

"So you say," said Mr. Crafft very gently.

"And I couldn't have given her any drug. And how could anyone be sure, if she had taken such a large quantity of a hypnotic drug, that she could come to the bridge? What was to prevent her becoming drowsy and deciding not to keep an appointment at the bridge, in the path of the car? Assuming," said Katie rather crisply, "that she had one."

"I think we must assume that," said the detective. "She certainly went of her own free will. And you forget the letter addressed to Steven Petrie."

"No," said Katie. "I didn't forget that."

"Look here, Miss Warren. Suppose it went like this: sodium pyratol was put in the tea which Miss Weinberg drank. She had already—for her handwriting was firm—written this letter. This mysterious telephone call came. Miss Weinberg made some appointment, went to her room with the letter, *which she left in her room,* got her coat and went to keep the appointment. An appointment which, I think, the letter fully explained—and, mark you, an important appointment. One she was eager to keep."

"But the tea was untouched."

"Oh, was it? Or was the teapot carefully refilled and the cups washed, to hide the fact that she had taken tea at all? And in the meantime Miss Weinberg had gone to keep an appointment just below the bridge. It was, I think, an appointment with someone who was to be driving a car, for it's evident that she stepped forward intentionally, in order to be seen by someone who was to meet her.—And she was dizzy and confused and could not think or act quickly.—Oh, it's not a usual murder.

"It is a murder which has been so carefully arranged that its accomplishment is like an automatic mechanism of some kind. The director of it starts it going by some simple, innocent-appearing act, and immediately the whole train of circumstances begins to fall into place. Charlotte makes an appointment at the bridge. It is an important appointment, don't forget that. It is made sufficiently important to insure Charlotte's meeting it and waiting, perhaps, to keep it in spite of any physical discomfort."

Katie shivered. She said:

"Charlotte would never have let anything keep her from keeping an appointment that was important to her. She was not—not that kind. She was wiry—was never tired—would fight down headaches or colds and keep on going on sheer nerve."

"So I judged," said Mr. Crafft. "Thus you, who knew her, realized."

"And that, of course, is another point against us," said Katie wearily.

"Against all of you," said Mr. Crafft somewhat grimly. "It was from the beginning evident that Charlotte's murderer knew exactly what she was apt to do. Knew, in fact, what all of you were apt to do and thus was able to start the train going. Charlotte would keep the appointment if it was humanly possible. You would be coming home through fog and sleet. Someone would have, for some reason, given Charlotte sodium pyratol. You would meet her at the most dangerous part of the road, on a steep slope. Charlotte would be confused, half asleep on her feet, in spite of her indomitable will to keep going. Then it would all be over. And the murderer would not appear at all."

"Then you don't think I killed her purposely," said Katie.

"I'm trying to find out," said Mr. Crafft. "Now,

then, how about it? Did Paul touch the gas throttle or not?"

"I don't know," said Katie. She added, with a touch of malice: "Would the murderer have foreseen that, too, and planned on it?"

"Possibly," said Mr. Crafft. "And there was the light in the summerhouse. That might have been to distract your attention."

"Yes, but I was busy and didn't turn to look. I'm sure of that."

"Still you thought of it and for a split second were thinking of that and not of what you were doing. But on the other hand—there was certainly someone in that summerhouse during the afternoon."

Katie's heart leaped.

"We are quite sure of that in spite of Madame Petrie's assurances that it was locked. After all, it would have been a simple matter to secure the key. Do you recognize this, Miss Warren?"

Katie looked at the small, slender object in his hand.

"Yes," she said huskily.

"You recognize it? It's a palette knife, as you see, with the end of it broken. Have you ever seen it before?"

"I don't know," said Katie. "There are many palette knives."

"Yes, of course. But can you tell us anything about this particular one? Look at it carefully—manufacturer's name Weber—smear of green paint on the handle——"

"It's—only a palette knife," said Katie.

He looked at it thoughtfully, turning and twisting

it in the light and touching the broken end of it with his brown fingertip.

"Well," he said thoughtfully, "Steven Petrie has one or two others of the same manufacture in his studio."

"That doesn't mean it belonged to him," flashed Katie.

"No—no," said the detective. "However, his fingerprints were on this steel blade. His fingerprints and those of Madame Petrie. And the knife was in the summerhouse!"

"Aunt Mina!"

He returned the palette knife to his pocket and verged sharply:

"Why did you come to speak to me just now, Miss Warren? Why had you so urgent a look?"

Katie remembered with, again, a shock. Steven, the palette knife, Mina, the capsules.

"These," she said and explained what there was to explain while Mr. Crafft took the box gingerly in his fingertips and opened it. He drew from a pocket a slender pair of forceps and delicately pulled one of the capsules apart and looked closely at the powder it contained. He smelled it but did not taste it. His face was a brown leather mask and told nothing except that there was an eager look about his nostrils. He said:

"Has the doctor gone yet?"

"I don't know."

"Don't touch this." He put the capsule carefully on the table and went to the door.

Katie leaned back against the cushion and took a long breath and waited. So they knew Steven had been in the summerhouse. Her careful guarding of that bit of steel had served no purpose; they had the knife from which it had been broken. How had it been broken? Was it accident? Or was it, too, part of the train of circumstances?

She thought of what the detective had said. One event had hinged upon another. Yet they had been so arranged as to synchronize perfectly. And to look like accident.

"Will you look at this, Doctor?" Mr. Crafft was back in the room, Dr. Mannsen, professionally bland and a bit hurried, following him. "This capsule. Is that the powder you prescribed for Miss Warren?"

The doctor looked, sniffed, tasted, and lost his professional bearing. He dropped his hat and his bag, snatched the top of the pasteboard box to look at it before Mr. Crafft could intervene, dropped it as if it were alive, sniffed the powder in the open capsule again.

"My God, no!" he said, in white horror. "Did you take one? Answer me. Quick. Telephone the hospital. Get a stomach pump! When did you take it?"

"Wait—wait, Doctor. She didn't take any!"

Dr. Mannsen looked at Katie.

He dropped blindly into a chair, reached vaguely in his hip pocket, drew out a handkerchief, and dabbed weakly at his forehead.

"You haven't got any brandy about, have you?" he said. "This's a shock."

"I take it, then, it is not the powder you prescribed."

"The powder I prescribed! Oh, my God!" moaned the doctor.

"What is it then?"

"That's a deadly poison. If I gave you that powder, Miss Warren," said Dr. Mannsen forcefully, "there's only one thing left for me to do and that's go home and shoot myself!"

"Well, don't do that," said the detective dryly. "You didn't give it to her." He glanced at his watch, and Katie had the impression that time was pressing. "See here, Dr. Mannsen, will you take one of these and give me a written record of what you gave Miss Warren and what you found in the box?"

"But how did poison get in those capsules?" demanded the doctor. "I gave them to her. I have a right to know."

"I don't know," said Mr. Crafft gently. "Can you tell us, Miss Warren?"

"No—no—I——" Katie paused, bewildered, and then her face flamed. "I didn't do it, if that's what you mean. If you think I brought that to you to divert suspicion from myself, you are entirely wrong. You——"

"There, now, Miss Warren. No need for explosions. No time for them, either. And Dr. Mannsen, while you are here will you answer a few questions regarding Madame Petrie?"

"If I can," said the doctor guardedly. He still looked dazed and watched the box on the table suspiciously, as if it might at any second produce further deviltry. A devil complete with horns and tail would be nothing, however, said the doctor's look, to what that box had already accomplished in the way of black magic.

"I'll try to word my inquiries so you may do so," said Mr. Crafft. He glanced at his watch again. "No, don't go, Miss Warren," he interpolated as Katie made a motion to rise. "How did you find your patient this morning, Doctor? Please reply as fully as you find it possible to do."

"Well," said the doctor slowly, "she is much better than I should have expected her to be. Isn't apparently suffering from shock."

"Nor grief?"

"Well, no," said the doctor rather uncomfortably.

"Do you feel at liberty to tell us the nature of the disease from which Madame Petrie is suffering?"

Dr. Mannsen moved uneasily.

"Well," he said hesitatingly, "it's rather difficult. It——"

"Yes?" urged Mr. Crafft as the doctor appeared to fall into a reverie.

Dr. Mannsen looked up with an air of sudden decision.

"I think it might be better to tell you exactly how it is," he said more briskly, although there was a worried look on his face. "And remember, first, that she's been to specialists and we've done everything that was possible to do. And we still don't know exactly what's wrong. Now that's the truth and kernel of it. I could give you a long résumé of tests and treatments and conclusions, but when you sift them all down that's what it amounts to. And yet, in spite of it all she steadily loses strength. It's as if she had simply made up her mind to die and was doing it."

Mr. Crafft studied the end of his cane as if he had never seen it before and felt obliged to analyze its minutest fragment.

"Thank you, Doctor," he said finally. "You've put

in a nutshell what it would have taken me considerable time to unravel. If, indeed, I succeeded in unraveling it at all. I suppose, then, in the last analysis it's—nerves?"

"Broadly, I suppose," said Dr. Mannsen hesitantly. "Of course, Madame Petrie is a rather difficult subject. She is—curiously stubborn about some things; in fact, she retains an impression of any kind, once she gets it, with amazing fixity. Thus, of course, she is at the same time susceptible and unsusceptible to suggestion. Do you understand me?"

"Then repetition does it?"

Dr. Mannsen looked quickly at Mr. Crafft.

"That's exactly it, Mr. Crafft."

Mr. Crafft smiled, for the first time in Katie's knowledge looking rather human.

"Doctor," he said, "you are a rarity. You can talk practical psychology to a layman and use a layman's vocabulary." His eyes narrowed thoughtfully, and he became, to Katie's mind, immediately less human, for he said: "You will be heaven-sent on the witness stand. Only don't forget, now and then, to throw in considerable chunks of weighty language. It's impressive. Flatters the jury. Besides, every once in a while somebody understands. There's nothing in Madame Petrie's physical condition, then, that gives cause for alarm? There is nothing definite, I mean? Nothing, perhaps," said the little brown man, eyeing the doctor intently, "of recent development? Any change—any kind of abnormality?"

The doctor stirred uneasily, looked at his feet, at the bag, at the box of capsules, which apparently overcame any hesitancy.

"Nothing," he said, "unless—well—she's begun to have hallucinations, you know."

"Hallucinations!"

"Yes. Queer sort of things. All nerves, you know, and weakening strength. She sleeps when she doesn't know it, probably, and dreams. It's hard to tell."

"Just what kind of hallucinations?" inquired the detective.

"Oh, the usual thing. Sees people she's known at some time or other. Maybe she's dreaming. She won't talk much about it. It's nothing really except that it marks a serious stage in her illness. Don't misunderstand me, Mr. Crafft, she is dying. Dying as certainly as if I could name the disease."

"I understand. Dr. Mannsen, you must have had a great many opportunities to observe Madame Petrie and Miss Weinberg. We have arrived at the conclusion that Miss Weinberg had a very strong influence upon Madame Petrie, and we are anxious to discover exactly the source of that influence. Can you help us?"

But Dr. Mannsen either couldn't, or wouldn't, do so. He had observed only that Madame Petrie depended upon Miss Weinberg's opinion in all matters and practically always followed it. Further than that he could not say.

"I see. Very well. Thank you, Doctor. I realize that you have calls to make and won't keep you longer."

"Glad to be of any assistance, Mr. Crafft. Any time. This capsule——"

He departed, his professional aplomb shaken.

The detective whirled toward Katie.

"Now then, Miss Warren, *what is it you know?*"

"I don't understand——"

"Nonsense. *What is it you know of such danger to the murderer that you cannot be permitted to live?*"

"I don't——" Katie took a breath and tried again to speak. "I don't know."

"You must know. Think. What is it?" He waited.

"But I've told you——" Katie hesitated, bewildered. "Mr. Crafft, I can think of nothing I know that could possibly be of danger to the murderer. I—I assure you that I'm telling the truth."

"Um'm. Well, that's bad, then. It's evidently something you don't recognize, yourself, as being significant." He paused, looking at her doubtfully. "See here, Miss Warren, we were speaking of the autopsy following Miss Weinberg's death. Do you know why Madame Petrie requested cremation?"

"No," said Katie, "unless because it was Charlotte's wish."

"It had nothing to do, then, with the fact that cremation would destroy every possibility of discovering that Miss Weinberg had taken a large quantity of sodium pyratol?"

"No—no!" cried Katie sharply. "That would be to say that Aunt Mina was implicated. That Aunt Mina knew of it. And wanted the evidence destroyed."

"And you don't think she did?" inquired the detective softly.

"Certainly not," said Katie, and then remembered Steven's voice saying: "Do exactly as Aunt Mina tells you to do. Don't cross her in the smallest thing." . . .

"Certainly not," she repeated, though less decidedly. "You don't know Aunt Mina."

"I doubt if you do, either, Miss Warren," he said pleasantly. "And I must get back to our clockmaker. I should have a further report on him very soon."

"Clockmaker?"

"Yes, of course. The late Herman Schmidt. We traced him without difficulty to his little shop. Now if we can discover why Miss Weinberg visited that shop ——" He glanced again at his watch, and Katie rose and approached the door. "You are a very confusing family, Miss Warren," said Mr. Crafft blandly. "Not one of you has an alibi for the time when the murder occurred."

"When was that?" inquired Katie, rather marveling at her own temerity. Yet the detective had certainly, for reasons Katie could not fathom, encouraged conversation.

"About six o'clock last night," said Mr. Crafft, his eyes looking luminous as they caught a reflection of the light beside him. "That is, as near as can be discovered. Our medical examiner says he'd been dead very close to twelve hours when he was discovered, and the chauffeur found him between six and seven this morning. Now if only one of you had an unshakable alibi for the time from four o'clock yesterday afternoon till about eight I should know where to look. These unshakable alibis are always suspicious. But none of you have one. You all seem to have been rather vaguely going your own ways. Where were you, Miss Warren? No one so far has mentioned your presence, and I've questioned everybody rather exhaustively. I take it if you made no alibi for another of the household, you haven't one yourself."

"You are quite right," said Katie, hating him again.

"I was alone in the park when I met—Herman Schmidt. And after he ran away I came back to the house and did not see anyone till dinner. Clarence and I ate dinner together, and then I went upstairs. I wanted to be alone."

"Just as I suspected," said Mr. Crafft. "Another person minus an alibi. Dear me—you are all so guileless. And yet——" The smile on his brown face was not pleasant. "And yet—the killing of Herman Schmidt is indissolubly a part of the murder of Charlotte Weinberg." He paused thoughtfully.

Katie did not move.

"A part of it," repeated the detective deliberately. "But an unexpected part. It was not foreseen by the murderer. There was, for some reason, no time to arrange circumstances—no time," said the detective very softly. "To arrange a train of circumstances which would insure accidental death."

"Accidental—death——" said Katie in a kind of whisper. His eyes held her own.

"There was no time," he repeated. "The little clockmaker knew too much and had to be silenced. If there had been more time—we should have read of it in the papers—a traffic accident, perhaps—or suicide, even—or death resulting from a hold-up—or a Herman Schmidt becoming somehow involved in a gang feud and being taken for a ride and found out in Cicero somewhere. But there wasn't time. He had to be silenced at once. So he was shot with a revolver from this house. Which is another evidence of the need for haste."

"Do you think—I did that?" said Katie with difficulty.

"I don't know," said Mr. Crafft, suddenly detached and bland again. "But if you didn't, Miss Warren—I think I had better warn you that—accidents—may occur at any moment."

"Accidents," repeated Katie.

"Yes, of course. That's a curious affair of the water wings last summer, you know. One wonders how many other accidents Miss Weinberg escaped. And if you had taken a poison last night—well——" He shrugged again. "You would have taken it yourself. Suicide of murder suspect.

"Another question or two, Miss Warren," he said briskly, not apparently at all disturbed by the thing he had suggested. "And I might tell you that it is rather important. You will immediately perceive why it is important. On your way home from the concert did you see anyone you know? Anyone, I mean, besides Paul Duchane and the desk clerk?"

"No one," said Katie slowly.

"No one on the safety island?"

"No one."

"Certain?"

"Yes."

He was not satisfied. His eyes stared through her; round, and shining and blank, like Friquet's eyes. "And I don't suppose you know," he said softly, "whether or not—*anyone you know saw you?*"

"No—I don't know. I——" Katie stopped, in sheer bewilderment.

"I suppose you don't. Well, find Steven Petrie for me, Miss Warren," he said airily. "Good-morning."

He went quickly past her and into the passage. He vanished, and then as Katie stood there staring rather incredulously through the doorway and seeing only polished wood panels beyond, his brown face returned to peer, as if suspended against those dully gleaming panels, back at her. "And don't leave the house and grounds. There'll be policemen on guard to prevent anyone's leaving. But it will be pleasanter if you don't try."

Then he was actually gone. Katie sat down again dazedly to think and sort out what he had said and what conclusions she had drawn. But there weren't any conclusions. There were only questions which had no answers.

Jenks, coming to the doorway to announce, as lugubriously as if he were announcing a death, that lunch was served, aroused Katie from the seething tumult of speculation into which she had plunged. There were, she thought rather wearily, following Jenks, few conclusions to be drawn, but there were at least a hundred lines of reasoning, and it was her ill fate to follow all of them so animatedly and with such fertile imagination that each one seemed tenable.

Happily no one tried to talk during the meal. Chris and Paul were both there, Chris brooding rather sullenly and Paul abstracted but composed. Fanny was there, too; she ate heartily and said practically nothing, and her hard blue eyes would fix themselves on a spot on the white tablecloth and shine eagerly, and she looked collected and poised ready for a spring again.

Clarence, however, shared none of their composure. He was frankly uneasy. He started whenever Jenks, who was assisting Melissa by serving the meal, approached him, ate little, and had, overnight, developed a queer little habit of glancing over his shoulders. He would do it suddenly, jerkily, with a kind of pounce as if, that time, he would catch something lurking in the corner of the room or behind his chair.

It was not a nice gesture. Katie felt her hair stirring on her neck and a kind of thrill inside her elbows, and she had an uncomfortable longing to jerk her head suddenly around, too, and see what was in the corner nearest her. Her neck muscles twitched and her hands felt cold, and just then Clarence shied away from the celery like a startled horse. Jenks went on passing celery imperturbably, although the back of his thin neck was very stiff, and Katie forced herself to look away from Clarence's puffy, haunted eyes and to eat.

In spite of the grisly incident of the capsules, she did not feel afraid of the food. It was true that common sense impelled her to eat only foods that the others were eating. But she was not actually afraid. Not of that. It wasn't reasonable or logical, but it was true.

But presently, when she thought no one was observing her, she turned her head and looked into the corners of the room. There was nothing there, of course.

"It's getting darker," said Fanny suddenly. "Fog's coming in again. Turn on the lights, please, Jenks. Do you know," she went on conversationally, "I shouldn't be at all surprised if Steven's murdered, too."

Lights sprang up suddenly, and Clarence's glass of water went over with a splash and a clatter of glass. Jenks hurried forward, and Clarence said peevishly:

"What do you want to go talking about murder for, Fanny?"

"Might as well talk it as think it," said Fanny. "Steven's been murdered himself. Or else he murdered Charlotte and has escaped."

"Then who shot this man on the beach?" said Clarence.

Chris looked up, glowering, but Fanny continued without glancing at Clarence:

"The detective—that ugly one with the brown face —as good as admitted it to me this morning. He said they had to find Steven or Steven's body."

"The corpus delicti," murmured Paul, looking at his plate.

CHAPTER XVII

THE fog came in again. It was heavy and black, and it rolled up from the lake with an oddly sinister silence and darkness. It blotted out the lake and surrounded the house again and crawled through the park and hung in gray shrouds from the trees and black, wet shrubbery. It hid the gash of the ravine below the bridge, and the road became slippery, and the house itself was dark and still and it waited.

By four o'clock, the last lingering remnant of men from police headquarters with all their paraphernalia of detection had gone. A bevy of reporters, very practised and a bit bored, had been dealt with by Chris, who managed somehow to thrust his own angry preoccupation into the background and who talked suavely and pleasantly but did not leave, Katie thought, a very favorable impression. She wondered if he had been too suave regarding the mystery of the revolver, when he said they were all shocked and completely mystified by its appearance at the scene of the crime, and added quickly that Herman Schmidt was entirely unknown to any of the household. There was a kind of silent skepticism in the air.

"See here, Mr. Lorrel," said one of them. "This fellow, this Herman Schmidt—do you think he was killed on the beach?"

"I don't know," said Chris. "I'm sure I can't say."

"Well, he might have been killed, say, somewhere else and brought there?"

"I suppose so," said Chris. "I can't say."

"In the park below the house, for instance," pursued the reporter. "And then carried down to the beach. They say there weren't any clear footprints."

"So I believe," said Chris.

"Or," went on the reporter in a careless manner as if he thought little of what he was saying, although his eyes were very sharp, "he might even have been brought in by a launch or a boat of some kind and dumped there."

But Chris did not rise to the bait.

"I don't know," he repeated, untempted. "You'll have to ask Mr. Crafft."

"Well, of course," murmured the reporter, "there's the revolver from the house here. That seems to connect it pretty strongly with the house. Even if none of you knew the man that was killed. Strange, isn't it?"

"Very strange," said Chris coldly. "Now if you gentlemen will excuse us——"

They thanked him, not very warmly, and went away, and Chris got out a handkerchief and touched his forehead and sighed wearily.

Katie thought of the little German clockmaker and his troubled blue eyes. He had known only two names —one was Charlotte Weinberg, and he had known her face. And he had inquired for Steven.

Yet he had been frightened and had turned and vanished with the swiftness of a frightened rabbit when he saw Paul and Chris walking down the road. Katie said slowly:

"Think, Chris. Are you sure you never saw Herman Schmidt?"

His eyes were little dark slits in his great face.

"Good heavens Katie, what's wrong? Didn't you hear me say I didn't know him?" He was angry. That was evident. But there was a timbre of something like fright under that anger, and he went quickly away from her into the bookroom, and Katie remembered certain unforgettable things, and the house was very silent and dark and secretive, with the fog pressing in at the windows.

She went to the windows and looked out through the ferns to the wet, dreary lawn and the dim line that was the wooden railing, and above a sea of impenetrable fog. A figure came out of the fog and passed close beside the window and vanished. It was a policeman, with his cap pulled low over his eyes and a long black mackintosh cloak shining with moisture. It seemed to Katie she could feel the jar of his heavy regular footsteps. There was something inexorable about that regular, unhurried pace, and something frightening. Still, Katie told herself, with policemen about the house, surrounding it, things ought to be safer.

She whispered the last word to herself.

"Safer."

The house had again, with the fog, taken on that curiously pregnant silence. It was as if the fog itself carried threat and it crept inside the house and drifted into its shadows and settled itself into the vacant rooms and permeated everything, the walls, the thick rugs, the dark spaces where the fog made shadows, and the very air they breathed.

Something caught in Katie's throat, and she whirled. She didn't know what she had heard, if anything, or what she expected to see. But she felt with a kind of shrinking of her bones that some formless moving thing might have drifted swiftly from the shadow under the stairway and have found shelter again in the shadow of the passage just before she looked.

There was nothing, of course.

Nothing but—Katie sniffed—something burning somewhere. It was a faint, acrid odor, barely perceptible, drifting through the dark spaces of the house.

It was not cigarette smoke. It was not a pastry burning in the kitchen oven. It was not paper or wood or coal. It was not anything that ought rightly to burn.

Katie sniffed perplexedly. There might be a fire in the grate in the bookroom.

There was a fire there. Or rather there had been.

And the acrid, bitter odor, somehow repugnant, was more distinct.

Katie bent over the warm heap of wood ashes. They had been raked together quickly. The small shovel in the brass stand was still warm. But she could not discover what ashes smelled so strangly. Smelled like—— She hesitated. Like rope burning! Was that it?

But no one now was in the bookroom. No one at all.

And all around lay that silent, secretive house. While rope—if it was rope—burned in the fireplace and became ashes.

Friquet, hidden in the shadow under the table,

scudded out suddenly and slid out the door and away with a flash of green eyes and a great blue tail.

What had frightened the cat? Nothing, probably. Nothing at all.

Katie turned blindly. In the hall she snatched a wrap. She opened the front door boldly, missed a patrolling policeman by twenty feet, and flashed across the gravel toward the park so lightly that he did not look, and she saw his dark bulk vanish momentarily around the corner of the kitchen wing.

But today the park was no better than the house.

The air was moist and cold on her face. Katie pulled the scarlet-lined hood up over her head and walked rapidly along the twisting path. She could see for a distance of perhaps thirty feet around her where the trees and shrubbery opened and permitted it. And the heavy fog was closing steadily down and dimming that decreasing area. Her face felt cold and her eyes tired. But there was no need to fear. There was a guard of policemen about the house and grounds. No need to fear.

It became a kind of rhythm to which her feet walked.

The trees were brown and wet and bare, clad only in fog wraiths. The path underfoot was wet, too, and slippery, and there was a damp smell of leafmold and wet soil with, under it, a faint tingling odor of balsam.

She left the path presently and crossed the road below the bridge. There were two policemen standing at the bridge. They were talking, their backs turned to the road below them, and Katie could hear the dull murmur of their voices.

She paused on the edge of the ravine, wondering

why she had come. It was good to get away from the house, yes. But it was no better there in the park.

The ravine was like a black gash through the grounds. But that day its blackness was veiled in fog that lay very heavy there below Katie's feet. Fog always sought the low places first, she thought idly.

The fog was rising, masking the shrubs, turning them into dark presences like people. Like—— Katie realized that the dark thing she was looking at there in the bottom of the ravine was not a shrouded shrub but a man bending low. A man whose figure was so familiar and so longed for that the cry on her lips which would have brought the two policemen from the bridge choked itself unuttered.

Katie peered through the fog, and the man straightened, became Steven. He saw her then, and she bent and began to scramble silently down the side of the ravine, silently so the police on the road should not hear. Steven must have known who it was, for he was coming nearer her, winding among the shrubs, and then he was immediately below her.

He pulled himself up the steep, fog-hung side of the ravine.

"Steady there, Katie," she heard his whisper. "Catch hold. Now—let go. I'll catch you."

She relinquished her grasp on the tough sumach she'd clung to and slid somehow through wet, slapping little twigs into his arms.

Tight, warm, secure. Somewhere she could feel his heart thudding, thudding.

Then he held her away and looked at her and grinned.

"Your chin is pink," he said. "A man's been kissing you very hard and very long. Does it hurt?"

Katie nodded. Her chin did hurt—it stung, tingled. She smiled but couldn't speak for looking at Steven and trying to realize that he was there. Steven safe—Steven alive—tall, strong, warm. Steven laughing at her. Steven holding her safe after all the loneliness and terror. Funny her eyes blurred when she was so happy.

He pulled her against him and put his cheek down on her face.

"Oh, golly, I love you, Katie," he said with a kind of sigh.

The fog was very still around them. He was kissing her again. Gravely this time, rather blindly feeling for her lips.

A man, away off in a forgotten world, called vaguely to someone on the road and was answered. It was a dull, far-away word or two muffled by fog.

Steven lifted his head, looked into her eyes again, and took a long, rather shaky breath.

"We've got to talk," he said unsteadily. "What are you doing out here? How are things at the house?"

"Steven, Steven, where have you been?"

"Hiding," he said promptly.

"Why?"

"Because I don't want to be arrested. Katie, what's going on at the house? What does it mean, this German clockmaker being murdered? Who did it?"

"I don't know, Steven. I don't know——"

"But there's Uncle Petrie's revolver. Did you hide it as I told you to?"

"Yes. In the umbrella stand in the coatroom. You

remember that dreadful bronze thing with a cherub holding out its arms?"

"There?" Steven grinned again and sobered. "You'd have thought it would be safe there. I can't imagine anyone willingly approaching the thing. You didn't touch the gun again?"

"No. But they found my fingerprints on it."

"Oh, good Lord!" said Steven. "And I told you to hide it! What did they have to say?"

"Oh, they've not charged me with murder yet, if that's what you mean. They are just waiting to find you. They think we are accomplices. You see, Charlotte had been given a drug before she came out on the grounds that afternoon. She didn't quite know what she was doing. She was fuddled and confused and——"

"*What do you mean! Who gave it to her? Tell me.*"

Katie told it quickly, watching Steven's grave, suddenly intent face. Then, more slowly and still watching his face, she told of the broken palette knife.

"So that was what you were doing that night in the summerhouse?" said Steven when she'd finished. "I was watching you. I was the man in the fog. I was so near I could actually hear you speak. It worried me—your wandering around on the grounds."

"Then it was you at the window?" cried Katie.

Steven looked suddenly blank.

"At the window! No. I stopped there at the bridge."

Katie could feel again that nameless menace that stalked them.

"Did you escort us back to the house again?"

"No. I went on along the edge of the drive and waited while you went by the path. Waited till I saw the door open and heard you enter."

"Then who else was in the park? Who was it I followed instead of Paul? I got confused," went on Katie hurriedly, at Steven's look. "Followed someone else instead of Paul who was ahead of me. Then he called and I found him again."

"Oh, my God, Katie!" said Steven in a kind of groan. "Don't—don't go out at night. Don't—leave the house."

"But Steven, that house—someone tried to poison me! There in the house. I don't know who."

"Tell me——" said Steven in a voice Katie never had heard before.

When she finished, he said nothing for a moment.

"You can't go back there," he said finally in a labored way. "I don't know——" He stopped, and a flame leaped and smoldered and leaped again in his eyes, and then he said: "Katie, I've got to tell you. It's not safe. You can't go back there. But I can't take you with me."

"What—Steven, why—— Why did you say over the telephone that terrible thing? That you knew Charlotte was going to be murdered? Why did you go away like this?" Katie's voice was beginning to choke. "I've been nearly frantic, Steven. What did that letter mean? What are you doing?"

"You see, Katie—I'm trying to be a sort of red herring. I didn't kill Charlotte and had nothing to do with her death. Except that—as I told you, I knew it was going to happen! But I couldn't, God help me, stop it!"

"I don't understand—you must tell me——"

"So you see that makes me a kind of accessory. I knew it was going to happen. And I was here that afternoon. And I was in the summerhouse. And I used that palette knife in the door. It had stuck. And I happened to have the palette knife in my pocket because I'd intended to stop and order another exactly like it—it was a good palette knife."

"You said you knew that it was going to happen!"

"Yes." Steven's eyes went swiftly along the ravine wall and returned to Katie. "Talk low, Katie—someone might hear—the police. Katie, do you know why and how Charlotte ruled Aunt Mina?"

"No."

"Well—look here."

Katie looked. He drew from an inner pocket a long, folded paper. Unfolded, it revealed a curious arrangement of concentric circles and lines and emblems. There was a second sheet, with words written on it. Katie looked, read, and gasped incredulously, and Steven said:

"Exactly. I couldn't believe it, either. It's Aunt Mina's horoscope. Embraces the whole year, or rather it's supposed to embrace the whole year. But it doesn't. It stops the last week of February. The 26th. That's tomorrow. It stops very suggestively."

Again a fleeting memory was evoked in Katie's mind. A little blue book dusted with gold. A little blue book, dotted with stars.

"Why, of course," cried Katie. "She was interested in astrology years and years ago. I'd forgotten. Do you mean that Charlotte——"

"Do you see how it coincides with Charlotte's note?

'Mina knows her destiny too well to be swerved by a shadow.' Wasn't it something like that?"

"Yes—as I recall it. But, Steven, that letter was addressed to you."

"I know," said Steven grimly. "Katie, the thing is, it doesn't matter at all what you think of astrology. You may consult the stars all you please or not, just as you choose. *But it was, in this case, a tool in the hands of an unscrupulous woman.* Charlotte furnished Mina with this horoscope. And Aunt Mina showed it to me, and I took it to an astrologist and also compared it with a new book forecasting the movements of the stars for the present year. *And this horoscope is all wrong.*"

"Wrong? Then Charlotte——"

"Charlotte manipulated it. Of course," added Steven. "The astrologist and the book didn't exactly agree, either. But they came a lot closer to agreeing than this horoscope of Charlotte's agrees with anything. And it's a most suggestive horoscope. It's all put in veiled phrases, but reduced to its simple terms it's this: 'It is an unfortunate year for a person falling under this sign.' Here's the hour and date of her birth. 'Illnesses are apt to be chronic, even fatal!' 'There are in the early part of the year family disturbances and unwelcome and self-seeking guests. The family disturbances become serious.' 'Anyone having legal documents to draw up should do so before the last week in February.' 'There is one loyal friend during this period.' "

"Steven, I cannot believe it."

He nodded. "Neither could I. Read on. Listen. 'This loyal friend may be completely trusted.' 'A young person will seek to influence and should be strongly resisted.' 'Legal documents should be made before the last week in February.' See, that's repeated. And look here, Katie, down at the last. 'This horoscope is not clear after February twenty-sixth.' What's that but death?"

"And Aunt Mina believed all this?"

"Why not? The point is, *it's not the right horoscope.* Charlotte made it, told her in so many words to distrust her family, trust Charlotte, resist your influence and mine and Paul's, and draw up her will before the last week in February. And then indicated that after February twenty-sixth there was no horoscope. In other words, that Aunt Mina was to die."

"Charlotte—did—that!"

"Charlotte. Playing on Mina's credulity. Making astrology merely a tool in her own unscrupulous hands. I daresay it's been done before. And Charlotte did it very cleverly. Mina was, of course, a perfect dupe. Shrewd, stubborn, dreadfully credulous about things of which she was ignorant."

"But Steven—Charlotte was killing Aunt Mina!"

"Yes, of course," said Steven more cheerfully. "That's just what she was doing. Told her she wouldn't live past February 26th. Told her that it was ordained in the stars. And for all these years Mina has believed implicitly in what the stars said. Or rather what Charlotte *said* the stars said. So now, if she was to die, she would die, and there was Charlotte to see that she did it. I don't know whether Charlotte would have succeeded or not. I rather doubt it; still stranger things have happened."

"That agrees," said Katie slowly, "with what the doctor said."

"What was that?"

She told him briefly.

"I wonder," she said, finishing, "what's going to happen. Charlotte is dead; she can't impose her will upon Aunt Mina any longer. Whatever you say about all this horoscope business, it was basically Charlotte's will imposed upon Aunt Mina's. Now will Aunt Mina live tomorrow? Or—die——"

"Live, probably," said Steven. "That is," he added soberly, "if the decision remains with her. Look here, Katie, how does she seem?"

"Why, she seems much stronger."

"As if a burden had been removed?"

"Well, yes. Perhaps. Steven, you said that you knew Charlotte was going to be killed."

"Yes. Yes, I did. That's the dreadful part of it. I tried to prevent it. Thought I had. I'd better tell you about it, Katie. You see, that afternoon, the afternoon Charlotte was killed——"

"Yes——"

"Well, Paul had been up at the studio. Paul and some other fellows. He hadn't any more than left when Aunt Mina telephoned. She told me to come out as fast as I could. She—she's always so self-contained, you know. Her voice so flat. But it wasn't that afternoon. She sounded—queer. Scared. I don't know why, but I felt—well, scared, too. I turned the fellows out and left. Got my car and came out here as fast as I could. The fog wasn't quite so thick then, and I made pretty good time. I didn't know what in hell was going on. She'd said not to come to the house but to park the car outside the grounds and meet her at the summerhouse.

"So I did. Nobody saw me. It was cold and wet, and she was waiting there on the porch of the summerhouse because she couldn't get the door open."

He stopped, searching Katie's eyes. He looked pale again and curiously baffled.

"It was queer, you know, Katie. Rather awful. She just stood there in some kind of dark cloak, her face white, with her eyes sort of burning out of the whiteness. And she said she was going to die. That the stars said so. It was all ordained. But that she was going to kill Charlotte. I tried to soothe her, but it didn't help. It was dark and wet, and I was afraid she'd catch cold, so I opened the door; she had the key. The door stuck after it was unlocked, so I reached into my pocket and worked at it with the palette knife.

"But it didn't break in the door, Katie. Aunt Mina broke it. Broke it with her hands. A flexible steel palette knife. It—I don't know. It made me sort of—sick. It was dark, you know, and cold. And her white face. And she took that knife and said: 'It isn't sharp enough. It's no good.' And then she broke it. And stood there staring at me!"

Katie whispered something.

"Oh, yes," said Steven. "Oh, yes, Aunt Mina murdered Charlotte."

CHAPTER XVIII

"THAT's why I got away," he went on presently. "You see, I knew who had killed Charlotte. And I know that they have a little evidence against me. Not enough, unless I've overlooked something important, to hang me on. But enough to confuse the issue. And if Mina actually dies—why, let her die in peace. I'll stay away long enough for that. They won't be apt to make an arrest until they can find me. They know about my car having been parked that afternoon secretly outside the grounds."

"And—that letter," reminded Katie again.

"Yes. That letter," said Steven. "See here, Katie, does Aunt Mina still confide everything to Chris?"

"Why—I think so," said Katie considering it slowly. "She seems to. Steven, did you know that Chris was pressed for money?"

Something flickered back in Steven's gray eyes.

"*Chris* hard up! What on earth makes you think that!"

"He——" Katie hesitated. "He loaned me money on an all but worthless note, without saying a word. But Steven, he tried just the night before last to borrow money from Paul."

"Would Paul lend him any?"

"No."

He sheered abruptly.

"I see by one of the papers that they've even unearthed someone who saw me leave the car and enter the grounds."

"I didn't know that."

"You should read the papers. I thought, you see, that I would just vanish and that very fact would lead them to think I was guilty. The search would go on, I would stay hidden—Aunt Mina could die in peace. You see, I didn't realize then, when I talked to her, that her fixed idea of death was based on so slim a foundation. In fact, I wouldn't have believed that it was possible; that an idea could be implanted in a person's mind so firmly, could grow so formidably, could take such a hold that it actually made a physical mark. Aunt Mina's been growing weaker and weaker and—why, everyone thought she was dying. Charlotte said so. Aunt Mina thought so. And as a result—she is dying. I would never have believed it had I not seen it. I'm not sure I believe it now."

"You should study psychology," said Katie. "It's not at all uncommon."

"Nonsense. Studying about something and then seeing it happen right under your very eyes are two different things. Anyway, it happened. There you are."

"No," said Katie soberly. "There's still tomorrow. February 26th. What did Aunt Mina tell you?"

"She broke down—talked wildly but still didn't say much. I thought it was irrational. I thought, really, that Aunt Mina was hysterical. Or worse. She'd been ill so long, you know. Living a queer sort of life with Charlotte. The only life, if I'm beginning to see the truth of it, that Charlotte would let her live. She wanted——" Steven paused and said, as if he had to force the words out: "It's pathetic, Katie. It's terrible

and sad and—and it muddles up life. You don't know
what to think. You see, she wanted me to help her. She
said she was afraid she couldn't do it alone. She
said——" Steven swallowed. "She said Charlotte was
so wiry."

Katie shivered, and Steven added, trying to speak
in a more natural voice: "Yes. I know——"

Katie said huskily: "Go on. What did you do? It's
all our fault. We ought to have seen."

"Charlotte would never let us see. We hadn't a
hint of it. Oh, I knew she stood between us and Aunt
Mina, but I didn't realize that she had Mina bound
so tightly. That it was anything like this. I thought it
was just jealousy. Wanted Aunt Mina's affection for
herself. And, of course, I knew she expected Aunt
Mina to reward her in her will. Well, anyway, I tried
to get Aunt Mina to tell me why she thought Charlotte was killing her. But Aunt Mina was queer—flat,
white. She just kept saying that Charlotte was making her die. That she couldn't escape. That she'd got
to die, and it was on account of Charlotte. She seemed
to be desperate. Afraid—poor soul—of the dark."

Afraid of the dark—and of the cold and lonely
journey Charlotte had said she'd got to make.

"Did you tell her not to be afraid?"

"Yes. Told her we'd get other doctors. She said it
wouldn't help. That Charlotte was killing her. That
she was going to kill Charlotte. She had it firmly fixed
in her mind that if she killed Charlotte it would somehow release her. Don't ask me why. Go and study your
psychology. That's what she felt. I talked to her a
long time. Talked and reasoned and thought I'd got
her out of the notion. I didn't, I swear, think she was

dangerous when she left me. In fact, I never thought really that she was dangerous at all, except when she —broke the palette knife. Anyway, I finally took her back to the door. She was quiet, and I thought I'd got her talked back to herself again. I thought I'd go and see the doctor."

"What time was this?"

"I don't know. But it must have been only a short time before you came along in the car. Anyway, there at the door she turned around and handed me—this horoscope. I didn't know what it was. She just said, 'Take this and look at it.' I said all right and for her to go and lie down and rest. Told her to call Melissa to get her something hot to drink. I would have gone in myself—you don't know how I've regretted that I didn't—but, you see, I was anxious to get to the doctor. That was all I could think of. It—I was sort of —upset."

"What did you do then?"

"I left her at the kitchen door. She wanted to get up the back stairway unobserved, and I wanted her to, for she looked—queer. Shattered. Then I went back through the grounds to my car. I had this horoscope in my hand, and when I got to the car I turned on the dashlight and started to look at the thing. Right away, of course, the phrasing struck me as being singularly apropos to Charlotte's purposes. And I realized then what instrument Charlotte had been using all these years as a lever. Well, I sat there—I don't know how long. Then I drove down to the corner drugstore, several streets back. I tried to telephone the doctor but couldn't get him. Finally I came back here. Left the car outside the gate because I wanted to walk. Then I saw the police car and the ambulance leaving, and I knew—or was afraid I knew—what had happened."

"Do you mean Aunt Mina gave Charlotte the capsules to—to confuse her—bewilder her—make it easier for Aunt Mina——" Katie stopped because she could not readily utter the words that made up her thought. They were not, however, necessary.

"I don't know. It's entirely possible."

"But who telephoned to Charlotte? If it was Aunt Mina, who arranged it so her death would appear to be an accident? How did she get Charlotte to come out here in the road?"

"Easy," said Steven. "Aunt Mina has got a telephone in her rooms that doesn't connect with the house telephone at all. That would be simple. Or, as to that, there's also the kitchen telephone which might have been used."

"I'd forgotten that," said Katie. "But Steven—they are sure I did the telephoning on account of what Jenks heard. And Paul could have done it; he had stopped to get cigarettes at exactly the time Jenks says that the call was made. So you see—we can't be sure. There's even Chris; though that's rather absurd. And Steven, the afternoon you telephoned to me just before you disappeared——"

"Yes——"

"There was something in the dining room. Watching me. Listening. I don't know what. It was dark in there. I couldn't see. I could just hear a sort of tinkle —and the cat——"

The cold damp air was penetrating Katie's very bones. She shivered, and Steven said:

"You ought not to be out here. You'll get pneumonia or something.—Who was there, Katie?"

"I don't know. When you rang, I went and turned on the lights, and there wasn't anyone. But there had been. And Steven——"

"Well?"

"It's that house, you see," said Katie illogically. "Anyway, why should Aunt Mina kill the little German clockmaker?"

"That's what brought me here," said Steven. "Who was he and what connection does he have with Aunt Mina?"

"He inquired for you," said Katie.

"*Me?* But I've never seen the man. Not to my knowledge, anyhow. Do you mean he asked for *me?* By name?"

"Yes. And he had Charlotte's picture."

Katie, shivering under her cape, told him the story briefly, watching his face and his dark gray eyes shining from under the low brim of his hat. It was growing steadily darker, and their isolation in the fog and darkness the more pronounced.

"And," Katie concluded, "Sergeant Caldwell tells me I'm as good as under arrest right now. For Charlotte's murder and because I saw and talked to Herman Schmidt and my fingerprints are on the gun."

"Oh, no," said Steven grimly. "They aren't going to arrest you. Not after I tell what I know. I'll see to that. I didn't dream it was so bad for you. The papers were very cautious, and they've been my only source of information. No, my dear, they won't arrest you. But—but I don't understand, Katie. There's something——" He paused. His face in the gathering twilight was white and thoughtful, and his eyebrows a straight, forbidding line. "Aunt Mina didn't shoot that little German. There's no sense to that. And why did Charlotte go to his shop?" He paused again, deep in thought. Then he took Katie's hands. "You mustn't stay out in the cold any longer. You're going with me. I've got a launch—if I can find it out there off the point. Came across in a rowboat."

"Oh—I heard a launch last night——"

Steven laughed, mirthlessly. "That was I—nearly got lost in the fog. A dumb thing to do, but I thought maybe I could get closer to the house. Police have been close around it every time I tried to get near. Come on, honey."

"No, Steven—I—I've got to go back. Don't you see? If I escape, too, it will be, in their minds, as good as a confession. And besides—I can't leave Aunt Mina until—until after tomorrow."

"Very well," said Steven after a moment. "I'm going back to the house, too. I won't give myself up now. But I'll be in the house tonight."

"No——"

"Do you think I'm going to let you go back to that place alone? After what has happened?" There wasn't, Katie realized, much use in resisting. "Come," he said. "We'll follow the ravine to the beach. Then along the beach, and you can slip in the door of the lounge. Take my hand. And don't make any sound."

It was a strange journey through the fog and darkness, with Steven's hand the only safe and stable thing. Darkness had fallen by the time they reached the sandy beach, and Katie had lost all sense of direction. Steven, however, walked along steadily through the mist and darkness. Several times Katie could hear the muffled lapping of waves. Then he had found the steps, and they were ascending very cautiously, so that the patrolling police should not hear them. At the top of the steps they could see, across the lawn, a glow from the lounge windows.

Steven stopped there and took her briefly into his arms.

"I'll be in the house tonight," he whispered. "I can get in all right. If you are frightened about anything —*anything*, mind—don't wait, scream. I'll be there."

As she opened the door to the lounge, a heavy hand fell upon her arm.

"Hey there, who——"

She turned so the light was on her face. The policeman gasped.

"How did you get out here?" he thundered.

"I've just been for a walk," said Katie sweetly. "Good-night, officer."

She closed the door.

Immediately the heavy silence of the house fell upon and surrounded her. The lounge, funereal in its black wicker and its green ferns, was empty. The mirror above the desk reflected the lighted but empty space of the dining room. Katie pushed her hood back wearily and put her wet cape over her arm. Then she went to the mirror and leaned very near to look fully at her face. Her hair was disheveled and had mist caught in tiny silver beads against the soft black. Her chin *was* pink. She touched it and thought of cold cream and rather approvingly of her face, and vaguely of the obscure impulse that sends a woman so directly to a mirror after she has seen a man she loves. She thought of all three things at once and then knew that eyes were meeting hers in the mirror.

Clarence stood in the dining-room doorway. His eyes, meeting her own, looked at that double distance small and malignant.

"Why," thought Katie with a kind of shock, "he looks as if he hates me."

She turned, slowly drawing her eyes away from that mirrored gaze to the real figure.

But the malignant, ugly look in Clarence's eyes had gone—if it had actually been there. He wavered a little in the doorway and then approached her on somewhat unsteady legs. His face was pink and puffy, and he carried a pungent aroma along with him.

He was, however, quite sober and collected; it was only his neatly graceful legs that betrayed him.

He was already dressed for dinner and, being Clarence, managed to look elegant in a dinner jacket and not collegiate. His curly brown hair was neat, his tie just right, and his neat small face was smiling agreeably. He had something of Paul's caressing charm.

"Hello, Katie," he said. "It's a gala occasion. Mina's coming down to dinner."

"Mina!" said Katie in a little gasp. Mina—and tomorrow was the twenty-sixth. The day when Mina had supposed she was to die. Was it, then, a gesture of defiance on Mina's part? A glove tossed to fate?

"Yes. Fanny's dressing now." One small, graceful hand went to his chin. He said with sudden irritation: "These safety razors are the damnedest things. Borrowed two blades from Paul, and still I can't get the hang of it. My chin feels like it'd been butchered.

Katie———" He paused and continued in a low voice, as if they shared some secret, and just for a moment something strange and alive and ugly peered out of his eyes. "Katie—what do you suppose has happened to my razor?"

"I don't know," said Katie. A swift vision of Mina's thick white hands flashed across her; Mina's thick white hands breaking a flexible steel palette knife. And Mina's flat voice saying it wasn't sharp enough. "You've lost it somewhere."

"No, I haven't lost it," said Clarence slowly. "But I wish I'd never come here. Fanny made me, you know. She makes me do everything. If she gets Mina's money she'll have me under her thumb the rest of my life. Only a slave," said Clarence morosely. "Hitched to her chariot wheels. A bird in a gilded cage." He paused reflectively, and Friquet scooted suddenly across his toes and was gone like a flash up the stairway. "Good God!" said Clarence, startled. "What was that?"

"Only the cat."

"Oh," said Clarence. He touched his forehead with his handkerchief. "There's something queer about that cat. It—it sits and stares. Just stares. Sometimes at me. Sometimes at nothing. Only you feel, if you understand me, that it isn't nothing. It makes me," said Clarence, "nervous."

"All cats stare like that," said Katie. "And it makes me nervous, too."

He looked at her doubtfully.

"I'd have wrung its neck long ago, if I'd thought it would have done away with the cat," he said darkly.

"But it would have come popping to stare at me.
Katie, Mina doesn't look to me like she's dying.
What's the matter with you, Katie?" He broke off
abruptly, and his eyes narrowed again and scrutinized
her. "Where have you been? You look——" He
paused and then said slowly, "You're in love and
you've been seeing him. Is it Paul?"

"Is what Paul?" They both looked upward, Clarence spinning about in order to do so and clutching at
a chair to steady himself. It was Paul, descending the
stairway. Paul, too, was ready for dinner; his olive
face looked dark and smooth above his white shirt
front, and his hair glistened above perfectly tailored
black shoulders. "What's that about Paul?" he repeated, reaching the lower step and strolling toward
them.

"Nothing," snapped Clarence, suddenly peevish. "I
asked Katie if she was in love with you, but I don't
think she could possibly be!"

"I could ask for nothing better," said Paul, smiling
at Katie. "How about it, darling? I could easily fall
in love with you. Particularly when you look as you
do now. You're—really—beautiful, you know. Come
on, Katie—let me love you. I think I do." He was
smiling, very certain of his own charm, very sure of
himself.

"Well, don't," said Katie crisply, gathering up her
cape. "I try to conceal it, but I've got a shrewish
nature!"

Paul followed her to the stairway and stood there,
his hands on the newel post.

"Katie," he said, and she paused to look down,
"just how shrewish?"

Katie did not reply for a moment. Then she said soberly: "Shrewish enough to ask questions."

Something closed back of Paul's dark eyes. He kept on smiling.

"Questions?"

"Yes. Paul—when you went into the drugstore for cigarettes, did you telephone to Charlotte?"

Paul laughed. Curious, said something in the back of Katie's mind, that his laugh did not dispel the somber silence of the house.

"So that's what you're holding against me," said Paul. "To think that was going on back of your blue eyes. What earthly reason had I to telephone to Charlotte! And anyway, my dear, though I don't like reminding you, especially in view of tonight's papers, it was certainly you who were driving the car."

"Tonight's papers?" said Katie slowly.

Clarence sputtered in the background: "Don't look at 'em, Katie. The police are only trying to draw Steven out of his hiding place. If he's hiding. I think, myself, he's probably murdered, too."

"Let me see," said Katie.

"I'm sorry, Katie," said Paul instantly. "I ought not to have said that. Aunt Mina's looking at them now. It's as Clarence says. The police are hanging the thing on you in order to draw Steven out, I'm sure. This Crafft seems to think that Steven's rather—fond of you. Won't see you charged with murder if he's got any evidence that will save you."

"Oh——" said Katie weakly.

"Do go along and get dressed, Katie," said Clarence pettishly. "It's just as Paul says. The situation hasn't changed any, and they've no new evidence.

Except your dressmaking bills and that thirty-five hundred you owe Chris on Charlotte's account. They've got hold of that somehow. Must have been going through Chris's business affairs. That was mean of Charlotte—reneging on her order like that. She was," said Clarence reflectively, "a thoroughly tiresome and disagreeable woman. Well out of the way. Go on and get ready for dinner."

Katie went. After all, it was no more than she had expected. And it was only evidence that she had need of money, not evidence that she had murdered Charlotte. Mina had done that.

Or had she? What about the murder of Herman Schmidt?

Dinner was actually, as Clarence had said, a gala occasion. A strange and terrible gala, with Mina managing to impart a gruesomely festive air to the long, glittering table, and Clarence elegant but jerking his head now and then to look back of him toward the corners of the room, and the others puzzled and waiting and unable to follow Mina's lead, and all of them aware of something rather horrible about the room. Something quite intangible, yet always there, in the food they ate and the air they breathed and the veiled way their eyes met one another's eyes and turned quickly away.

Not a little of the strangeness was due to the fact that Mina had managed to withdraw from some forgotten wardrobe an old ivory satin evening gown heavily embroidered with gold which she wore. Because of its high bust and narrow waist and a stiff puffed suggestion of sleeves on her shoulders, it was weirdly and unbelievably fashionable. It was also

faintly wrinkled and smelled heavily of attar of roses
and thinly but pungently of mothballs. It was also
astounding, although Mina seemed quite unaware of
the fact. Katie had only the dimmest memory of seeing Mina in anything but the trailing, sober black she
had worn for many years. And Fanny gasped when
she saw the ivory satin, opening her mouth and click-
ing it shut again like a steel trap, and Clarence just
stared, and Chris opened his eyes wide and complimented Mina.

"You're looking well tonight," he said.

"Thank you," said Mina imperturbably. She settled
herself, stiff and thick and white, in the high-backed
chair at the head of the table. For all the tarnished
elegance of that old ivory satin she still looked
hunched and tired and as if she'd had to work very
hard for many years. Her black hair was in its tight
little bun, and her black eyes still burned with that
secret fire. But in her white cheeks was an ominous
little flame of red. And she ate nothing, which was in
itself astounding.

But she would have them talk. She would have them
talk though she only sat and stared into their faces
with that feverish look.

Throwing her glove to fate, thought Katie, and
tried to talk and did. Talked so gayly that Chris gave
her a slow anxious look once or twice, and Paul, sitting beside her, began to smile at her and once below
the tablecloth took her hand and held it and pressed
it slowly before Katie could pull it away and she
realized that she, too, must look and sound feverish.
But none of the rest of them knew what Mina was
doing.

Where was Steven?

Had he got into the house? Was he there some-where? Could he hear their voices going on shrilly?

Fanny's green wisps of chiffon floated and her bracelets jingled as she leaned to speak to Mina. Katie could suddenly see them in a curious kind of picture which included herself and yet from which she was re-mote—entirely detached.

There was the long table sparkling with silver and crystal, with candles wavering so that the shadows in the corners advanced and retreated, and a great mass of crimson roses in the center, red as blood against the white.

Behind them Jenks was coming and going silently. And there was Mina thick and stiff and haunted in her ivory satin, and Fanny tinkling and floating green chiffons—and Chris big and bulkier than ever in a dinner jacket with his shirt front bulging and his face so tired and haggard in the light from the candles. Clarence, elegant and sulky and nervous. Paul, dark and smiling, talking to Mina. She could even see her-self, slim with white shoulders and arms emerging from lace that was as delicate as the petals of a Reine d'Or; a slender sheath and a touch of froth above which her hair was black and her eyes very dark and her mouth crimson from lipstick. It was lucky, she thought, looking at Mina, that Clarence had warned her and she had dressed to suit Mina's grisly need.

Mina—fighting murder at the cold hands of a wo-man three days dead.

Katie shivered and tried to hide the little ripple her shoulders gave. And Clarence's neat head jerked, and he looked backward suddenly into wavering shadows.

Mina gave some directions to Jenks. Then she looked around the table, gathering them with her hot black eyes. She was going to speak. Katie's hands clutched each other in her lace lap, and she felt rather than heard the quick breath Paul drew. Mina said:

"There is something I wish to ask of you, my family—my friends, my guests. I am an old-fashioned woman. There is something I wish you to do for me. For reasons——" She paused, and Katie was aware that Jenks was serving coffee there at the table and with it delicate glasses. Wineglasses, very old Venetian, gold-flecked, beautifully wrought. "For reasons which need not be given, I should like you to—to drink a toast to me—and to tomorrow. The twenty-sixth day of February."

There was a complete and utter silence. It was a fantastic climax to an already fantastic dinner. And the others had no explanation of it. The fragrance of port, like a strong, warm perfume, drifted to Katie's nostrils. She rose.

"To Aunt Mina's—good health and long life," she said clearly without stumbling over the unaccustomed phrases. "And to the twenty-sixth day of February."

They got somehow to their feet, bewildered. Somehow they drank that strange toast.

"Thank you," said Mina deliberately. "Will you come with me, Katie?"

Katie, still in a kind of daze, obeyed, offering her cold arm for Mina to lean upon. But Mina had no need for assistance that night. And when she reached her room, she drew Katie inside and closed the door.

Friquet leaped lightly from a chair and strolled toward the door, pausing to stretch; the temptation to sharpen her claws was irresistible and she did so, tentatively—with a wary glance at Mina—on the rug.

"I've just heard about Charlotte and the bonds she told you to sell, Katie," she said calmly. "Mr. Crafft came to see me this afternoon, and I—I have had rather a shock."

There was no shock in her voice.

"It seems that Chris has—has used a great deal of my money——"

"*Chris!*"

"He was caught in the crash. I feel sure he didn't realize that he couldn't recover. He doesn't know yet that I've been told."

"Did Charlotte know?" (The letter to Steven! Had she meant it for Chris, after all?)

Mina looked at her slowly.

"I don't know," she said. "He wouldn't have told her, of course. But the point is, Katie, when it's all cleared up there may not be much left. And I want to write a check for you now. Hush—not a word."

The room was bare and hot and bright with electricity. Mina, in that incongruous ivory satin, sat down at her tall desk and drew a fat checkbook forward.

Katie stood quite still in her slim lace gown. She felt queer—the wine had been old and too fiery. It was nauseating. No—it wasn't that—it was something wrong in the room. Something wrong——

There was no light. It went suddenly, completely. There was only hot darkness and Mina somewhere across the room.

Katie tried to move and couldn't. Tried to speak and her throat was stiff.

A cold breath of air came from somewhere, and then the incredible thing happened.

Something passed her in the darkness. A hand brushed her hand.

There was the raucous scream of a frantic cat.

And Mina, across the room, cried out in a strangled voice: *"Charlotte! Charlotte!"*

CHAPTER XIX

Out of the confusion of darkness came sounds. The hot black air was filled with motion. But after Mina's choked cry there was no sound of a voice.

Sheer terror held Katie rigid. She had a kind of dazed feeling that, if she remained quite still and stiff, the sounds that swirled through that blackness might swerve from her without engulfing her. . . . "The air was filled with a beating of wings" . . . but they would be dark wings, black wings. . . . She jerked herself back to a semblance of sanity. She must do something—stop whatever was going on there across the room.

She was confused, groping for the door. Where were lights? Where was the door? Her hands were shaking—what had Steven said?

Someone was screaming. Someone had broken through a paralyzing barrier and was screaming.

It was, incredibly, Katie, standing there screaming in her soft lace gown with hot blackness everywhere.

But quite suddenly the blackness was very still. The sounds of motion were gone. Katie took a breath. And in the silence she heard, very distinctly, a door closing across the room.

Then there were people in the passage. Fanny was screaming, and her thin screams were coming closer and closer. Chris was shouting something in his great deep voice. Paul was crying out something about a light.

They were there crowding at the door. Someone held a flashlight. It made a circle of light on the dark taupe carpet, and in its faint glow there were faces white and eerie and afraid. Then Steven brushed past Paul's hand and the light and took Katie into his arms. His voice was strange and shook and he kept saying, "Katie—Katie—Katie——" over and over again and touching her face and her arms anxiously as if to assure himself she was not hurt.

"Mina——" Katie realized that she had been trying to tell them to go to Mina and that she could not make herself heard in the confusion. "Mina—across the room."

The circle of light broadened.

There was the dark desk. There was Mina's ivory satin. She was sitting, staring downward. There was Friquet, with her ears laid back and her tail lashing—and her great eyes staring, too, at something that was crouched, curiously, at Mina's feet.

"Melissa——" Fanny was half sobbing, half screaming. "Melissa—she's dead! She's murdered!" She kept repeating it thin and high, like a mechanical toy that can't stop: "Murdered, she's murdered——"

"Stop that, Fanny. Somebody get lights. Telephone for the doctor——"

Chris, a huge black bulk, emerged into the circle of light.

Mina turned a still white face upward toward Chris and pushed her chair back. And Clarence leaned forward:

"There's my razor," he said shrilly, pointing.

Katie turned in Steven's arms and put her face against his shoulder and let the warm sense of security flow over her in waves. Somewhere away off there were suddenly lights and a voice saying distinctly:

"But she's not dead yet. If we get the doctor here soon enough——"

"Hey," said someone from the doorway. "What's going on here? What's—— Mother of God!"

"She's not dead yet," said Chris rapidly. "If you can get a doctor——"

A shrill long police whistle pierced and cut off Chris's voice and shrilled and echoed through the whole heavy house.

Afterward Katie realized that, with the shrill notes of the police whistle, things began to take on a weird sort of order. She was never sure just what happened, although she was always to recall the queer color of Dr. Mannsen's face as he hurried past them into Mina's room—they were, then, clustered in the hall just at the top of the stairway. And she remembered that a button was gone from the blue tunic of the policeman who stood there with them, and how one of Melissa's soft brown hands dangled limply as they carried her through the passage and past that quiet, huddled group.

And she remembered that her throat ached painfully when Dr. Mannsen nodded to Chris's inquiry. Melissa—poor, tranquil Melissa.

"She may live—there's a chance," said Dr. Mannsen, not looking at any of them and hurrying as if afraid they would force him to pause. He was uncomfortable, acutely embarrassed.

But, of course—Dr. Mannsen knew—the police

knew—everyone knew; it was as if one of them had become suddenly and secretly infected with some horrible, dangerous disease and they did not know which one it was. They only knew it was there.

Paul was looking at Steven. "So you're back," he said. And that was the only mention any of them made of Steven's unheralded appearance then or later. "You'll all," said the policeman, "go downstairs, if you please. The sergeant and Mr. Crafft are on the way."

The lounge was cold and drafty, but the bookroom was warm and, unbelievably, had not changed at all. Nothing had changed, which was entirely incredible. And it was only ten o'clock.

As the clock finished striking, Mr. Crafft stood in the doorway. A djinn out of a bottle, a brown tiger out of a jungle.

And then that rapid inquiry began. It was a repetition of a nightmare.

"But you didn't hear any voices?" Mr. Crafft persisted.

"No—no," said Katie wearily. "Just sounds."

"A struggle?"

"Perhaps—yes, it might have been."

Mr. Crafft glanced at Mina. She was sitting very quietly in one of the tall chairs. Her eyes burned, and the little spots of flame trembled against her white cheeks. She still looked feverish. Mr. Crafft's topaz eyes flicked the ivory satin, became fixed and rigid at a small crimson stain on its hem, and then went back to Mina's face.

"What did you hear, Madame Petrie?"

"Nothing more than that," said Mina flatly. "I did

not move. There were sounds of people in the room. I realized that Katie was screaming. Then I heard a door close somewhere back of me. It must have been the door into the passage that goes to——" She choked, put both hands to her throat. Her chin sank lower toward the ivory satin folds on her high bosom, and she finished: "To Charlotte's room."

Mr. Crafft whirled, pouncing.

"Did you hear a door close, Miss Warren?"

"Yes. It was very distinct."

"You think someone went out that door?"

"Yes. But I think someone entered the room by the door to the corridor. I was standing, you see, between the door and Aunt Mina. And just after the lights went out, I felt a current of cold air on my face and then——" Katie's voice wavered upward. Steven, standing just behind her chair, put his hand on her shoulder, and the detective's eyes went to Steven and flickered and came back to Katie. "Then someone passed me. I felt something touch me."

A cold, ominous little breath went over the room.

"Touch you?" repeated Mr. Crafft. "What was it?"

"I don't know," said Katie slowly. "But I think it was someone's hand. It touched my arm. And passed me."

Steven's fingers were digging into her bare soft shoulder.

"I should think," Steven was saying hoarsely, "that with all of your policemen around the place you could give some kind of protection. You've kept this girl here, and you let this happen to her and you——"

"It didn't happen to her," said Mr. Crafft. "It

happened to Melissa. No need to get all worked up now about it, Mr. Petrie. Now suppose you tell us where you have come from."

"I met Katie this afternoon, and she told me how things were here, and I came back. And a hell of a lot of good I did."

"Um'm'm," murmured the detective. "That remains to be seen. Well, now that you are here, I suppose I shall have to place you under arrest."

"I expected that," said Steven. "On what charge?"

"Murder," said Mr. Crafft. "Where were you when Miss Warren's screams alarmed the household?"

"I was in my own room. Thought it was not a likely place for anyone to look for me."

"What did you do?"

"Hurried out. There were no lights. I ran. Somebody had a flashlight, and they were all crowding there at the door to Aunt Mina's room. And I pushed past them and went in."

"O'Brien tells me a main switch had been pulled and that the fuse box is behind that panel on the landing of the stairway. It's quite clear that Melissa must have been just at the door to Madame Petrie's room. That her murderer knew where she was and what she was about to do—pass some kind of information on to Madame Petrie, I suspect. Her murderer pulled the switch, ran up the stairs, reached his victim probably at the door, and followed her into Madame Petrie's room." Mr. Crafft was speaking in short, clipped phrases. No longer gentle, no longer purring.

"Melissa tried to defend herself, I suppose. Now, then, Petrie, to go from your own room to Madame

Petrie's you were obliged to—pass the room which was formerly used by Miss Weinberg?"

"Yes."

"The room which connects with a passage from Madame Petrie's room?"

"Yes."

"And it was the door to that short hall between Miss Weinberg's room and Madame Petrie's rooms which you heard close, Miss Warren?"

"Yes," said Katie. "But anyone might have escaped through Charlotte's empty room and joined the others and no one would be the wiser. The hall was entirely dark."

"Oh, doubtless," said Mr. Crafft. "I daresay none of you are equipped with that useful thing called an alibi?"

He was, it developed after somewhat lengthy and involved inquiry, quite correct in his surmise.

Clarence had been in the dining room; the lights went out, and he just stood there waiting for them to come on again. Then he heard screams upstairs and realized something was wrong and ran upstairs.

"Finding your way along in the dark?" interrupted Mr. Crafft.

"Yes," said Clarence, his eyes narrowed and malignant, with pink puffs under them.

Chris had been in the bookroom reading the papers when the lights went out. He had thought immediately that a fuse was gone and had got up to call Jenks. When he got into the lounge he saw that the whole house was dark and immediately thought of Mina and started upstairs.

"I was at the top of the stairs," said Chris, "when

I heard the screams. I turned toward Mina's room, and then Fanny joined me. She was scared—I knew it was Fanny on account of her bracelets jingling—and then she screamed, too. And Paul came from somewhere and had a flashlight."

"From where?" said Mr. Crafft.

"I don't know," said Chris. "He was just there."

"Well, Duchane?"

"I was in my own room," said Paul. "I was hunting, if you want to know, for a stud I had dropped before dinner. The lights went out—as you have already heard a time or two; I waited, thinking they would come on again. Then I heard a woman scream. I grabbed for a flashlight that was on my table and hurried out and came upon Chris and Fanny and Clarence in the hall there at the turn."

"You had to pass the door to Miss Weinberg's room also, did you not?"

"Yes."

"When did you turn on the flashlight? While you were in your room, I suppose?"

"Why, yes, naturally."

"But apparently you and Petrie followed the same way through the corridor and still saw nothing of each other until you reached Madame Petrie's room!"

"My room is beyond Paul's," said Steven.

Mr. Crafft considered this, then returned to Paul.

"Then if anyone had come from Miss Weinberg's room into the corridor you would have seen him?"

"I suppose so. I don't know. It was all rather confusing. I thought some terrible thing was happening."

"A terrible thing *was* happening," said Mr. Crafft, suddenly very grave. And again that cold little breath of air went through the room. Melissa—poor, tranquil Melissa.

Fanny said unexpectedly:

"But I saw Melissa."

Something opened and closed in the detective's luminous eyes.

"You saw Melissa, Mrs. Siskinson? What do you mean? When?"

"When I went upstairs. Just after dinner. It was chilly, and I wanted my shawl. So I started upstairs for it. And as I got to the top of the stairs I—I——" Fanny was hesitating. A purple wave was crawling steadily over her face. Then she said: "I thought I would walk down the hall to Mina's room. I knew Katie was with her, and I thought——" She hesitated again and recovered herself. "I felt a little uneasy about Mina. She'd looked rather ill during dinner. Not like herself. I thought she might need someone."

"But Miss Warren was with her."

"Yes—yes, I knew that."

You wanted to listen, thought Katie; you wanted to know why Aunt Mina had asked me to go with her. You wanted to know if she was going to give me anything.

"I was merely uneasy," said Fanny.

"I see," said Mr. Crafft. "You were uneasy. Go on, please."

Fanny's eyes flashed sharp blue fire.

"I was about to say," she went on, biting off her words, "that I saw Melissa. Just as I turned toward Mina's room. I stopped there, hesitating a moment, and was just all at once conscious that someone was standing near me. You know how you feel when eyes are looking at you. I whirled around, and it was Melissa. And she—— You can say what you please, but Melissa knew she was going to be murdered."

"Fanny!" It was Mina, stirred quite out of her flat stillness.

"Yes, she did, Mina. And I ought to have made her—made her do something. I don't know what," said Fanny helplessly. "Call the police, I suppose. Much good they would have done," she added viciously.

"What did you do, Mrs. Siskinson? Why do you think Melissa was—frightened?"

"Because of her color. She was like—like a plum," said Fanny with a burst of imagery. "Even her mouth was sort of blue. And she just stood there looking at me. I was shocked—surprised. She was so silent, and I hadn't known anyone was near. It gave me a sort of start, you know. I felt for an instant that she'd been —well, spying on me. Watching me."

"But I don't understand," said Mr. Crafft softly, "why Melissa should have been watching you."

"Neither do I," snapped Fanny. "But there's a lot of things going on in this dreadful house that I don't understand. Do you want to know what Melissa did or not?"

"Certainly. Do go on."

"Well, I asked her what she was doing. I may have spoken a bit sharply, as I was considerably startled. She said she'd come up to turn down the beds. I said then to do it and not stand there looking at me. Then I turned away toward—toward my own room. And Melissa put out her hand and—and caught my wrist. Yes, she did. And her hand was shaking, and I was so surprised that I just stood there staring at her. And there were," said Fanny in a suddenly hoarse and strident voice, "little queer drops on her forehead. Drops," said Fanny hoarsely, "of sweat."

She coughed once, noisily.

"And she asked me if anyone was upstairs. If I had seen anyone. I said, 'No.' And she said, 'Where is Miz Petrie? I've got to tell her something.' And I told her that Madame Petrie was in her own room. And I felt upset and queer, and I—I brushed her hand away," said Fanny uncomfortably. "And—and I went to my own room."

"And left her standing there afraid," said Mina in as flat a voice as it would have been had the words held no meaning at all. "She was appealing to me, Fanny. You ought to have helped her. You ought to have brought her to me."

"Do you know anything of what she might have wanted to tell you, Madame Petrie?" said Mr. Crafft.

"No," said Mina, moving her head slowly from side to side. "No, I don't know. I didn't know that Melissa was there until they brought the flashlight. I thought it was—someone else."

"Who?"

"I thought," said Mina slowly, her eyes burning into the detective's face, "that it was——" She checked herself abruptly, began again, and said blankly: "Tomorrow is the twenty-sixth. I thought she'd come to make me——"

"Mr. Crafft," interrupted Steven crisply, "I know that you intend to question me at some length later. Won't you do so immediately? There are some things I think you should know."

Katie wondered what was going on back of the ugly brown face that turned so slowly and so consideringly toward Steven. Whatever it was, it must have been somehow gratifying to the detective, for he said, purring:

"Certainly, Mr. Petrie. As you say, there are a number of things we have been anxious to question you about. In a few moments. Now then, what about this razor?"

A number of voices spoke at once; Katie was vaguely surprised to hear herself joining.

"So it belonged to you, Mr. Siskinson?"

"Yes," said Clarence savagely. "It was mine. Everybody in this room knows it was mine. But it's been gone for days!"

"What happened to it?"

"I don't know. But I knew," said Clarence darkly, "that something was going to happen with that razor loose around here."

"You knew it?" repeated the detective softly.

"But I didn't have anything to do with it. It's my razor, but everybody knew I'd lost it. I told everybody."

"Why did you tell everybody, Mr. Siskinson?"

"Because I wanted 'em to know it. And if you want to know what I think, I think Melissa took it to protect herself with. That's what I think. And I think that if she hadn't been murdered just when she was, she'd have told who killed Charlotte. And that German fellow."

There was again the most singular sensation of a cold little wind about that room. So cold that Katie shivered. And she saw Fanny move restively, and

Chris rose and began to float up and down there in the shadow between the table and the bookshelves.

"She knew she was going to be killed," reiterated Clarence, looking at his feet. "And I wouldn't be at all surprised if there was a bunch of woolly black hair——"

Dr. Mannsen stood in the doorway. He fixed his eyes carefully upon the detective. He looked pale and shaken and avoided seeing anyone else.

"Is she—dead?" asked the detective.

How still it was suddenly in that room! Chris stopped his restless motion and was a great black shadow. Steven's mouth was grim, and his fingers were pressing into Katie's shoulder again. And Katie somehow knew, without looking, how keen and still were Paul's veiled dark eyes and that Clarence's lips had stopped moving as if stricken dumb, and that Mina was turning slowly, so slowly, a thick, gleaming column of ivory satin, to look at the doctor. The detective, brown and ugly, waited, too, and all at once in the stillness there was a faint regular tinkle and Katie looked and saw, inconceivably, that Fanny was wringing her long, strong hands, and the bracelets on her wrist kept sliding and tinkling against each other.

"Well?" said the detective.

"I—beg your pardon, Mr. Crafft. I—this is a rather shocking thing. I—really didn't hear your question. I was—thinking."

Thinking, thought Katie swiftly, which one of us did it.

"Is Melissa dead?" repeated Mr. Crafft.

"Not yet," said the doctor.

"Will she die?"

"I don't know. I'm afraid so. I've done everything I can do."

"Will she—talk?"

So still, so still. Even Fanny's wringing hands stopped in each other's clutch.

"Perhaps."

Mr. Crafft looked at Sergeant Caldwell.

"Guards," he said shortly. "At once."

"Yes, sir."

Sergeant Caldwell vanished.

Mina said flatly: "Nurses. She must have nurses. Everything that can be done, you understand, Dr. Mannsen."

"Yes, Madame Petrie," said the doctor, not looking at her. He extended an open hand toward the detective. "Here was something in her pocket, Mr. Crafft. It looks like—well—a little bit of crinkly black hair."

After a long tremulous moment, Clarence got to his feet.

"I've got to have a drink," he said blindly. "I don't care what anybody says, I've got to have a drink."

CHAPTER XX

"THAT'S my handkerchief," said Mina. "I wrapped it in my handkerchief. Why did Melissa take that bit of hair?"

"I don't know," said Mr. Crafft. "But I think we are about to find out. Dr. Mannsen, would it be asking too much to ask you to stay here in the house——"

"I intended to," said the doctor. "My patient needs me. Now if I may be permitted to telephone——"

"Yes, of course." Mr. Crafft's eyes met for a fleeting instant the gaze of the policeman who stood at the door and gave consent. "Now, Mr. Petrie, I should like to talk to you alone. Will you follow me, please?"

The detective turned toward the door, where he stopped to give a low order or two to the policemen who stood there. Steven bent over Katie.

"I'm going to tell everything we know. If it was Mina—the thing was done right at her feet. I'm afraid I've got to tell." He was whispering urgently.

Then the door closed behind the detective and Steven's blond head and grim face, and Katie shivered. So they were to wait there, all together, in that room, at the tiger's pleasure. The door opened again to admit two more policemen, who went to stand in opposite corners of the room and were very quiet but not unobtrusive. Clarence, who had been standing hopefully, gave the newcomers a baffled glance and sank down into a chair again and put his head in his hands.

And Chris, big and savage and angry, prowled up and down there before the books.

Something swirled against the windows, and Katie realized that, without their knowing it, the fog had been swept away by a sudden lashing rainstorm, blowing in from the lake.

No one moved, except Chris, and Paul, who smoked. No one spoke. Once Katie looked up at the nearest policeman and saw his gaze traveling curiously over them, and she wondered what he thought of them. What he thought of Mina in her ivory satin with the small red spot on the hem of it, of Fanny with her jewels and wild white hair, of Clarence neat and elegant and graceful as a ballet dancer. The policeman met her eyes, and Katie knew that he was thinking of her. What's that girl doing here? said his puzzled gaze. Puzzlement changed to a distinct approval before Katie looked away.

They were all of them strung together. They were like marionettes on a single wire, and when the door opened they all started and then tried to hide that little ripple of alarm.

It was Sergeant Caldwell, pink with excitement. And he asked Miss Warren to be so good as to step this way. He ushered her into the lounge.

Steven and Mr. Crafft were standing in the doorway between lounge and dining room.

"She said," Steven was saying as Katie approached them, "that it was a sort of tinkle. Quite clear. Like a dish touching another dish. But that when she got to the dining room there was nothing at all. No tray— no——— Oh, there you are, Katie."

Mr. Crafft turned to glance at Katie, and something away down in her was stirred to a deep, strange excitement. The detective's eyes were glowing; there was about him an air of tense eagerness. Like a cat, thought Katie vaguely, in view of his mouse and about to leap upon it. His claws unsheathed for the spring.

He said, quietly enough:

"There's only one thing in this whole room that could possibly tinkle. That is, except a piece of china or glass. And that's——" He stopped, jerked his head upward toward the gleaming chandelier hung with crystal prisms of glass, and turned to Sergeant Caldwell.

"A chair—something—anything to stand on."

Steven sprang forward, pulled a chair near the table, and was on it, reaching up toward the chandelier.

"There's a little hollow rim just around the top of the lights—where the ornamental rim cups up—see it?—Look, there——"

"I can't find anything. Not in this one. Wait—I'll try the others——"

There was a sudden small tinkle as two of the small prisms swung together and kissed each other lightly.

"That's it—that's what I heard—so small a sound——" breathed Katie, watching Steven's exploring hand.

"Here's something. I don't know what. It feels like—here it is."

He drew out something very small, slender, and crystal clear and put it in the little detective's eagerly upstretched hand.

"Here's more of them. Seven or eight——"

"It's what I expected," said Mr. Crafft. "Good! Good! Get 'em all, Steven. Get 'em all."

Katie thought: He's excited. I've never seen him excited before. And then she realized that her own breath was coming swiftly and jerkily and her hands were clutching tightly at each other.

"That's all," said Steven. The light shone on his blond head, and he got down from the chair and bent over the little crystal-clear cylinders in the detective's hand.

"What are they?" cried Katie.

"These?" said the detective, rather impatiently, as if she ought to know. "Why, I suppose it's sodium pyratol. Put up in glass ampules. Simplest way to give it. Break one end with your fingernail and there you are, a liquid which is instantaneously dissolved into another liquid."

"But who? Who put it there? Why?"

"Melissa, I suppose," he said, again impatiently. "And because it was a very simple and easily accessible hiding place."

"But was she—was she going to—give it to me when I heard——"

"I don't know, I don't know. Perhaps. But I don't think so. Not then. It wasn't till you told of the grape hair that you became actually dangerous. It's possible that she became frightened and decided to remove the ampules and get rid of them. After what had happened to Miss Weinberg after the stuff had been dropped in her tea, Melissa may have grown suspicious."

"Do you mean Melissa murdered——"

"Come, come, Miss Warren, I didn't say anything

of the kind. Mr. Petrie has told me a number of things which would have helped me quite a lot, if he had told them sooner. Still—things go as they go. Can't be helped. This astrology affair: that puzzled me. There was a distinct suggestion of it in the letter Miss Weinberg had written. Yet the only connection I could discover consisted of a quantity of books and notes about astrology which were found in Mrs. Siskinson's possession. I suppose she must have taken them from Miss Weinberg's room almost immediately following Miss Weinberg's death. But that rather threw me off."

Katie thought of the bolster, opened her mouth and closed it again. After all, there was no need to tell it.

"So that's the meaning of the twenty-sixth," said the detective, turning his hand so that the tiny glass ampules rolled this way and that. "We found the coat, Miss Warren."

"The coat!"

"Yes, of course. One more link, Miss Warren, and think carefully. You remember the voice you heard in the fog, from someone standing on the safety island where you met Mr. Duchane? Someone saying something about grape hair? In a strong German accent?"

"Yes—yes, of course," said Katie. She felt bewildered, uncomprehending; she was still exploring the possibilities of some coat which they had found, and of the slender crystal-like ampules in the detective's small leathery brown hand.

"Well,"—his impatience was growing more pronounced—"have you ever before or since heard that voice?"

"No," said Katie, staring at the blankly shining

eyes of the detective. The pupils were large and deep. Like a cat's. Like Friquet's. "No," she said again puzzled.

"Think, now, Katie." It was Steven, speaking urgently. "Are you sure?"

"Why, yes, I——" Katie checked herself. A voice came suddenly out of foggy, cold air, talking to her. Speaking to her about a shop, and about Charlotte Weinberg. Blue Bavarian eyes turned up to a gray sky.

"Herman Schmidt!" she said, catching her breath.

"You're sure?" The detective leaned forward to clutch her arm eagerly. "Sure?"

"Yes. Oh, yes. I ought to have known long ago. But I didn't."

The detective and Steven exchanged a brief look.

Mr. Crafft drew a paper envelope from his pocket, slipped the slender ampules into the envelope, and folded it carefully, before putting it away in some inside pocket. In the same motion he drew out two sheets of paper; ruled sheets, they were, torn along one side as if they'd been removed from a book.

He glanced at them, thoughtfully.

" 'Item, one brown toupee sold to Christopher Lorrel,' " he said in a musing way as if speaking to himself. "That's this top sheet. And this one is: 'Item, one masquerade costume sold to Steven Petrie.' " He turned suddenly to Katie: "Miss Warren, when I questioned Mr. Siskinson regarding the occurrences immediately following the death of Miss Weinberg, he said something about your face—it seemed to impress him that there was something wrong with your face. What exactly was it?"

Katie repressed a notion that the little detective had gone out of his wits and replied, rather dazedly:

"I suppose my face—well, I'd been running through the park, you see. And it was so foggy and dark I couldn't see, and I bumped into a shrub or two. Scratched my face. Fanny said there was even grease on it, although I don't know where on earth I could have got grease——"

"Thank you, Miss Warren." The detective's voice was crisp, sharp, thin.

A policeman stood suddenly near them, and Dr. Mannsen was in the doorway.

The detective's eyes opened and closed inwardly as if the pupils had flickered.

"She—she's conscious, Mr. Crafft," said the doctor hoarsely.

"Can she talk?"

"I'll let you see her," said the doctor, without committing himself further.

"Wait in the lounge, please," said the detective.

The black wicker was dismal and caught highlights. The ferns clustered but did not hide winking black window panes. Two policemen came quietly forward, and Katie watched the doctor and the little brown detective disappear into the shadows of the stairway. The doctor, tall and pale and tired-looking. The detective, little and brown and tireless, padding along silently on the padded steps.

They turned the landing and were gone, and Katie looked at Steven and looked at the policeman. Each of them was standing with his right arm crooked in a curious posture. It was a moment before Katie suddenly realized that each had his hand on his revolver.

Heavy revolvers, they were, in thick brown leather holsters. How often she'd seen them swinging along on the street! How useless those weighted brown holsters had always seemed! Now they were menacing, indescribably threatening. They were there, these two men, to see that neither she nor Steven escaped. She turned to Steven:

"What did he mean by grape hair? How did he know?"

"I told him," said Steven. "I heard you telling Paul about it in the fog that night. I was quite close to you. Heard it all."

"But what does it mean? What is the connection? And this masquerade costume? *And—and Chris*—why does he have the bill for a toupee?"

"Why, you see, this little Herman Schmidt also made wigs, did a bit of costuming. Apparently he made Chris's toupee."

"But Chris said he didn't know him."

"Yes. I know. He—he—it's not very pleasant, Katie—" He paused thoughtfully and fell silent. The policemen exchanged a glance which Katie caught, but neither spoke.

In the bookroom the rest of them waited. And did not know that Melissa was conscious.

What would they do if they knew? Would that agony of suspense be more than one of them could bear?

The house was silent; there might have been no living thing within it. Upstairs Melissa, with her strange red hair bright against bandages and her dark face haunted and tragic and pain-ridden—dying, perhaps—would be telling them who had killed her. And why.

It was intolerable, sitting there so still, waiting. Katie made a motion to rise, although she did not know what she intended to do. But the policeman near her tightened his grip suddenly on his revolver, and Katie sank back again.

Rain slanted against the black windows and ran down in quick streams. Katie stirred presently, and Steven at last looked at her and tried to smile.

"Don't look like that, Katie," he said. "It'll be all right."

"What—time is it?" She found it difficult to speak. Her voice sounded husky and unnatural.

Steven turned his wrist, and a policeman came nearer. "Oh, I'm only looking at my watch," said Steven wearily. "It's nearly eleven, Katie. That's all."

More minutes dragged along.

"Do you suppose," said Katie, "that Melissa can— talk?"

The policemen exchanged glances. One of them cleared his throat uncertainly and said:

"No talking is permitted."

"*No talking!*" said Steven. "Why on earth not?"

"Well," said the policeman uncomfortably, "you're both under arrest, you know. For murder, Mr. Petrie. And this young lady's the accessory before the fact." His eyes went to Katie and lingered there, and he added unexpectedly: "Though I must say she don't look it."

"They never look it," muttered the other. "Shut up, O'Brien."

"It's no harm to compliment a pretty face," said

O'Brien. "It's only those that—— My God, what's that?"

No need to ask.

Revolver shots thundering against the walls. Thudding and pounding incredibly loud and shocking inside the bookroom. Deafening in their quick, shattering reports. Revolver shots.

There were many of them. Suddenly they stopped. Someone started to scream, and that stopped, too.

They heard the door to the bookroom open and close again. A policeman with a streak of red across his face and his hair awry came running from the passage into the lounge.

He saw them and opened his mouth and then looked up toward the stairway and checked the speech on his lips. Katie followed his gaze and saw Mr. Crafft standing there on the landing. He was brown and very still, and was not smiling. Katie thought: She's dead.

For perhaps thirty seconds no one moved. The brown silent man on the stairway held them in a queer breathless spell. It was only half a moment, but Katie was never in all her life afterward to forget those fleeting seconds.

Then he moved and came on down the stairs while the policeman waited at its foot. He stopped and spoke in a low voice to the policeman. Even in that silence Katie could not hear what he said or what the policeman replied. Then Mr. Crafft turned and walked quickly toward them.

"I'm hungry," he said unsmiling. "Do you suppose there's anything in the refrigerator, Miss Warren?"

CHAPTER XXI

IT WAS, perhaps, the last thing in the world that Katie expected him to say. It was not until long afterward that she realized that he had, somewhere within him, a desire to shield her from the ugly thing that must be done.

She turned dazedly toward the dining room. Dimly she knew that Steven was following them and that the two policemen at a quick nod from Mr. Crafft disappeared toward the passage leading to the book-room.

Katie led the way through the long butler's pantry with its shining chromium-steel sink which reflected like a misted mirror the soft lace froth of her gown.

It was there in the kitchen, with its shining white walls and tables, that Katie heard the story. Mr. Crafft, little and brown and ugly and very, very tired, sat on the high stool with a plate of cake on the table near him and a bunch of grapes in his hand. He looked amazingly human and ordinary, spitting out the seeds, and gradually less weighted with the knowledge of tragedy.

Katie said: "I'll make some coffee," and she was measuring the last tablespoonful of coffee when Mr. Crafft began to talk.

"Well," he said and sighed, "it was as I said. Poor Melissa was a tool. It all worked like a piece of machinery. All he'd got to do was start the thing going. Other 'accidents' like the water-wings affair had apparently failed. This one might easily—oh, so easily—have failed. But it worked. If it hadn't, another would have been arranged."

"Then it was——" Steven was white and grim and tense.

A wordless intelligence went from the detective's eyes to Steven's. Katie, standing there beside the white-topped table, with the homely fragrance of coffee in the room, listened and watched and dreaded the knowledge that was suddenly alive between the two men. Yet she must know.

"Who——" she said in a kind of whisper.

Mr. Crafft looked at her, sighed again, then took another grape.

"I guess you'd better know," he said. "It's quite an even line of reasoning. It's a well-linked chain going from one thing to another. And Melissa—has given us the proof of it all. If I'd only unearthed the particular Andrews, the cleaner, a bit earlier in the afternoon. But it might not have helped even then, without what Steven has told me." He paused to explore for an elusive seed and removed it carefully. "I'm on a diet," he informed them. "Grape seeds very bad. Yes, a nice chain it is, going straight from grape hair to hallucinations, to the proof Charlotte mentions in her letter, the coat that went to the cleaner's, and the grease on Miss Katie's pretty face.—And of course, the picture I saw in Madame Petrie's room. A very interesting picture. And to Mr. Lorrel's attempt to borrow money."

"Chris——" said Katie.

The detective paused as if to listen, his ugly little

brown head tipped on one side and a grape suspended in the air. There was a faint stir somewhere in the front of the house. Feet and a low voice or two.

Katie said suddenly, without quite realizing that she was speaking: "There was rope burning. This afternoon. In the bookroom."

"No," said Mr. Crafft. "No, Miss Katie, it wasn't rope. It was, probably, grape hair."

"*What's that?*" cried Steven sharply, rising. "Listen."

Feet shuffling beyond the door of the butler's pantry. Steven crossed, and Katie made a motion to follow him. The detective put his brown hand on her arm.

"Don't go," he said gently. "It's better not to go."

"*What——*" Katie's mouth was stiff.

Steven was suddenly back in the room again.

"If he——" he began and stopped.

"There's nothing you can do," said the detective.

"You remember, Miss Warren, what you told Steven, and he passed on to me, about your trip through the dark one evening to the summerhouse. The night when you found the broken end of the palette knife. And you told him that it seemed to you someone was following you—watching you. Well, that night—you walked as near death as one may walk and escape unscathed." He paused again, swallowed, and added: "The murderer was in the park that night."

Steven took a long step or two towards Katie and took her in his arms.

"The murderer walked with you," said the ugly

little brown man slowly. "It was, of course, Paul Duchane. You must have known."

She did not question it; it wouldn't have helped.

And the hot fragrance of coffee filled the room, and the white light shone down and left no shadows in the corners, and a djinn out of a bottle munched grapes and told the story of it.

"He had to have money, you see. And he wanted to inherit from Madame Petrie. He had a very pressing need for money, for what he told Chris Lorrel was the literal truth. Every cent he had was in a real estate development and was going to go unless he could somehow bolster it up. He had to have money. But Charlotte Weinberg had such great influence over your aunt that Duchane had to discover some very strong influence to combat Miss Weinberg's. It was quite simple. He realized that your aunt was in a state of mind to believe practically anything if it were presented to her in the right way. His only hold on her was through an early sentimental—er—attachment."

He paused to look at Steven and then at Katie and then to select another grape with an air of detached speculation.

"Attachment," he repeated. "To Paul's father. By the way, Miss Katie, do you know what grape hair is? Or rather, allowing for Herman Schmidt's accent, crêpe hair?"

Something dimly connected with masquerades and amateur theatricals struggled for recognition in Katie's mind.

"He hadn't been paid, it seems," said the little detective. "And he met Paul where Paul was waiting for you, Miss Katie. And when, as I suppose, Paul said he couldn't pay him, the little German replied, 'But I won't eat crêpe hair nor yet clocks.' In other words, he had to have money for the necessities of life. But as to crêpe hair——"

He took a small rolled object from a pocket.

"This," he said as they stared at the bit of woolly black hair, "is crêpe hair. It comes in braids. You buy it by the foot. You make—oh, false beards, false mustaches, false hair if you like. Stick it on with spirit gum. Paul had himself made a handsome beard— which I suppose he burned in the fireplace this afternoon—and, in it, looked exactly like his father. The resemblance is marked; the beard and the right clothes would make it irresistible to Madame Petrie. Particularly after Melissa——" He stopped, took another grape and a breath.

"Paul realized, you see, that his only hold was this attachment to his father. And that it was a dim attachment, already more than sufficiently presumed upon. Well, then, what more logical than to freshen it up a bit?

"So," said Mr. Crafft, looking very old and brown and wise, "Paul conceived the simplest plan in the world. But first he must pave his way. He realized that he must have someone in the household to assist him and to tell him how things were going. Melissa" —a gray shadow fell on his face, and he looked for an instant incredibly sad and world-weary—"Melissa was a maid in the apartment building where he lived. She got in a pinch of some sort and stole some money —unfortunately from Paul. Oh, it's an old and simple story; he got her this place out here in your aunt's home and threatened her with prison—thus she followed his demands. Which were, at first, rather easy to follow. It was only when she realized that death followed one of his instructions that she began to grow suspicious and frightened. It was then that she began to watch, secretly, everything that was done. It was she who followed you in the park the night you went to the summerhouse. She, rather, whom you followed, I suppose. It was she who, acting under Paul's orders, gave Charlotte sodium pyratol in her tea, and then, to make it look as though Charlotte had not taken tea, refilled and rearranged the tea tray. She knew very well how to give the stuff in tea, for it was her duty on certain occasions to administer rather large quantities to your aunt. On certain," said Mr. Crafft, looking at the cane, "occasions."

"When?" said Steven tensely.

"It's over now, Steven," said Mr. Crafft still looking at the cane. He sighed and began on another bunch of grapes. "Occasions when Paul impersonated his father," he said casually.

"What!"

Mr. Crafft glanced at Katie in surprise.

"Why, yes, of course. I told you that he realized that Madame Petrie's attachment to his father had grown dim—and he resolved to freshen it up a bit. He hied himself to a costumer's———"

"Herman Schmidt!" said Katie, without realizing she had spoken until the detective nodded impatiently.

"Of course. Took an old photograph of his father along and had himself made up to resemble it, black beard and all. On subsequent occasions he did it himself. Then, with your aunt strongly fortified against becoming too broadly roused and inquisitive, he appeared. A vision," said Mr. Crafft, looking disapprovingly at a soft grape, "whether you believe it or not. Hallucinations, said the doctor. It took Charlotte to discover the truth and the proof of it. He took no chances at all. He knew your aunt's mental make-up. Shrewd and suspicious if he had approached her openly. Gullible as a child about things of which she was ignorant. And more than half turned toward the supernatural already, for Charlotte's interpretation of the stars was convincing to your aunt. It is perhaps unnecessary to state that this hallucination assured your aunt of its distant but immortal affection and its tender hope that she would be kind to its earthly offspring. Oh, yes, it was very simple. You know, young man, if you'd stayed where you belonged this thing would have been more rapidly settled. That is," said Mr. Crafft honestly, "it might have been. You can never tell. However, the coat he sent to the cleaner's the morning after Charlotte was at last successfully and 'accidentally' disposed of, which the cleaner says was spotted with glycerine, and the grease which was also glycerine and was on Miss Katie's face make a nice bit of evidence."

"Glycerine?" said Katie.

"Glycerine and alcohol. The fluid in the brake drum. Hydraulic brake on the car, you know. He pretended to clean the headlights. Really he had pliers ready. It took about ten seconds to twist the screw with the pliers (it's called, by the way, the bleeding screw and it's inside the right front wheel), on the brake drum. The fluid, glycerine and alcohol, was released, and thus when you used the footbrake, Miss Katie, there was no pressure at all."

"Oh," said Katie. "Then——"

"Then he slipped the nut and the pliers in his pocket. It was very simple, but by accident he managed to get the fluid on his coat sleeve, and it smeared on your face, Miss Katie, when he leaned across you, pretending to pull on the handbrake. Sergeant Caldwell's and William's insisting that the brake was all right put me off. Then I realized that Paul had been left alone with Charlotte while Miss Katie came to the house for help. He had thus plenty of time to replace the screw, toss the pliers into a pocket of the car and pump the brake a time or two to distribute more fluid from the master chambers. That done the brake system was working again."

He ate a grape slowly and a bite of cake and went on:

"When Paul had once succeeded in meeting you, Miss Katie, and telephoning to Charlotte to arrange a meeting which Charlotte was all too eager to keep, and at the same time telephoning by way of the kitchen telephone to Melissa, there wasn't another thing to do but manipulate the brake. Of course, it might not have worked—other things had failed. But this one worked. He knew Jenks had a toothache and that Melissa could serve the tea. Melissa dropped sodium pyratol in the tea, slipped out and closed the gates to the drive, returned and cleaned the teapot. In the meantime Steven had brought Madame Petrie back to the house and Charlotte had taken the tea and gone upstairs, where she left the letter addressed to Steven and got her wrap."

"The letter——" said Katie.

"Its content is self-explanatory," said Mr. Crafft. "However, I've got something to show you." He reached into his pocket, pulled out a paper, handed it to Steven, and went back to his cake.

Katie and Steven read it together.

"Dear Steven," it began surprisingly.

"Steven?" said Katie.

Mr. Crafft nodded and mumbled through cake: "Got 'em mixed up. Wrote to Paul and to Steven and got 'em confused in the envelopes. She was beginning to feel drowsy, I suppose."

"Dear Steven," said the note. "I think you should know that owing to a most unwise and wicked attempt on Paul's part to influence your aunt in his favor, your aunt is in a very serious condition. I have asked Paul to cease the dreadful thing he is doing and he has refused. Won't you see me about it? Your aunt needs your help. C. W."

"She meant," said Mr. Crafft briskly. "That *she* needed your help. Melissa found the note on the floor. It was addressed to Paul, so she kept it—after Charlotte was killed she began to be afraid of her own part in it. So she kept the note in the weak hope that it might protect her against Paul. She said, too, Miss Warren, and I believed her, that she didn't know it was poison that she put, at Paul's orders, into the capsules for you."

"Why—was that?" whispered Katie.

"You knew too much, too," said Mr. Crafft. "He was not a strong soul, was Paul. He had to kill Charlotte when she told him that she would tell Madame Petrie what he was doing. He could set the ball rolling and plan its course. But when things happened he couldn't face them. He was in a panic. He only knew to kill and to silence those who knew. As he silenced the little German. As he tried to silence Melissa when he overheard, as I think he did, her conversation with Mrs. Siskinson and realized that she had decided to tell what she knew."

"The little German . . . Herman Schmidt— how——"

"Paul saw him talking to you and realized his danger. He had caught a glimpse through the window of you hiding the revolver. There was nothing simpler than to take it in gloved hands; I'm inclined to think that the little German did not actually leave the grounds after he talked to you, Miss Warren. It was probably not difficult to discover him, talk to him, lead him down to a deserted and out-of-sight spot on the beach, and murder him. Paul had to do it for his own safety. That paper with Charlotte's picture on it was death to the little German. Apparently Paul had given your name, Steven, to the clockmaker. But the little clockmaker knew too much. You see, Charlotte had discovered what Paul was doing. She went to the shop of Herman Schmidt—heaven knows how she discovered him, but I gather she was indefatigable—and talked to him. He had thought it was only a joke of some kind. But Charlotte came away with proof of her knowledge."

"Charlotte's proof," said Steven. "The little wisp of black hair in her hand when she went at Paul's request to meet him and arrange—a truce."

"A truce until after February twenty-sixth. May I have some more coffee, Miss Warren? You aren't drinking your coffee. Drink it immediately. You look like a scared little ghost."

Katie put out a nerveless hand and took the cup and gulped hot coffee.

"Your danger, Miss Katie, after the night in the park when you told him idly, never dreaming what it meant to him, about the crêpe hair, was—well——" The little detective checked his own words, smiled once at Katie, put down a shredded grape stem, said briskly, "It's over now," and turned toward the dining room.

In the lounge with its shining wicker chairs and green ferns and a gilt-framed mirror over a small writing desk, Mr. Crafft turned again toward Katie.

"I might tell you," he said, "that, a little while ago, Paul—tried to escape."

There was a long pause. Rain whispered against the winking black windows, and a policeman came slowly from the passage to the bookroom and stopped when he saw Mr. Crafft.

"With the result?" said Steven finally in a very quiet voice.

"With the result," said the detective, "that there will be no trial."

"Oh!" said Katie in a strange little gasp. "I—I must go to Aunt Mina. It will kill her."

"Nonsense." The little brown djinn looked at her wisely and rather kindly. "May I offer advice, Katie Warren? It's sad and tragic and terribly human. But it's done, and life is still to be lived." He smiled again. And added with abrupt heartiness: "And as for Aunt Mina, she'll be a damn sight better off."

Like a sharply definite period, the telephone at his

side began to ring. Absently he picked it up and answered it and said, yes, yes, he was Crafft.

A single, masculine voice at the other end of the wire was suddenly swept away by a shrill flood of sounds that babbled and flowed and raged like a torrent.

"But——" said Crafft in a defensive way. "You are——" and once got as far as a rather half-hearted, "Come, come——" But the torrent mysteriously increased both in volubility and violence. Increased until Mr. Crafft, with a very queer look on his face, gently replaced the telephone on its cradle.

There was a soft click, and then silence.

Mr. Crafft took out a handkerchief and touched his forehead. He looked at the policeman.

"Officer Getch needs help," he said. "Will you tell Sergeant Caldwell that"—the djinn choked slightly but continued—"that he has eleven Hilda Hansens at the G Street police station. And they all wish to be released. They wish it," said Mr. Crafft with faint discomfort, "vehemently."

He walked, a small brown figure, to the door of the passage. He turned then and was suddenly remote. A djinn out of a bottle who knew many things.

"The charges against you both are dropped," he said. His eyes shone and were luminous. Then he was gone.

Beside Katie the mirror gleamed. She saw herself, pale above soft yellow lace. She saw Steven's blond head and met his eyes.

"It was Melissa, then, who watched me—I was sitting here at the desk. Here where Charlotte sat and wrote her letters just before she died. Her face with its wrinkled eyelids was reflected, I suppose, in the mirror. Her curled dark hair. Her eyes. Perhaps she looked up when she heard Melissa bringing her tea. Perhaps there was that little crystal tinkle. Perhaps she looked at herself before she went out in the fog to death. I wonder——"

In the mirror she saw Steven's arms around her.

"It's done," he said. "And there's life to be lived."

The mirror, silently, secretly, in its gilt frame went about its beginning record of a new page. A page that was, on the whole, rather exciting and handsome and gay.

THE END